Olivia lunged o ...
against the clos ...

Agent West cursed, ro ...
and pinned her arms to ... he took the
opportunity to knee him ... the groin.

He doubled over, wincing in pain. "What is wrong
with you?"

She frisked him, checked his pockets, then pulled
open his shirt. Nothing. Nada. No witchcraft tools.
"Your eyes were glowing earlier, and now here you
are, in the room where my dad killed himself. That's
too damn weird for me."

"My eyes? They've always been like that."

"They're your power."

He made a face. "Well, thank you very much, but
I'm not feeling particularly powerful right now."

She thought about her premonition, the vision of
them kissing in her loft. No damn way was she
going to let that happen "Truce, then. But if you
try anything funny, I'll kill you."

"Likewise." He got to his feet, doing his best to
maintain his machismo. "Now get the hell out of
here."

Olivia almost smiled. "See you around, Agent West."
With that, she left him alone, knowing this was the
first time a woman had knocked him on his ass.

Dear Reader,

What do you plan to accomplish in 2005? Let Silhouette Bombshell jump-start your year with this month's fast-paced lineup of stories featuring amazing women who will entertain you, energize you and inspire you to get out there and get things done!

Author Nancy Bartholomew brings on the heat with *Stella, Get Your Man*. P.I. Stella Valocchi is on a missing-persons case—but with a lying client, a drug lord gunning for her and a new partner who thinks he's the boss, Stella's got her hands full staying cool under fire.

The pressure rises as our popular twelve-book ATHENA FORCE continuity series continues with *Deceived*, by Carla Cassidy, in which a computer whiz with special, supersecret talents discovers that she's on the FBI's Most Wanted list and her entire life may be a lie.

Reality isn't what it seems in the mystic thriller *Always Look Twice* by Sheri WhiteFeather. Heroine Olivia Whirlwind has a unique gift, but delving into the minds of crime victims will bring her ever closer to a ruthless killer and will make everyone a suspect—including those she loves.

And finally, travel to Romania with Crystal Green's *The Huntress*, as an heiress with an attitude becomes a vampire hunter on a mission for vengeance after her lover is captured by those mysterious creatures of the night.

Enjoy all four, and when you're finished, please send your comments to me c/o Silhouette Books, 233 Broadway, Suite 1001, New York, NY 10279.

Sincerely,

Natashya Wilson
Associate Senior Editor, Silhouette Bombshell

Please address questions and book requests to:
Silhouette Reader Service
U.S.: 3010 Walden Ave., P.O. Box 1325, Buffalo, NY 14269
Canadian: P.O. Box 609, Fort Erie, Ont. L2A 5X3

SHERI WHITEFEATHER

ALWAYS LOOK TWICE

BOMBSHELL™

Published by Silhouette Books

America's Publisher of Contemporary Romance

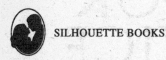

SILHOUETTE BOOKS

ISBN 0-373-51341-0

ALWAYS LOOK TWICE

www.SilhouetteBombshell.com

Printed in U.S.A.

SHERI WHITEFEATHER

lives in Southern California and enjoys ethnic dining, attending powwows and visiting art galleries and vintage clothing stores near the beach. She believes in the power of being a woman and thoroughly enjoys creating kick-ass heroines for the Bombshell line. But she also thrives on emotion-steeped romances, writing for Silhouette Desire, as well.

Sheri's husband, a member of the Muscogee Creek Nation, inspires many of her stories. They have a son, a daughter and a trio of cats—domestic and wild. Visit her Web site at: www.SheriWhiteFeather.com.

To Tara Gavin, Melissa Jeglinski, Leslie Wainger, Natashya Wilson and Lynda Curnyn (the editorial Bombshells at Silhouette) for making this project happen. To Irene Goodman (my agent) for her enthusiasm and advice. To Judy Duarte (my critique partner) for her unwavering support while Crystal Green and I wrote our first Bombshell novels. To Crystal (my other critique partner) for being wonderfully neurotic with me. To Katherine Garbera (fellow Desirable and Bombshellite) for her expertise. And to my readers for their interest in this story, even while I was in the process of writing it. For those of you curious about the supernatural elements, I researched American Indian witchcraft and added my own spin, blending fact, fiction and imagination.

Chapter 1

The stainless steel table was cold. Olivia Whirlwind could almost feel the chilled metal beneath Denise Red Bow's lifeless form. Her body had been gutted, from top to bottom, through a Y-shaped incision that crossed her chest then ran down to the top of her pubis. She looked waxy, inhuman, as surreal as a hollowed-out mannequin.

Death didn't become her.

And neither did the autopsy room: a row of operating tables, water sloshing in sinks, surgical instruments clattering upon deaf ears.

Olivia wanted to rescue her, but it was too late. She wished she could go back in time, before the pathologist had wielded his precision blade. Before Denise Red Bow had been the third victim of the Indian Slasher.

"Special Agent West should be here any minute."

Detective Steve Muncy's voice interrupted the image, bringing Olivia back to the present, back to a conference room at the Los Angeles Street Police Station.

She rubbed her eyes, blinked, did her damnedest to clear her senses.

The autopsy was hours ago, but Olivia hadn't been present. That privilege had been reserved for the Homicide Special Section detectives and the FBI profiler who'd been assigned to the case.

She sat back in her chair, knowing Agent West intended to give her a hard time. She'd yet to meet the elusive fed, but his reputation preceded him.

He didn't like working with psychics.

So much so, he'd banned her from the autopsy room, convincing the pathologist that she didn't belong there.

Although Olivia had been involved in the Indian Slasher investigation for months, this was West's first day on the case. He'd arrived just in time for the autopsy, just in time to see Denise Red Bow flayed out on the table.

Well, bully for him, she thought.

Muncy bumped Olivia's shoulder. "Riggs thinks the special agent's a hunk."

At the mention of her name, Detective Joyce Riggs turned, flashed a pretty smile, then told her partner to piss off.

Olivia couldn't help but laugh. Muncy and Riggs were an unlikely pair.

At forty-eight, he was short, rumpled and happily

married. A dedicated detective, Muncy lived by his own set of rules, determined to solve every case the department dropped in his lap.

Riggs was just as tenacious. Only, she came in the form of a single, flirt-for-the-fun-of-it blonde. Olivia nicknamed them Columbo and Cagney, after the TV cops they reminded her of.

Suddenly the door to the conference room opened, and Olivia looked up. A striking man in his midthirties wearing a dark suit and slightly scuffed cowboy boots took center stage. He stood tall, with tanned skin, thick brown hair, chiseled features and disturbing eyes. An obscure shade of gray, they assessed her with cool reserve.

Special Agent Ian West.

There was no damn way she was going to let him intimidate her.

He greeted everyone with a nod, including Olivia. Then he slid some photographs on the table in front of her. "Ms. Whirlwind, I presume."

"That's right." She didn't bother to glance at the pictures. She knew they were from Denise Red Bow's autopsy. "I've already seen them. In my mind," she added, reminding him that she was an established psychic. That banning her from the medical examination hadn't made a difference.

Detectives Muncy and Riggs remained silent, watching her and West.

He left the photographs in front of her. Finally she picked one up, studied it, saw that Denise's scalp was pulled down over her face. The front quadrant of her skull had been cut away and removed. Standard autopsy stuff.

"Denise doesn't like this," she said, pretending the victim was making contact with her. "She preferred her brain the way it was."

Agent West wasn't amused, but she knew Detective Muncy appreciated her offbeat humor. They'd met ten years ago, on the night of her father's suicide. He'd seen her at her worst.

"I heard you were a smart-ass," West told her.

"And I heard you would try to discredit me." Los Angeles was her turf, her city, the place where she'd been born and raised. She had every right to help the police apprehend the Indian Slasher. The faceless woman in the photograph deserved that much.

West didn't respond. Tension buzzed between them, zapping the room like fireflies. The flag in the corner didn't dare wave, in spite of a strong, hard blast from an air-conditioning vent.

"Olivia is FBI, too," Muncy said, catching the profiler's attention with a silly joke. "Full-blooded Indian."

"I'm aware of that." He leaned forward, putting his hands on the conference table, looking straight at her, his voice laced with a Southern-boy slant. "I assume you're concerned about helping our people."

"Our people?" She raised her eyebrows. He wasn't claiming to be Indian, was he? Olivia hailed from an Oglala Lakota father and a Chiricahua Apache mother, both of whom were long gone from her life. A younger sister was her only family.

"Let me guess. Your great-great-grandmother was a Cherokee princess," she said, poking fun at the oldest, most ridiculous wannabe claim that ever existed.

A cynical smile ghosted across his lips. Apparently he was familiar with the princess scenario. "I'm a card-carrying Muscogee Creek, Ms. Whirlwind."

Who relied on his heritage when it suited him, she thought. A special agent, ready to save the day, with one-sixteenth or possibly one-eighth Native blood flowing through his veins.

But, hey, he was registered with his tribe.

"I'm impressed," she told him.

"So I see," he mocked. "And considering you have a lot in common with the victims in this case, you should be. A young, attractive Native American woman living and working in Los Angeles County. I'd be careful if I were you."

"But you're not me, are you?" Olivia knew damn well that she could shoot a flea off the back of a gnat's ass faster than West could pull out his peter to pee. "I can take care of myself."

He dropped his gaze to the base of her throat, where a noticeable scar made a mysterious statement. "You sure about that?"

"Positive." Was the special agent wondering if someone had tried to slit her throat? Olivia knew how her scar affected most people and what their speculations were.

Of course, he was different. He'd probably figured it out already. He'd probably seen enough wounds to know how they were inflicted. But even so, she lifted her chin, allowing him a good hard look.

He took an unabashed gander, but he didn't let his gaze slip lower, even though her curve-clinging jumpsuit attracted plenty of attention. Olivia enjoyed dressing like a designer-clad dominatrix. It fit her daring personality, the part of her that refused to be tamed.

"Why don't you brief me on the case?" West said, his tone a tad too condescending.

She glared at him. "I'm sure the detectives already brought you up to speed."

"I'd really like to hear it from a psychic's perspective."

"Fine." She accepted his challenge and glanced at Muncy, who leaned back in his chair, keeping his emotions in check. Riggs, on the other hand, managed a small smile. But whom the smile was intended for wasn't quite clear.

Olivia came to her feet, walking to the front of the room. At twenty-nine she worked hard to keep her body fit, taking pride in the beauty that came from being a woman. Bulletlike, her spiky-heeled boots sounded on the floor, as deadly as her aim. A ladylike bondage belt was slung low on her hips, resting to one side. And although the Glock she routinely carried was in plain sight, she'd snagged a permit to carry a concealed weapon, something next to impossible for a California civilian.

West didn't take a chair. He parked his butt on the

edge of the table, and when Riggs cleared her throat, a blast of sexual energy ripped through Olivia's body.

Well what do you know? The lady cop really did think the profiler was a hunk. Olivia wondered if fraternization was allowed, or if FBI agents were banned from boffing pretty blond detectives.

She glanced at his left hand, then got a quick flash of the wedding band that used to be there. She shrugged away the energy connected to it, the hurt and anger, the nights he spent alone.

West crossed his arms. "Any time you're ready."

Needing a distraction, Olivia messed up her hair, scattering the short, choppy layers, blocking out the profiler's private life. "There's been three female victims in this case," she began. "The first two were slashed inside their L.A. homes, stabbed repeatedly, with no forced entry and no sexual assault. The third, Denise Red Bow," she added, indicating the autopsy pictures, "was killed in the same manner. But even though she lived and worked in Hollywood, she was stabbed while house-sitting for her parents on their reservation, about 120 miles south of L.A." Olivia paused, cursing the law. "And that's why you were brought in. Indian Country falls under federal jurisdiction."

"That's right." He uncrossed his arms. "And now here we are, one big happy family, working on this investigation together."

She looked at Muncy and noticed the strain around his mouth. The LAPD did its own profiling. They didn't need the FBI's assistance.

Olivia continued the briefing, reciting information West already knew. "The killer's calling card is an arrowhead encased in a valentine-style heart. He draws this symbol on the victim's abdomen, on the right side, using an average black marker."

"Have you gotten a reading on the artwork?" he asked. "Any vibes that enhance the investigation?"

Was he testing her skill? Or just hell-bent on giving her a hard time? Either way, she was used to proving herself. Most law enforcement officials—skeptical by nature and suspicious by training—didn't believe in her ability. And those who did, like Detective Muncy, didn't admit, at least publicly, that he consulted a psychic. The press would have a field day if they knew how many investigations she'd been involved in.

She finally answered West's question. "No, I haven't gotten any vibes about the Slasher's calling card."

"So what's your opinion? Do you think we're dealing with a serial killer?"

"Yes," she responded, knowing full well she was talking to a highly educated man with several advanced degrees. But that didn't make her opinion any less valuable. Olivia's gift gave her an edge.

"Why?" he pressed. "Why a serial killer?"

"Because he perpetrated random murders, with an emotional cooling-off period in between. The victims were unrelated. They didn't know each other," she clarified. "And each had been slain in a different location." She shuffled the autopsy pictures, stacking them like a deck of cards. "So far, the Slasher has gone after married women." But that didn't mean he wouldn't change his MO, she thought. Single girls could be at risk, too.

"Two of our victims were cheating on their husbands," West remarked.

"But Denise wasn't. At least not that we know of."

"So you think this is one killer? One man?"

Olivia nodded. "That's the feeling I have. My intuition."

"Why not multiple offenders? The forensic evidence is inconclusive." A frown marred West's forehead, carving a groove into his skin. "In fact, it's downright weird. Footprints that appear then disappear, hair samples that test human one time and animal the next. Nothing makes any sense." He shifted his weight. He was still perched on the edge of the table. "Do you have an answer for any of that?"

"Actually, she does." This came from Muncy, who rose from his chair. "Olivia thinks the killer has supernatural powers."

"Really?" West's frown remained, deep and dark and troubled. "And do you agree with her analysis, Detective?"

"I'm inclined to."

The profiler turned to Riggs. "And you?"

Her blue eyes locked onto his. "It's a baffling case."

The special agent nodded. "That it is." He tunneled his hands through his hair, quietly perplexed. Then he addressed Olivia. "Do you think the killer is a skinwalker?"

She tilted her head. "It's hard to say. There are other tribes besides the Navajo that have witches among them." And his attitude confused her. Why would a man who believed in supernatural beings resent working with a psychic?

Because he envied her power, her mind answered. West wanted what she had. The ability she possessed.

"You better be careful," he said, reminding her once again that the Slasher was attacking American Indian women.

Like her. And her sister.

She thought about Allie, about how gentle her younger sibling was. Then she glanced at West.

Suddenly his eyes, those odd gray eyes, were glowing.

Like a witch.

Twenty minutes later Olivia took the 101, engaging the gas petal, gaining speed, switching lanes, snarling at the late-day traffic.

She kept telling herself that West's eyes were a trick of the light, an illusion. He wasn't powerful enough to be a witch.

Darting past a poky compact, she accelerated again, her vintage Porsche purring with elation, the wind whipping through the convertible, stinging her face. And then she wondered what the hell she was doing.

Why was she on the freeway? She lived in a loft downtown, just minutes from the police station.

Suddenly her vehicle chose its own path, forcing her to fight the wheel.

Battling the entity inside her car, she screamed at it,

warning it to leave her alone. Sounds from the road sliced past her ears, fast, furious, overwhelming.

Her tires hugged the lane, spinning like black holes in space. But when she saw the Highland exit, she knew.

She understood.

A ghost, a *wanagi* in her father's language, was taking her to him. Not to his grave, but to the motel where he'd blown out his brains.

"All right," she whispered. "I'll go there." The wheel on the Porsche was no longer locked, but her destination had been forged just the same.

She drove to the motel, a place she'd been avoiding for years. Aside from a fresh coat of paint, it looked the same, an attractive building on a side street off Sunset Boulevard, with yellow trim and a swimming pool surrounded by empty lounge chairs.

She parked in front of Room 112 and stared at the heavy beige drapes in the window.

Now what? she asked herself. What difference did this make? She'd been having visions about her dad since the night he'd killed himself.

She'd seen it happen before he'd pulled the trigger.

But her mad rush to save him had failed, even with Detective Muncy's help. They'd called a list of motels in the Hollywood area, working in alphabetical order, checking registries, trying to pinpoint the location in her vision.

Olivia stared at the drapes again. The Z-Sleep Inn had been the last place on their list, a motel they'd never gotten the chance to call.

Instead, another guest had heard the shot and reported it to the front desk.

In the end Joseph Whirlwind had been found, alone on the bed, blood gushing out of his nose and mouth, the back of his head splattered on the wall behind him, chips of his skull imbedded in the plaster.

A biohazard removal company had cleaned up the mess, but no one could erase the recurring vision from her mind.

She looked up at the sky, knowing it was going to happen. Unable to stop it, she waited, her heart pounding with anxiety, with memories tangling like vines.

Then suddenly the familiar image sluiced through her brain, as vivid as a horror film bursting with surround sound.

She could hear her father's erratic breathing. He paced the room, passing the unmade bed. The quilt was a pleasant shade of blue, mottled with a green-and-yellow design. Joseph wanted to shred it.

Edgy, he glanced at the .44 Magnum on the nightstand. It was an old gun, a weapon he'd had since the seventies. *Dirty Harry* style, he thought, wishing he'd had a career like Clint Eastwood.

But Joseph was Lakota, an actor who refused to play parts that stereotyped his people. His agent kept telling him to get over it, to take whatever work he could find.

Joseph shook his head. He had pride. And honor.

He picked up the note he'd written to his daughters,

studying it one more time. He'd tried to word it simply, to refrain from the drama that had destroyed his life.

Steeped in emotion, he tucked it into an envelope, holding it, ever so briefly, against his heart. His girls were adults now, young women old enough to take care of themselves. He wasn't abandoning them. He was freeing them from the depression that swallowed his soul. Besides, he told himself, he was already dead. He'd ceased to exist on the day his wife had left him for another man.

When he climbed onto the bed and reached for the pistol, Olivia's heart went weak.

Don't do it, Daddy.

She opened her eyes, but the image wouldn't go away. She wanted to hate her mother. Except, it was her father placing the gun barrel in his mouth and pulling the trigger.

The high-powered blast reverberated in her ears, killing Joseph Whirlwind instantly.

She waited for his spirit to leave his body, praying he would find peace. Yet there was nothing but the aftermath of his suicide haunting the room.

Olivia went straight home, anxious to see her sister. She found Allie in the kitchen, humming to a Beatles song on an oldies radio station. The kitchen, like the rest of the loft, was decorated in Allie's eclectic style, with thrift-store treasures and shabby-chic collectables.

Allie was a full-time artist and a part-time art teacher

at a senior citizen's community center. She had a way with elders. With kids and animals, too. She spoiled a black cat, a stray she'd named Samantha that hissed at everyone but her.

Olivia stood back, watching her younger sibling. Although they were only a year apart, eighteen and nineteen when their dad had died, she'd always been protective of Allie.

And for good reason. Most of the time, Olivia's sister floated through life, ignoring her surroundings. At the moment she wasn't paying attention to anything except the health-food groceries she was arranging in a walk-in pantry.

"What if I was the Slasher?" Olivia said.

"What?" Allie spun around, her waist-length hair whipping across her body. She wore an ensemble of Southwestern-style clothes, gauzy fabrics decorated with turquoise jewelry she'd bought at a pawnshop.

"You didn't even hear me come in," Olivia told her. "I could have been the killer."

"The door was locked. You have a key." Allie stacked several cans of vegetarian chili on an already crowded shelf.

"That's not the point. You're oblivious."

"I have street smarts." The younger woman gestured to a nearby window, where designers, retailers, manufacturers and apparel marts converged in the Fashion District. "Look where we live."

Olivia shook her head. Their loft was located above

a trendy little shoe store and a gourmet coffee bar that baked fresh muffins throughout the day. Even now, the aroma of banana-nut bread wafted through the air, along with the scented candles Allie routinely burned. She existed in a dream world, right along with the fantasy creatures she painted.

"I'm going to teach you to shoot."

Her sister's dark skin paled. "No. Not after what Dad did."

"You need to learn to protect yourself."

"Not like that." When Allie cocked her hip, the shiny belt cinched at her waist made her look leaner than she already was. She was tall and graceful, stunningly lithe. Their mother had been a dancer when she was young. Olivia and her sister had inherited Yvonne Whirlwind's long shapely lines. Of course Olivia had inherited more than that.

Their mom was psychic, too.

The woman who'd walked out on them, she thought. The woman who'd purposely disappeared.

"It's bad enough that I have to put up with your arsenal," Allie said. "Most girls collect pretty trinkets. But no, not my sister. She collects weapons."

Enough of this, Olivia thought. "A *wanagi* was in my car today."

Allie's skin went pale again. A sun catcher in the window bathed her clothes in a prism of dusk, giving her a gypsy-in-the-mist quality. "What did it want?"

"It led me to the motel."

The younger woman hugged herself. Then she walked out of the kitchen and into the living room, where the massive loft nearly swallowed her whole. The walls were covered with a mural she'd painted, with unicorns and fairies and an armor-clad knight slaying a winged dragon.

Olivia followed her. "Don't shut me out, Allie."

"I'm not." She rubbed the goose bumps on her arms. "Sometimes ghosts bring messages. Dad used to say that."

"I know. But I'm not sure what this *wanagi* was trying to say."

"Maybe we should leave some food out for it, the way our ancestors used to do. If we don't, we might offend it."

Olivia thought about the vegetarian chili Allie had packed in the pantry. "I don't think it would like that healthy crap you eat."

They looked at each other and laughed, breaking the tension. To the Lakota, ghosts were *wakan,* hard to understand. Sometimes they haunted people, twisting their mouths and eyes. And sometimes they whistled outside someone's home. Olivia's ghost had done neither.

"Maybe it just wanted me to confront the motel," she said. "To quit avoiding it."

Allie sank onto a velvet sofa laden with embroidered pillows, a fat white candle flickering on the wrought-iron table beside her. Shadows swirled on the walls, making her mural come to life. "Maybe the *wanagi* was Dad."

The room nearly tilted. Olivia hadn't considered that possibility. She glanced at the gun cabinet in the corner. She still had the .44 Magnum he'd used. "Why would he make me go there?"

"To stop those visions you keep having of him," her sister said.

"If that was his intention, it didn't work."

They sat quietly for a moment, lost in thought. The banana bread aroma was gone, but vanilla-scented wax filled the air, like a milkshake melting over a flame.

"Who do you think is staying in that room?" Allie asked.

Olivia recalled the heavy beige drapes in the motel window. "I don't know. Lots of people have stayed there."

"But who's there now? Who was the ghost trying to make you aware of?"

Olivia's heartbeat blasted her chest. And suddenly she knew.

Ian West.

The special agent with the glowing eyes.

Chapter 2

Olivia parked her Porsche around the corner and entered the office of the Z-Sleep Inn, where the woman behind the counter gave her an empty smile.

Good, she thought, the clerk's mind was on something else, and preoccupied people were easy to fool.

Olivia had covered her jumpsuit with a long black sweater, a bulky cardigan that toned down her look. But that was part of her ploy.

"May I help you?" the other woman asked.

"Yes. My husband is checked into Room 112. His name is Ian West."

The clerk merely nodded. She was a color-treated blonde with wire-rimmed glasses, an averagely attractive girl in her midtwenties whose name tag identified her as Carla.

When Olivia's sixth sense kicked into gear, she realized Carla was new to the area. That she was trying to sell a screenplay.

That was even better.

Olivia opened her sweater, exposing the skintight jumpsuit. "I flew in to surprise Ian. He's here on a business trip." Next she adjusted the bondage belt around her hips, flashing an I'm-going-to-handcuff-my-husband-to-the-headboard smile.

Carla's eyes grew wide, but she didn't overreact. This was Hollywood, after all. And she was trying to fit in.

"I need the key to his room," Olivia said.

"Oh, oh…of course." The clerk took a moment to do her job, fiddling with her computer, making sure Ian West was registered to Room 112.

Bingo. Olivia saw the recognition on the other woman's face. She secured the key and thanked Carla, leaving the blonde staring after her.

Agent West was still at the police station, where he intended to remain for a while. That much Olivia could feel.

With a deep breath, she entered the room, closing the door behind her. When it clicked into place, her pulse jumped to her throat.

The decor had changed. The Z-Sleep Inn had updated their color scheme, using light woods and maroon accents. It didn't look like the place where her dad had taken his life.

But it was.

Olivia went to work, trying to get a reading on West, hoping to uncover something that revealed more about him. He was annoyingly tidy, making her job more difficult. He would notice if she left something out of place. His belongings were carefully unpacked, his underwear and T-shirts tucked neatly into a dresser that doubled as an entertainment center.

She went through the drawers, searching for witchcraft tools, possibly a vile of blood, a black candle or a bundle of dried herbs.

Nothing, she thought, as she restacked a handful of printed boxers. Strange, but she'd pegged him for a white-briefs kind of guy. Yet there wasn't a pair of bunhuggers in sight.

She paused, glanced around, then poked through West's toiletries on the vanity counter outside the bathroom. He used disposable razors and a generic brand of shaving cream. His designer cologne was a bit more costly. She removed the cap and sniffed. Nothing suspicious there. It actually smelled pretty good.

So what was the deal? Olivia frowned, wondering why West was staying in her father's old room. There had to be a mystical reason, something the special agent was hiding.

Finally she opened the closet. He favored dark suits, pale shirts and narrow ties. Apparently, the only shoes he'd brought were Western boots.

Stupid urban cowboy.

She checked the pockets of his suits, digging around for magic stones. Onyx, jet or a sturdy hunk of geode. Geode, a mysterious rock formation with a hollow cavity, promoted psychic ability, something West coveted.

His pockets were empty, not even a piece of lint. Maybe he wasn't so stupid after all. He hadn't left behind one shred of witchlike evidence.

Olivia closed the closet door and turned to look at the bed. Should she try to invoke the *wanagi* to help her? She knew that calling upon a ghost was a dangerous game.

Was the entity her dad? Was he trying to warn her about West? Or had West conjured the ghost? Was it part of his magic?

Suddenly she heard a vehicle.

Damn it.

She knew it was West's rental car. She could feel his energy connected to it. The son of a bitch had tricked her. He'd left the station earlier than he'd originally planned.

There was no escape. Motel rooms weren't equipped with back doors. Olivia darted into the bathroom, which wasn't much bigger than a photo booth. She glanced at the commode. The seat was up.

Because flushing herself down the toilet wasn't an option, she drew her gun and hid behind the door, leaving it slightly ajar, the way it had been before.

She sure as hell hoped that West didn't need to use the bathroom. Or he wasn't hankering for a shower.

With any luck, the special agent would dump his

briefcase, change into some casual clothes and head back out to grab a cheap meal. She doubted the FBI had given him a luxurious per diem.

Olivia heard him enter the motel room: the click of the door, the dead bolt sliding into place. She waited, listening to his footsteps.

Then she cursed. Something was wrong.

There was no time to ground out another expletive. He'd stopped breathing, stopped moving. She could feel his pulse, feel him reaching for his gun. Damn him all to hell.

He knew someone was in his room.

Olivia didn't have a choice. At this point, catching him off guard was her best defense. She waited, listening to him scan the room. And just when he focused on the closet, she swung open the bathroom door, taking aim.

He was just as fast. Within a heartbeat, his gun was pointed at her, too.

They faced off, an even match.

"I smelled your perfume the minute I came in," he said. "I suspected it was you."

What was he? A wolf? Her fragrance wasn't that strong. "Holster that thing, West."

"You first."

She didn't budge. "What compelled you to stay here?"

"What are you talking about?"

"This motel. This room. One-twelve."

"I still don't know what you're talking about." And his gun was still pointed at her chest.

She blinked, but she didn't stumble. A vision flashed across her mind. West was in her loft, kissing her, pushing his tongue into her mouth. And she was kissing him back, putting her hands all over him, dragging him to her bedroom.

No, she thought. *No.*

Olivia steeled her emotions, tempted to aim the Glock at his fly. "I asked you about this room."

"Humor me." He watched her. Aware, it seemed, that she'd nearly lost her composure. "Give me a clue. Tell me why this motel matters."

"My father committed suicide here."

"Christ." His gaze shifted, but only for a moment. "In this room? I'm sorry. I didn't know."

He seemed sincere, but she wasn't going to back off. Not until she found a way to frisk him, to check his pockets for magic stones, to search for an amulet around his neck, something, anything that could be used against her.

"When?" he asked. "When did it happen?"

"Ten years ago."

"How he'd do it?"

"A .44 Magnum."

"Christ," he said again, only this time he sounded as if he were praying. "Can we put these away now? Or are we going to keep this up all night?"

"Fine." She agreed to holster her weapon at the same time as him, waiting for another chance to strike.

She stepped out of the bathroom, inching closer to him. He remained where he was, studying her through those bone-chilling eyes. They weren't glowing, but they looked right through her, nearly penetrating her soul.

"Who told you I was staying here?" he asked. "Muncy? Riggs?"

A blast of betrayal gripped her hard and quick. "They knew?"

"They could have found out, I guess. I gave the lieutenant the name and number of this place. Right before I left the station tonight."

Which meant Muncy and Riggs didn't know. "Casper warned me that you were here."

"Who?"

"The friendly ghost."

West frowned. His tie was loose, and a strand of his hair fell across his forehead. His features were taut, strong and serious. She wondered if his wife had left him for another man.

He blew out a rough breath. "My grandfather says that when you pass a graveyard, you should chew a little ginseng, then spit it out on each side of your mouth, four times each way."

"That drives away the ghosts?"

"He thinks so. He never said anything about motel rooms, though."

"Your grandfather is a superstitious man."

"A lot of Indians are."

Olivia could see West's profile in the vanity mirror.

For all she knew, his grandfather was a witch. "I heard about an ancient Creek belief. Supposedly they wouldn't allow their children to congregate where old people were conversing because the elders might bewitch them. Is that true?"

"Yes, but that's because some of the old men had been through so many fastings in their lifetimes, people thought they might be wizards."

Exactly, she thought, as she lunged at him, knocking him against the closet door.

He cursed, rolled over on top of her and pinned her arms to the floor. She took the opportunity to knee him in the groin. Hard. As hard as she possibly could.

"Shit!" He doubled over, wincing in pain.

She frisked him, checked his pockets, then pulled open his shirt.

Nothing. Nada. No witchcraft tools.

"What the hell is wrong with you?" He found the strength to shove her away.

"Your eyes were glowing earlier, and now here you are, in the room where my dad killed himself. That's too damn weird for me."

"My eyes?" He braced his back against the closet. He was still wincing, still feeling the brunt of her attack. "They've always been like that."

"They're your power."

He made a face. "Well, thank you very much, but I'm not feeling particularly powerful right now."

"What about this room?"

"Maybe Casper drew me here."

"Why would he do that?"

"To tie us together. To help you trust me."

She thought about her premonition, the vision of them kissing in her loft. No damn way was she going to let that happen. "Fine, we'll call a truce. But if you try anything funny, I'll kill you."

"Likewise." He got to his feet. He was doing his damnedest to maintain his machismo, to pretend that his balls weren't still throbbing in his brain. "Now get the hell out of here."

Olivia almost smiled. "See you around, Agent West."

With that, she left him alone, knowing this was the first time a woman had knocked him on his ass.

Later that night Olivia couldn't sleep. She tossed and turned, gazing at the window, where moonlight glinted through lace sheers, sending a filigree pattern across the floor.

After she climbed out of bed, she slipped on a pair of sheepskin slippers, warming her feet from the linoleum. The loft was a little chilly at two in the morning. But just a little.

She smiled to herself. That was the beauty of living in Southern California. While other parts of the country were banked in snow, L.A. offered mild temperatures, even in February.

Olivia went into the kitchen, where a twenty-watt bulb above the stove served as a nightlight. She fixed herself a cup of mint tea and noticed conversation-heart candies dotting the counter.

Allie had left them for the ghost.

She picked one up, read the Be Mine inscription, almost ate it, then set it back down. Allie used to leave cookies and milk for Santa Claus, too.

Olivia tasted her tea. She'd never believed in Santa Claus or the Easter Bunny or any of those childhood myths.

Allie had believed in everything.

Taking her cup, she walked to her sister's room and peeked in. A low-burning lamp bathed a collection of fancy dance shawls with an amber glow, making the retired powwow regalia look like oversize butterflies with fringed wings.

Olivia expected to find Allie in bed, sleeping like a castle-bound princess, but the pink-and-gold chamber was empty.

She closed the bedroom door and headed to Allie's studio, knowing that was where she would be. Sure enough, her sister was working. The smooth side of a buffalo hide was stretched across a table, with Allie leaning over it, drawing a design she intended to paint.

"Couldn't that wait until morning?" Olivia asked.

Allie looked up. She wore white pajamas and pair of cat-shaped slippers. Samantha, the real cat, slept on a nearby shelf cluttered with art supplies. "No. I have to do this now."

"Why? What's the hurry?"

"It's going to be a portrait of Dad, so he can travel the Ghost Road. If I paint a tattoo on his wrist, the old woman will have to let him pass."

Olivia moved farther into the studio, still clutching her tea. In the early Lakota days, the Ghost Road was a path taken by spirits. To the south the road branched, where an old woman inspected the tattoo of each spirit. Those without tattoos would be pushed over the side of a cloud or a cliff, condemned to roam the earth as ghosts.

"Spirits don't get a second chance on the Ghost Road, Allie."

The younger woman continued sketching. "Dad might."

Olivia wished her sister's artwork had the power to free their father. He'd taught them about the old ways, but he'd lived a modern life. A tattoo for the Ghost Road wasn't something he'd considered. "Do you really think it's him?"

Allie glanced up. "Who else could it be?"

"I don't know." Olivia laughed a little. "I've been calling it Casper."

Her sister laughed, too. "At least Casper was on TV and in the movies." Her mood turned solemn. "Do you think Mom knows that he's dead? That he killed himself?"

"I have no idea." Joseph Whirlwind wasn't a well-known actor. His suicide hadn't made the papers. He'd disappeared into the bowels of Hollywood, like so many others before him.

Allie smoothed the hide. "I wonder where she is."

Olivia didn't want to think about their mother, about the betrayal that still left her empty inside. What kind of woman walked away from her family? Discarded them like trash?

She changed the subject, focusing on Allie's project instead. "Are you going to paint some weapons for him? A lance? A shield?"

Her sister nodded. "I'm going dress him in the traditional way, too. Eagle feathers in his hair and beaded moccasins with fully quilled soles."

"That's a good idea." There were only two times when moccasins with quilled or beaded soles were made. When a baby was born and when a loved one died.

"So did you find out who was staying at the motel?" Allie asked.

Olivia sighed. She couldn't seem to shake West from her mind. "It was the special agent assigned to the Slasher case."

"An FBI guy?" Her sister stopped drawing. Her hair was loose, falling in a thick black curtain, glimmering under the studio lights. "Wow. That's wild."

Yeah, wild. "He confuses me."

"Why? Because Dad drew him to that room?"

Olivia frowned. West had implied the same thing. "We don't even know if the *wanagi* is Dad."

"It is. It has to be. And after the Slasher case is solved, he's going to travel the Ghost Road."

After it's solved? Olivia glanced at the buffalo hide,

at the rough image that had begun to appear. She sipped her tea, needing warmth, needing reassurance.

Then without the slightest warning, Samantha opened her eyes, arched her sleek black body and hissed at a shadow on the wall.

Leaving Olivia chilled once again.

At daybreak Olivia drove to an area in the high desert where the Manson gang once dwelled, an area where methamphetamine labs brewed illicit drugs, and relocated sex offenders pretended to be part of society.

She parked beside a house encompassed by a chain-link fence. The front yard was littered with old car parts, broken-down swing sets, wagon wheels, goofy-looking lawn jockeys and bearded gnomes. Several outbuildings stored even more salable junk, things exposure to the elements could damage. A metal aircraft hangar sat behind everything else, taking up a noticeable portion of the seven-acre property.

Olivia approached the perimeter of the front yard and waited for the rottweiler on duty to snarl and bark his fool head off.

He did just that, baring his teeth until he realized who she was. Then he wagged his docked tail and whined for attention.

"Clyde, you big baby." She unlocked the gate with her key, entered the property and knelt to pet him. "Where's Bonnie?"

Just then, a miniature dachshund came around the

corner, her long, low-slung body wiggling. She looked like what she was—a wiener dog Clyde could consume for breakfast. But he wouldn't dream of it. Bonnie and Clyde adored each other.

Olivia tapped the dachshund's pointed nose and received a sappy grin in return. "Okay, you guys, I'm going to wake up your master."

She walked passed the junk, where a sixty-year-old house with a sagging porch made a run-down statement.

Once again, she used her key, hoping Kyle wasn't in bed with his latest lover, whoever the unfortunate girl might be.

His house was a mess, almost as cluttered as his yard. She passed the kitchen and winced. Food-encrusted dishes were piled in the sink and stacked on the counter, leaving little space for much else.

Kyle Prescott was a decorated Desert Storm soldier, a half-blood Apache who looked like an indigenous god, but he was also the biggest slob on the planet.

She tore open his bedroom door, and he awakened with a start. He was alone, as big and broad and surly as a brown bear.

"Olivia." He cursed her name. "Do you know what time it is?"

"I need to blow off some steam."

"Oh." His demeanor changed. He smiled and patted the empty space next to him. "In that case, I'm all yours."

"Not that kind of steam."

"Figures." He climbed out of bed, unabashed and completely naked.

Olivia had seen his bare butt before. She had been his on-and-off lover for nearly three years, a mistake she didn't intend to repeat. He was a bit too bizarre to make a woman feel secure.

"Go make some coffee and I'll meet you in the kitchen," he said. "Then we can get started."

He stumbled down the hall to take a shower, and she battled the dishes in his sink, searching for cups that were worthy of washing. He had three coffeepots, and all of them were thick with caffeine-laced drudge. Finally she found a fourth unit. A reconditioned model, it was clean and shiny and stored in a generic box. But what did she expect? Kyle was a junk dealer.

By the time he finished his morning routine, Olivia handed him a cup of his favorite brew. His blunt-cut, shoulder-length hair was held in place with a cloth headband, styled after the Mexican Period in Apache history.

Bare-chested with jeans and knee-high moccasins, he was an Indian groupie's dream, a gorgeous sight to behold. But in spite of his mixed-blood roots, Kyle didn't sleep with white women.

Olivia had met him through AIM, but somewhere along the line, he'd outgrown the American Indian Movement. These days he belonged to an underground warrior society, a militant group the government wouldn't approve of.

Not that the feds approved of AIM, she thought.

Kyle called the FBI the Federal Bureau of Ineptitude, and men like Special Agent West, fibbies.

"I shouldn't let you use me like this," he said, taking his coffee to a Formica-topped dinette set near the window. "I should make you return my keys."

She plopped down in the chair across from him. "We can't be friends if we're not sleeping together?"

He shrugged, feigning indifference. Olivia wanted to kick him. She knew he enjoyed being her instructor. The power-blasting rush probably gave him a hard-on.

"What's got you so wound up?" he asked.

"Everything." She blew a weary breath. "The Slasher, my sister's passive nature, the FBI."

That caught his attention. "What FBI?"

"The agent assigned to the Slasher investigation. I had a premonition about him. We were kissing, pawing each other, getting all hot and nasty."

"That's sick."

"He's registered with the Muscogee Nation."

"A Creek?" Kyle sipped lazily from his cup. "I knew those civilized tribes couldn't be trusted."

And she knew he was being smart. "This isn't a joke."

"I didn't say it was. An Indian fibbie is some serious shit." He frowned at her, and the sharp, rugged expression made him look even more handsome. "Why'd you kiss him?"

"I just told you, it was a vision. A premonition. It hasn't happened yet. And it's not going to," she added, even though the idea had begun to arouse her.

"Maybe it wasn't a premonition." He leaned back in his chair, scraping the metal legs against the floor. "Maybe it was somebody's fantasy."

"Somebody's? You mean his?"

"Or yours."

Trust him to bait her, to accuse her of being the guilty party, to figure out that she was attracted to West.

Olivia yanked away his cup, nearly spilling the rest of the hot brew. "I'm tired of shooting the breeze."

He came to his feet, six foot four of raw, rugged muscle. "Then what do you want to shoot, Liv?"

She gave him an exasperated look. No one but Kyle called her Liv. And no one but Kyle offered her the tools, techniques and tactical training she craved.

She needed him.

And he damn well knew it.

Chapter 3

Olivia followed Kyle outside, where they took his Jeep to the aircraft hangar, a ten-thousand-square-foot structure designed to his specification.

They reached the metal building, and once they were inside, he smiled at her, looking a tad wicked in the compound he'd created.

Kyle claimed it was nothing more than a sophisticated, indoor, laser-tag course, equipped with a montage of movie props and set changes, including lifelike audio tracks and things that varied the weather, creating heat, rain, ice or wind.

But to Olivia it was more than that. The other people who came here—mercenaries and militants—played war games. But she was a psychic honing her skills, using her mind, instead of her eyes, to locate a target.

Kyle, of course, was the great and powerful Oz. He controlled the environment, modifying the course when necessary, putting new obstacles in each participant's path.

"Ready?" he asked.

She nodded, handing him her pistol. He placed the Glock in a gun case and fitted her with a laser pack, then a laser gun. Next, he readied himself, using the same type of gear.

At the moment, the course was prepared for low-light combat. The hangar was dark, not pitch-black, but dim and shadowy. Only that wasn't Olivia's agenda.

Kyle came up behind her, placing a blindfold around her eyes.

"How long will I have this time?" she asked.

"Thirty minutes."

She nodded. Soon Kyle would become her target. The man she had to locate, the human predator she had to kill. They'd been working on this exercise for months, but she'd yet to catch him.

"On the thirty-first minute, you're fair game," he said.

"I know." He would be able to see her, she thought. He would have the advantage. But that was her choice, her challenge, the reason this drill mattered so much.

He leaned into her again, adjusting the blindfold, making sure it was secure. "Is that good?"

"Yes."

"How good?" he asked.

Confused, she frowned. "What?"

"Is it as good as when he touches you?"

She shook her head. She didn't need this testoster-one crap. She knew Kyle was talking about West. "Don't be an idiot."

"I'll bet you can see him in your mind right now, Liv. I'll bet you can feel him rubbing against you."

"Not a chance," she said, but her denial came too soon.

There was no time to think, to stop it from happen-ing. Within a heartbeat, within one breathless moment, an erotic image flowed through her blood, sending chills along her spine.

The vision seemed so real, so lifelike, forcing her to react. She moistened her lips. Warm, wet, much too eager.

West was going to kiss her.

She could see him, tall and tan, his obscure eyes a silvery shade of gray. She reached out to touch him, to feel the texture of his clothes. He moved closer, and her knees went weak. She could smell his cologne.

Beneath the blindfold, she rebelled, battling her de-sire, trying to will it away. But she couldn't. The en-chantment was there, deep inside her, like a—

"Now!" A pair of strong hands shoved her, and she went sprawling, falling to the ground, losing her weapon in the process.

She snapped out of the vision, cursing herself for fall-ing for Kyle's scheme, for letting him trick her. She could hear him running through the building, his foot-steps echoing, then disappearing into a maze of silence.

Her thirty minutes had begun.

She took a deep breath and focused on her missing gun, on the laser pistol that had skidded across the concrete floor.

There, she thought, using her ability to retrieve lost objects. To the right.

Olivia stretched her arm, found it, smiled like a siren. She was going to blow Kyle Prescott to smithereens.

She moved forward, zeroing in on the energy around her. Pickle barrels, shelves with canned goods, a pallet of paper products.

Confident, she continued on the same path, then nearly lost her footing on a rock that got caught under her shoe. The terrain had changed.

Dirt, boulders, instant sounds from the night. Crickets chirping, owls hooting. Her nostrils flared. Trees. Tall, realistic props, scented with evergreen.

Olivia put her hand out, making sure there was nothing in front of her, nothing blocking her way.

Then something growled, and she nearly jumped out of her skin. She turned, took aim, fired the laser gun.

An alarm sounded her victory. She'd hit one of the booby traps.

Elation streamed through her body like mist from a waterfall. She felt giddy, warm.

Sexual.

No, she told herself, as the forest turned quiet. She needed to stay on guard. No more hot-blooded visions, no more wax-melting moments.

She kept walking, sensing the terrain, the vines clinging to breakaway walls. She needed to zero in on Kyle's pulse. She needed to find him.

But she didn't. She tripped, nearly fell, realized she'd almost stumbled into a pond. Frustrated, she cursed beneath her breath. She should have been aware of the water.

Time passed. Too much time. She could feel it ticking, leaving her vulnerable to an attack.

She stopped, knowing she had to take to the shadows, to keep Kyle from seeing her. But where were the shadows, damn it? Where was the darkest point, the area that would shield her?

Something flew over her head. A booby-trapped bird, an electronic device tracking her location. She turned, fired, missed it.

And then she sensed him. Her enemy. The man she was supposed to shoot. He was watching her.

The way the killer had watched Denise Red Bow.

In the next instant an alarm sounded, shrieking in her ears. Too late. He'd shot her instead.

Just like that. Olivia was dead.

The police station was in its usual glory. Or gory, Olivia thought. She'd stayed away for a week. She had another life, after all. A day job, so to speak. She had a list of prominent clients who consulted her for private readings.

She glanced at the desk sergeant. He was ogling her,

checking out her leather skirt and thigh-high hose. Her legs were a mile long, a fact that made the micromini look even shorter.

The station was bustling with activity, with sights and sounds and smells that made her wrinkle her nose. A prostitute pushed past her, a big-busted woman drenched in cheap perfume and carting around a rear end the size of Texas.

The desk sergeant had been ogling her, too.

Cops were a strange breed. Almost as strange as FBI, she decided. Special Agent West had requested her presence today. And not only that, but he'd wangled an office, taking over the digs of a vacationing lieutenant.

She proceeded to the designated location and found the door open. West sat behind the pressed-wood desk, poring over a stack of paperwork, the monitor on his laptop casting a bright glow. She suspected he had accommodations available at the FBI field office, too.

He looked up. "Hey, gorgeous."

Olivia stalled. What had gotten into him?

"Don't panic. He's talking to me." Detective Riggs approached the doorway. "Aren't you, West?"

"Yep." He smiled at the blonde, then scratched his head, giving Olivia's outfit a curious study. Riggs scooted by, carrying another mound of paperwork.

Olivia entered the room, her stiletto heels sounding on the linoleum. "You two got awfully chummy."

The female detective shrugged. "I'm chummy with everybody."

"Maybe you ought to try it," West told Olivia, looking like the lord of the lieutenant's manor.

And maybe he should go jump in the lake, she thought. "Why did you ask me to come here?"

He ran his gaze up and down, cruising the length of her body, settling on her itty-bitty skirt. "For a ménage," he said, without the slightest bit of humor.

She raised her eyebrows. She knew he was trying to get her goat. "With who? Me and you and Muncy?"

Riggs laughed at that. She was in her Cagney mode, behaving like the TV character. Tough yet feminine, with chin-length hair and strong-boned features. "Muncy's wife might have something to say about that."

Olivia wasn't in the mood to laugh. She was still smarting over getting annihilated by Kyle last week. She didn't need to get taken down by West, too.

He came around the front of his borrowed desk and sat on the edge of it. Then he gestured to a chair, indicating for her to sit. She did, but not without crossing her legs and flashing the hooks on her garter belt, giving him a screw-you peep show.

He didn't miss a beat. He saw it all, even angling his head to get a better look.

Riggs took the other chair. She wore a simple blouse, pleated slacks and sensible shoes. "Just for the record," she said, scolding West in a malice-free voice, "I'm not the threesome type."

Olivia's tone wasn't nearly as forgiving. "Me, neither."

"Really?" He gave her a pointed look. "And here I thought you liked all that kinky stuff."

"Excuse me?"

"I found out how you conned your way into my motel room, Ms. Whirlwind."

She uncrossed her legs, let him take a second look, then recrossed them, thinking how predictable men were. He couldn't seem to get enough. "I did what I had to do. And cut the Ms. Whirlwind crap."

Riggs scooted to the end of her chair. Intrigued, it seemed, by their conversation. Then she leaned into Olivia and whispered in her ear. "He's kind of sexy, don't you think?"

Olivia almost laughed. West was frowning now. Apparently he didn't appreciate being the object of feminine scrutiny. "I haven't decided," she whispered back.

Riggs cupped her hand like a first-grader, making their secret even more obvious. "You should give him a chance. He's a pretty good flirt, once he takes that stick out of his ass."

"Would you sleep with him?" Olivia asked, still whispering.

Riggs turned, looked at West and sized him up. "Probably not," she said, loud enough for him to hear. "Would you?"

Yes, Olivia thought, as the memory of her vision washed over her. "No." Her voice was just as loud. "Not a chance."

"Okay, ladies," West interrupted with a scowl. He resumed the seat behind his desk, putting a barrier between them. "That's enough. You got me back."

"For what?" Olivia asked innocently.

"Yes, for what?" Riggs parroted, mimicking his accent, the Southern drawl that slowed down his words. "That little ol' ménage thing?"

His face nearly flushed. Olivia wanted to shoot Riggs a high-five. The lady cop certainly knew how to put a man in his place.

"What'd I miss?" Detective Muncy shuffled through the door, with a cup of burnt-smelling coffee and bed-head hair, even in the middle of the afternoon. His clothes, as usual, were wrinkled.

"Nothing," West said. "You didn't miss a thing."

Olivia and Riggs exchanged a glance, then remained, quite demure, in their chairs, waiting for the meeting to begin.

West took charge, removing a small stack of pictures from an envelope on his desk. "These were provided by Denise Red Bow's husband. I want Ms. Whirlwind—" he paused to correct her name "—Olivia, to look at them and tell me what she sees."

She accepted the photographs. She wasn't sure where West was going with this, so she studied them carefully. Denise in a long, silky wedding gown, Denise making a funny face at the camera, Denise at an Indian gathering, eating fry bread. "I see a beautiful young woman who shouldn't have died."

"Me, too. But there's more to it than that. Something

I can't put my finger on." He reached for the wedding photo. "She looks truly happy here. The others almost seem like a forgery."

Olivia glanced up at him. "Why?"

"I don't know. It's a gut a feeling, I guess. My ESP, if you will."

She merely nodded. Most investigators had strong instincts. But that didn't mean he was right. Or that he had powers beyond the norm.

Except for those eyes, she thought, as she searched his gaze. They were almost devoid of color today. Like clear quartz crystals from the earth.

"Does Denise remind you of someone in those pictures?" Muncy asked West.

The special agent shrugged. "Lots of people smile when they're troubled. Lots of people fake it."

Olivia glanced at the remaining photographs in her lap. She could feel West's energy, his displacement, the electrical charge swirling around him. "She reminds you of your ex-wife," she said. "That's the forgery you were talking about."

He gave her an annoyed look. "This isn't about me."

Olivia didn't back down. "Your ex was unhappy. Discontent. You spent more time on the job than you did at home, and she couldn't handle that."

West didn't respond, but he didn't have to. The scene was already set.

Muncy tapped the fry-bread picture of Denise. "She was married to a surgeon."

"And she probably felt neglected," Riggs put in. "Her hubby worked some rigorous hours."

"She didn't cheat," Olivia said, studying the dead woman's image. "She didn't have a lover."

"You sure about that?" West asked.

"Yes. But…" A sudden sadness ripped through her body. Denise's loneliness. The nights she dreamed about romance and flowers and a man whose touch would make her feel special. "She wanted to. She fantasized about having an affair."

West sat back in his chair, grabbed his bottled water and took a swig. Apparently Denise's fantasies had left a bad taste in his mouth. "The killer knew that. The son of a bitch knew."

Olivia agreed. "I think so, too." But she wasn't surprised. The Slasher's supernatural abilities were part of his MO, part of what drove him.

"I could use a drink," West said suddenly, discarding his water. "Something stronger than this."

Because he was still dwelling on his ex, Olivia thought.

"Sounds good to me." Muncy frowned at his over-brewed coffee. "Why don't we all meet at the Mockingbird later? After this long-ass day ends."

"I'm game." Riggs looked at Olivia. "How about you?"

She knew the Mockingbird was a cop-patronized bar downtown. And she knew Special Agent West was going to get tanked. Damn-the-consequences drunk. "Sure," she said, glancing in his direction. "I wouldn't miss it for the world."

* * *

At 6:00 p.m., Olivia had dinner. Nothing fancy, just a routine meal with her sister and Glenn Sabolich, a family friend who'd been part of their lives since they were children.

The trio met regularly at Mel's Diner, a legendary restaurant brimming with fifties nostalgia. This evening they ate on the patio, where a view of the Sunset Strip presented the glitz and glamour associated with West Hollywood.

Glenn munched casually on a Famous Melburger, his grayish blond hair blowing lightly in the breeze. He was more than a family friend, Olivia thought. He was also their landlord, the real estate mogul who owned the loft in which she and Allie lived. But Glenn had owned the rental house where they'd grown up, too.

At fifty-four, he was the same age as their dad. Or the same age Joseph would have been if he hadn't pulled the trigger.

Glenn and their father had been close, and when Joseph committed suicide, he'd helped Olivia and Allie pick up the chipped pieces of their lives. She was never sure what Glenn had thought of their mother, although he'd never said anything unkind about her.

He looked up and caught Olivia watching him. "What's wrong?" he asked.

"Nothing," she responded, wondering why he'd never remarried. Glenn's socialite wife had filed for a divorce ages ago, about six months before Olivia's mom had ditched her dad.

Allie finally decided to join the conversation. Until now she'd been people watching, gazing at the trendy pedestrians walking by. "We should tell Glenn about the *wanagi*."

"A ghost?" He recognized the Lakota word.

Olivia sighed. Allie was obsessed with the *wanagi*. "It made contact with me, but Allie thinks it's Dad."

Glenn's voice cracked. "That's not good. Your father deserves to have some peace. He…"

As his words faded into the atmosphere, his emotions knifed Olivia's heart. Shame. Remorse. A horrible secret. Stunned, she shifted in her chair, studying the man she'd always trusted.

Glenn was hiding something. Something he'd been hiding for years.

Allie reached for her tea, adding honey to the warm brew. "I've been leaving those little candy hearts out for Dad. Just in case he wants to communicate with us."

Olivia tilted her head. Suddenly everyone seemed mad. Not only did Allie expect the *wanagi* to eat the candy, she expected it to make sentences out of things like, Hey Babe, Get Real, Go Girl and Don't Tell.

Don't tell.

Olivia looked at Glenn, saw him struggle to finish his burger.

Dinner went downhill from there. Glenn remained

uncomfortable, barely speaking. Allie resumed people watching, her mind probably drifting on a cloud.

And Olivia? She checked her watch, anxious to leave, to have a drink with the detectives and the FBI agent investigating a trio of grisly murders.

Thirty minutes later she arrived at the Mockingbird, still wearing her minuscule skirt and the lacy garter belt she'd flashed at West. She'd added a biker jacket to the ensemble, warding off a self-induced chill.

What if Glenn had done something to intensify her father's pain? What if he had been part of her dad's despair? A link in his suicide?

It was a cruel thought, but it kept running through her brain, slinking and sliding like a poisonous snake.

Clearing her mind, she entered the bar. The Mockingbird was a down-to-earth watering hole, with a jukebox in front and a billiard table in back. The owner, a no-nonsense Irishman, didn't take any guff from his law-enforcement patrons.

Olivia found Muncy and Riggs seated at a scratched and scuffed table, drinking beer and eating peanuts. They looked up, greeting her in unison.

"Where's West?" she asked.

Muncy gestured with his thumb. "In the head."

She glanced in the direction of the men's room and took the chair across from Riggs.

"That's where West is sitting," the female detective said. "That's his drink in front of you."

"Oh." Olivia smiled at the other woman, picked up the glass and tasted the contents. "Strong stuff."

Riggs laughed. "You left a lipstick mark."

Olivia ran her tongue across her teeth. She wasn't used to bourbon. "It'll probably turn him on."

"Who? West?" Muncy made a curious expression. "I knew something was going on earlier. I knew I missed something."

Olivia took another sip of the special agent's drink, and he came out of the bathroom, catching sight of her hording his spot and his alcohol.

He approached the table. "What are you doing? Warming my seat?"

"Nope, it's my seat now. And your fly is open."

He bent his head to check his zipper, and Olivia winked at Riggs. His fly wasn't open, but she'd made him look.

"Funny girl." He snatched away his drink, studied the lipstick mark, then put his mouth directly over it and downed the rest of his bourbon.

Olivia felt as if she'd just been kissed. Or kicked. Or both. West never failed to leave her sexed up and irritated.

He grabbed an empty chair from a nearby table and placed it next to her, too close for comfort.

Muncy ate another handful of peanuts, but he was watching her and West, analyzing their body language.

"I picked this song," the special agent said.

Olivia listened to the lyrics playing on the jukebox. "You shot the sheriff?"

"No. The guy singing did." He rubbed the lipstick

mark with his thumb, smearing it. "Eric Clapton. Am I still on your shit list, Ms. Whirlwind? Olivia?"

"Yep."

"Mine, too," Riggs put in.

"You hit on both of them?" Muncy shook his head, chuckling beneath his breath. "Federal Bureau of Insanity."

West defended himself. "It was a joke." He signaled the cocktail waitress for another drink, and she arrived instantly. "Give us both one of these." He held up his empty glass and gestured to Olivia. "But make hers a double."

"I'll take a cola," she said, declining the bourbon. Alcohol diminished her ability, and now she wanted to remain on guard. West's eyes were on the verge of glowing, catching a flicker of candlelight.

Riggs scooted closer to the table. She still wore her sensible outfit, and her hair was still neatly styled. "I lost interest in him."

"I was never interested," Olivia said.

The lady cop merely smiled. She knew Olivia was lying. Everyone probably knew. Including West.

"I wanted him right away." Muncy joined in, making the girls laugh.

West rolled his candlelit eyes, then shot the jovial detective the bird.

Olivia decided they were an interesting group. A foursome. Not a threesome, she thought. No ménage.

Her soda arrived, along with West's hard liquor. She sipped. He guzzled.

"Still thinking about your ex?" she asked.

"Don't start. I'm sick of women."

"He's drunk." Riggs clucked her tongue. "Someone is going to have to pour him into bed tonight."

Olivia turned to look at the intoxicated agent. "I knew he was going to get wasted."

He made a disgusted sound. "'Cause you know everything."

She didn't respond. His psychic envy was showing. But he probably thought she had penis envy. Most macho men did. "I'll drive him back to his motel."

"Lucky me. What if I puke all over your Porsche?"

"You wouldn't dare."

He lowered his gaze to her throat, and she sensed that he wanted to touch her scar.

And then she got another eerie feeling.

Someone was watching them. Not someone in the bar. But someone with powers that rivaled Olivia's. Someone who could see them in his mind.

The Slasher, she thought, as her veins turned to ice.

The man prowling the city for another victim.

Chapter 4

West didn't puke in her Porsche, but he didn't say anything to her, either. The drive to his motel was steeped in silence. She hadn't told him about the Slasher watching them. But the empathic vibration hadn't lasted more than a second, making her wonder if it had been real.

Olivia's gift wasn't infallible. Sometimes fear got in the way, an emotion she did her damnedest to control.

She parked in front of West's room and killed the engine. His rental car was still at the bar.

Finally he turned to look at her. She could feel his heart thumping in his chest. The way she'd felt her dad's pulse on the night he'd died.

Strong and steady. Edgy. No imaginary trick.

"Do you want to come in?" he asked.

"What for?"

"So I can apologize."

She almost smiled. Now he'd intrigued her. "Sure. Why not?"

He didn't weave on the way to the door, but he fumbled for his key, cursing when he couldn't find it in his pocket.

"I still have mine." She opened her purse. "Good thing I kept it."

"Oh, yeah. Good thing." He leaned against the stucco wall and watched her. "I should have made them change the lock."

She opened the door. "But you didn't."

"No, I didn't." He reached across and flipped the switch, where the lamp flickered, illuminating the room like a strobe light.

She placed her purse on the dinette table in the corner and draped her jacket over a chair. Her silver-studded accessories looked sorely out of place in the simple surroundings.

Following her lead, he removed his sport coat. But he hung it in the closet. Neat and tidy, she thought. Even when he was drunk.

She glanced at the bed, then sat in one of the straight-back chairs. "Feel free to apologize anytime."

West grabbed the chair with her jacket, turned it around and straddled it. His face was shadowed in harsh lines and angles, making him look sensually surreal. "How'd you get that scar?"

"That's my apology?"

"I'm sorry for being an ass. Now, how'd you get that scar?"

She touched her own throat, using the tip of her finger like a blade. "None of your business, and your apology sucked."

He shrugged. "I think I already know. I just haven't figured out the details yet."

"So what?" She met his gaze, looking into those unnerving eyes.

"I'll bet you got that raspy voice from whatever caused your scar. Women with husky voices fascinate me."

"Too bad I prefer men who can hold their liquor."

"But I can." He laughed a little. "Most of the time."

She laughed, too. He had an odd brand of charm.

A moment later they both turned solemn. The misbehaving lamp flickered once again, making her wonder about the Slasher, about how strong his powers were.

"My ability isn't error proof," she said. "Sometimes I make mistakes."

"I didn't think you were perfect. But you were right about my ex-wife. She couldn't handle my job."

Olivia wondered if he would be telling her this if he was sober. "Did she cheat? Did she leave you for someone else?"

He nodded. "It was the worst experience of my life. The most hurtful, I guess. I liked being married. I liked having a woman to come home to." He studied her scar again. "We were together for six years."

"But did you love her, Agent West? Was she as important as your career?"

He pondered the question. He was still straddling the jacket-draped chair, still looking surreal. "I loved her, but my job is my life. It's who I am." He pushed his hair away from his forehead. "Does that make me a bastard?"

No, she thought. It just made him that much more appealing. Olivia's work was her priority, too. "How old are you?" she asked, realizing the simple things about him eluded her.

"Guess," he said. "Figure it out."

"Thirty-six."

"Nope. I'm thirty-five, and you're a lousy psychic."

That made her laugh. In spite of her imperfections, she knew she was good. He knew it, too. "Where are you from?"

He removed his wallet and tossed his ID on the table. "I live in Virginia."

"Of course you do. The National Center for the Analysis of Violent Crime is located there." She took a good look at his license, wondering if he'd meant to reveal his home address, to let it sink into her memory. "That's where you work, where criminal profiling is done. I was asking where you were from. Originally."

"I was born and raised in Oklahoma." He tapped the rail of her chair with his boot. "And for the record, we call it criminal investigative analysis now. Profiling is an outdated term for what we do."

"Fine. Have you analyzed the Slasher?" she asked, knowing the LAPD was trying to get a handle on the killer, too.

"Yes. But I'm going to return to the NCAVC on Monday to consult with my colleagues about it."

"You're a team player."

"We all are. We're supposed to be."

She glanced at his boots. They were the only scuffed part of him. "Do you trust me, West?" Or was he fooling her with his ID?

He blew out a rough breath, wafting the smell of alcohol in her direction. "I don't trust very many people. Seeing the cruelty humans are capable of makes me distance myself from them. But even so, I wouldn't want to do this alone. Looking at grisly pictures day in and day out gets to a man. Or a woman," he added.

"I should go." She still hadn't decided if she trusted him, either. "You need to sleep it off."

"I suppose you're right." He came to his feet. "Are you going to pour me into bed?"

She shook her head, gathering her belongings. "I'm sure you can do that by yourself."

He made a troubled face. "I'm not staying here when I get back from Virginia. This room gets too cold at night."

Her heartbeat pummeled her chest. "You've felt the ghost?"

"I don't know. Maybe."

"Too much death," she said.

"Yeah." He almost touched her scar. Almost, but not quite. His hand lingered, then fell away. "Be careful, Olivia."

"You, too." It seemed like a strange thing to say to a man who'd been analyzing killers for years, who knew what made them tick.

But as she left him standing at the door, battling a state of inebriation, she got the stomach-clenching sensation that Special Agent West was going to die.

Not tonight. But sometime during this investigation.

And she was going to be there when it happened.

The moment Olivia entered the loft, Samantha hissed at her. The living room was dark, but she could see a vague outline of the cat, a small black shape, a glint of green eyes.

She moved farther into the room, then stopped dead in her tracks. She could see another shadowy image in the corner.

Still, lifeless. Slumped over in a chair.

"Allie!" She screamed her sister's name and nearly tripped on the hissing cat when she attempted to turn on the light.

Finally she reached the lamp and illuminated the room. A bundle of blankets lay in the chair.

No body.

No blood.

No Allie.

Olivia tore through the loft like a maniac, going from room to room. Suddenly the place seemed like a maze, with its high ceilings and eclectic furniture. She brushed by a tall, leafy fern, felt it tickle her skin, felt goose bumps attack her arm.

Nothing. No one.

Yet she'd seen Allie's car in the parking structure.

"Where the hell is she?" Not knowing what else to do, Olivia went into the kitchen to check out the candy, to look for a message in the conversation hearts.

Surely, she was losing her mind.

She scanned the counter, reading each colorful piece. The hearts didn't say anything they hadn't said before.

Just as Olivia left the kitchen, the lock on the front door rattled, making an ominous sound. But Samantha didn't fret. She knew who it was. The cat sailed across the room to greet her mistress, nearly flying through the air like a feline on a witch's broom.

Olivia let out the breath she'd been holding. Allie entered the loft, balancing her keys, a small beaded purse and a plastic cup. A half-eaten muffin was stuffed in her mouth.

"You were downstairs," Olivia said.

Allie nodded, grabbed the muffin before it fell. "You look like you saw a ghost." She paused, glanced around. "Is Dad here?"

"No. No one is here." Samantha was purring, twining around Allie's legs. "No one at all."

"I had a craving for a mocha cappuccino." Her sister dropped her purse on a nearby table, discarding her keys with it. "It's decaf, with a shot of raspberry." She knelt to pet the cat. "Are you okay?"

"Who? Me or Samantha?"

"You."

"Not really, no."

Olivia sat on the sofa, and Allie took the chair with the blankets, dropping crumbs from the muffin onto her clothes. She'd combined a baggy sweater, tight jeans and slightly scuffed shoes.

Kind of like West's boots.

"I was with the special agent tonight," Olivia said.

Allie's eyes grew wide. "You slept with him?"

"No. We were just talking. But I've had visions about kissing him. And then this evening I had the horrible feeling that he was going to die."

"Oh, my God. Why? What's going on?"

"I don't know. Earlier I thought the Slasher was watching West and me. Keeping track of us in his mind. But I might be confused."

"West. That's the FBI guy's name?"

Olivia nodded. "Ian West. What if he dies? What if I can't stop it from happening?"

"Dad is trying to protect us. Maybe he'll try to protect West, too." Allie held her coffee, curling her fingers around the cup, clutching it to her chest. "If the killer is watching you, then why haven't you been able to see him?"

"I'm not sure. Maybe he's blocking me. Maybe he's messing with my mind."

"Then we have to stop him."

Olivia rubbed her eyes. Suddenly Allie looked like a moonlit mirage, a nighttime enchantress with her rain-straight hair and glittering jewelry. "We?"

"I can help you locate him."

"How?"

"In a painting."

The idea seemed absurd. Yet it made sense, too. Allie was beginning to believe that she could create magic with her art. And Olivia wasn't about to scoff at the possibility, especially now, when she needed her sister to be strong. "What are you going to paint?"

"His calling card. The heart with the arrowhead."

A shiver raced up Olivia's spine. "No one is supposed to know about that. The police are keeping it under wraps."

"I'm not going to exhibit the painting. It's just for us."

And for the killer, Olivia thought. For the man they were trying to locate. "It's an outline. A black drawing."

"Then I'll paint it like that. Is there something I can use as reference?"

"Yes. But they're crime-scene photos, Allie. Are you sure you can handle that?"

"Do I have a choice?"

"Not if you're determined to go through with this."

"I am," the younger woman said, lifting her chin. Beside her, Samantha meowed, supporting her mistress.

"Then I'll call Agent West in the morning. Maybe he'll agree to bring the pictures here."

And maybe, just maybe, Olivia would be able to see the Slasher in her mind.

As daylight filtered through the sheers in her room, Olivia reached for the portable phone. She sat on the bed, fighting a chill in the air. She sensed it was going to rain. The Chiricahua used to say that rain would come if a horned toad or a snake was killed and placed on its back, but Olivia didn't want to think about dead animals.

She grabbed the phonebook and looked up the number of West's motel, then asked to be connected to his room.

He answered on the third ring. "Hello?"

"I wasn't sure if you'd be awake," she said.

"I just made a pot of coffee. I feel like crap." He paused. "Why are you calling me?"

She wasn't surprised that he recognized her voice. Supposedly he liked the raspy tone. "I need a favor." She explained the situation, telling him about Allie, about her sister's idea to track the killer.

"That's weird," he said.

Olivia rolled her eyes. She could hear him pouring his coffee. "And the evidence in this case is normal? When's the last time a footprint disappeared from a cast? Or hair samples changed color? Or went from human to animal?"

"Fine. But you could have asked Muncy or Riggs for this favor."

"The killer isn't watching them. But he might be watching you and me."

Something clanked. A plastic spoon. His cup on the counter. A sound she couldn't quite define.

"Since when?" he asked.

"Since last night. But I'm not sure about this." Nor did she intend to mention that she'd sensed his death. At least not over the phone. She felt responsible for him, and that didn't sit well. She had enough to worry about. "So are you going to bring over the crime-scene photos or not?"

"I shouldn't be doing this. I shouldn't be involving your sister." He blew a frustrated breath into the receiver. "This is a hell of a favor."

Which meant he was coming. "Are you going to take a cab to the Mockingbird to get your car?"

"Yes. Then I'll pick up the pictures."

"Do you need my address?"

"No. I already know where you live. I'll be there in about an hour."

She hung up, wondering what else he knew about her.

Deciding it didn't matter, she got dressed, zipping into a pair of old jeans and a tight black top. She wet her hair and ran a glob of gel through it, giving the layered strands its usual choppy style.

Because Olivia always wore makeup, she smudged her eyes with a smoky black liner and applied a deep-red lipstick. In the mirror she saw a haunting resemblance to her mother. But that wasn't something she could change.

A moment later rain blasted the window, like a sign

from her mother's people. To the Chiricahua, a dark, heavy rain was male. Of course, Yvonne Whirlwind used to love the hard, driving force of a masculine rain.

By the time a knock sounded on the door, Olivia was more than ready to get this show on the road. Allie wasn't, though. Her sister was still in the shower.

Olivia answered the summons. As usual, West wore a dark suit. His hair, soaked from the rain, was combed away from his face.

She gestured for him to come in. He gave her one of those sinful looks and entered the loft. Apparently he noticed that she wasn't wearing a bra.

Samantha came slinking around the corner, and Olivia waited for her to hiss. Instead she crept up to West and rubbed her face against the top of his boot.

"Cute cat," he said, releasing his briefcase and scooping up the finicky stray.

"She belongs to my sister. And she's never that friendly."

"Really?" He stroked the feline's slick black fur. "Maybe she's in heat."

"She's fixed. And is that the only time females like you? When they're in heat?"

He released Samantha, then snared Olivia's gaze. "You ought to know."

She contemplated kneeing him in the groin, just to remind him that she'd done it once before. Just to remind him that she was good at it.

He broke eye contact. "Interesting place."

"We like it." She pointed to the sofa. "Why don't you have a seat and wait for Allie? She should be ready soon."

"Sure." He grabbed his briefcase and sank onto the couch.

While he studied the embroidered pillow next to him, giving it a guy-type examination, Olivia sat in a rocking chair she and Allie rarely used.

"Did you bring all of the pictures?" she asked.

He shook his head. "Just the ones with the symbol. Some of them are graphic, though. Bloody. Your sister won't get queasy, will she?"

"I don't know. Speaking of queasy. How's your hangover?"

"I'll survive."

Olivia glanced at his briefcase, where she assumed the photos were. She'd seen them, of course. But knowing Allie was going to view them made her edgy.

Finally her sister entered the room, wearing a gauze dress and a floral-printed scarf tied around her waist. West came to his feet and introduced himself. Allie shook his hand.

"You look like an FBI agent," she said.

"And you look like an artist."

They exchanged respectful smiles, and Olivia marveled at how easily West had morphed into a gentleman.

Federal Bureau of Ingenuity, she thought.

He didn't waste any time. "Ready?" he asked Allie.

She agreed and sat next to him. Much to her credit, Allie looked at the pictures without blanching. West explained who was who, speaking gently about the victims, pointing out the symbol that had been drawn onto each woman's abdomen on the right side, like a bikini-line tattoo.

"He didn't remove their clothes," Allie said.

"No. He just moved them out of his way to draw the symbol."

"I should paint those portions of their bodies, just like they are here."

Blood splatters and all, Olivia thought, wishing she could protect her sister from this.

"I can do it on one canvas," Allie said. "Close up, in three sections. Then I'll use a marker for the heart and the arrowhead. Like he did."

The special agent merely nodded, handing Allie the photos she needed to complete her project, to help Olivia see the killer.

After Allie disappeared into her studio, Olivia offered to fix West breakfast, to keep busy while they waited.

He sat at the glass-topped table in the kitchen, and she removed a frying pan from the counter beside the stove.

"What are you going to fix?" he asked.

"The Hangover Five-Alarm." She turned to see him watching her. "It's on the menu at Mel's Diner."

"That *American Graffiti* place?"

"Yep. Be ready for a chili cheese omelet."

He gave her a curious study. "Are you sure that's a hangover cure?"

"I'm going to add lots of hot sauce. It works like a

charm." And if it didn't, then she would ply him with antacids and hope for the best.

Twenty minutes later they ate the spicy concoction with buttered toast and orange juice. Afterward, they lingered at the table, with two cases of dragon breath. His stomach had handled the food just fine.

They waited for what seemed like forever. Rain pounded on the roof of the building, echoing through the loft.

And then Allie emerged with her painting. It didn't look like a murder scene; at least, not to the naked eye. The artwork was divided into three rectangular shapes, the victim's abdomens blown up to enhance the detail, creating abstract designs. But even so, Olivia recognized their skewed, bloodstained clothes, the arrowheads and hearts drawn onto their skin.

Allie hung the canvas on the wall, taking down another picture and putting this one in its place. Everyone fell silent.

Olivia wondered if they expected her to snap right into a vision, to see the killer's face or to get an image of him slashing his victims.

"This might take some time," she said.

Allie and West didn't respond.

Talk about pressure, she thought.

Finally Allie spoke up. "I'll clean the kitchen." She looked at West. "And you can help."

He rose from his chair. "Aren't you going to eat first?"

She shook her head. "I'll have a grapefruit later."

Olivia breathed a sigh of relief. While her sister and the FBI agent cleared the table, she gazed at the painting, trying to get a reading on the killer, trying to feel his emotions.

But nothing happened.

Nothing but Allie and West talking among themselves, trying to behave as casually as possible. Then West made a remark about the Valentine candies dotting the counters.

"I assume those are for the ghost," he said. "My grandfather taught me not to eat food that had been left overnight because ghosts might partake of it."

Allie perked up and began telling him about their dad, about how she thought he was trying to protect them. And then she blurted out that Olivia was worried that West might die.

He spun around to challenge the guilty party. "You're trying to kill me off?"

Olivia walked away from the painting. "It was a feeling I had. I couldn't help it."

"She had visions about kissing you, too," Allie said.

"Really?" Now West had the gall to grin. "That was before I died, right?" He paused to roam his gaze over Olivia's body, taking in every curve. "Somehow I don't see you as the postmortem type."

She wanted to strangle him, right after she strangled her sister. "Go ahead and laugh it off. But when you're six feet under, I'll have the last laugh."

He pinned her in place with those strange gray eyes. "You wish."

Peeking around his shoulder, Allie made a face. She looked like a kid who'd gotten caught with someone else's lunch money. "I think I'll have that grapefruit now," she said.

West remained where he was, a bit too macho for his own good, squaring off with Olivia. Sooner or later they would end up in bed. She knew her vision wasn't a lie. He seemed to know it, too. And it humored the hell out of him.

Too bad he didn't take the possibility of dying more seriously. That he considered it a joke, as well.

Ignoring him, Olivia turned away and focused on the painting instead, on the symbol the killer had drawn onto his victims.

Allie came over to her, still holding the knife she'd used to slice her grapefruit. "I'm sorry, Olivia," she whispered. "I didn't mean to—"

The rest of her sister's apology never reached her ears. The only thing she could hear was the rain, water pounding from the sky.

And then a horrifying image crashed into her mind.

But it wasn't the killer.

It was another victim. A lady with long black hair, a motionless woman positioned on an antique bed. Part of her body was draped with a white sheet, streaks of blood staining the material. On her abdomen she wore the signature of the Slasher.

His calling card. The heart. The arrowhead.

Olivia slid to floor, clutching her knees to her chest, fighting a bout of dizziness.

Allie knelt beside her. "What's wrong? What did you see?"

Olivia looked into her sister's soft, brown eyes, then glanced up at West, who towered over them like a tall, dark shadow. "The Slasher killed her," she said. "He killed our mom."

Chapter 5

Ian dropped to his knees, assessing the situation. Working with psychics was never easy, but this case was getting more complicated by the minute.

Olivia still sat on the floor, clutching her knees to her chest. Her sister remained beside her, just as stunned, just as emotional.

He searched Olivia's gaze. "I need to know exactly what you saw."

"She saw our mom," Allie said, tears flooding her eyes.

"I know. I'm sorry." He removed the knife from Allie's hands, nearly prying it from her fingers. "But I need details." He needed to know if Olivia's subconscious had conjured her mother's murder or if the woman was really dead.

He removed a small spiral notebook from his jacket. "Tell me, Olivia."

While she recited the details, he took notes, staying close to her and Allie, trying not to break the connection.

When she finished talking, he closed his notebook. He wasn't through taking notes, not by a long shot, but he didn't intend to conduct the rest of this investigation on the floor.

"Let's go to the other room." He reached for Allie's hand, helping her to her feet. Olivia refused his aid, managing on her own.

As tough as nails, he thought. As beguiling as a winter rose. The scar across her throat made her seem vulnerable. But he knew better. Olivia Whirlwind wasn't a damsel in distress.

They moved into the living room, where rain slashed against the windows. Allie lit several candles, then curled up on the couch. Olivia sat next to her, lending her support.

Ian remained silent, allowing them time to absorb the shock. The picture Allie had painted was still in the kitchen, still haunting the walls. But even so, he doubted either sister would destroy it.

Were all the women in their family steeped in magic? In danger? In death?

"What happens now?" Allie asked, directing her question to him, looking for hope, for answers he might not have. "Where do we go from here?"

"I'll investigate your mother's whereabouts," he told

her, knowing this was going to be tricky. "I'll consult the detectives on the Slasher case. But without a body, there's not much we can do." He turned to Olivia. "You know how this works."

She merely nodded. Apparently she'd been involved in police work long enough not to argue, not to fight him on an issue they couldn't change. Psychic evidence wasn't admissible in court.

"Will you tell me about your mom?" he asked.

"What do you want to know?"

"How about her name?"

"Yvonne Catherine Whirlwind."

"And her maiden name?"

"Nanchez."

"How long has it been since you've seen her?"

"Twelve years. I was seventeen when she walked away, when she left my father for another man."

He reached for his notebook. "That's what I figured. If she were still part of your life, you would have dialed 911, gone straight to her house, done what frantic people do."

Olivia lifted her chin. "I did that for my father."

"But it's too late for your mother?"

"It was too late for my father, as well."

And now I'm sleeping in his motel room, Ian thought. Getting cold at night, imagining his restless spirit.

"I didn't wish this upon her," Olivia said. "And neither did Allie. Our mother hurt us, but we didn't want her to die."

Contemplating her words, he stopped writing. He'd spent a week poring over police reports, autopsies, lab results, maps, sketches and photographs. He'd reconstructed the crimes, studied the victims, done his damnedest to analyze the killer. And all along, this case was connected to the psychic, to her family.

"What did that vision tell you?" he asked. "When did Yvonne die? Was she the Slasher's first victim? Was she his last?"

"I don't know." She glanced out the window as if she were trying to see beyond the sheet of rain. "I'm not sure."

When she turned back, their gazes locked. An unholy alliance, he thought. He was already in too deep, already wrapped up in a game Olivia Whirlwind had started.

She looked dangerously erotic with her sultry-shaped eyes and bad-girl clothes. She was toying with him, even now, in the height of her crisis.

Ian moistened his lips, fighting a sudden thirst. He was toying with her, too. Not about this case. But about the energy that bled them both dry.

He was lusting after a woman who'd accused him of being a witch, who drove him half-mad and claimed he was going to die. Things couldn't get much worse.

"Tell me about this man Yvonne ran off with," he said. "Who he is? How long had she been involved with him?"

Olivia sighed. "We don't know anything about him, not even his name. We never saw him. We didn't even know that she was having an affair, not until she packed her bags and disappeared."

"Did she leave a note?"

"Yes."

"Do you still have it?"

She shook her head. "Dad destroyed it."

Ian frowned. He'd considered destroying everything connected to his ex-wife, too. But in the end, he'd stopped himself from going that route, from making his marriage that important. He'd spent enough time nursing his bruised ego, imagining the woman he married in bed with another guy. "Is she the reason your dad pulled the trigger?"

"She's the reason his life fell apart."

Olivia rose from the couch, crossing her arms, hugging herself. Lonesome comfort, he thought. She was hurting more than she was willing to admit.

He glanced at Allie. She was blinking back tears, trying to come to terms with all of this. But she wasn't as delicate as she seemed. The little sister had inner strength. Somewhere deep down, she and Olivia were cut from the same cloth.

"Do you have any pictures of your mother?" he asked, waiting to see who would respond. "Or did your dad destroy them?"

Allie spoke up first. "We managed to salvage one. I'll get it for you."

After she left the room, he shifted his gaze to Olivia. The rain-drenched window framed her in a cloudy light, creating the perfect ambience for a psychic.

"Are you still going back to Virginia tomorrow?" she asked, reminding him that he was leaving on Monday.

"Yes, but I'll only be gone a few days. Muncy and Riggs can follow up on this until I get back." He lifted his eyebrows. "Why? Are you going to miss me?"

She ran her hands through her hair, spiking the choppy layers, creating sexy havoc around her face. "Not as much as you're going to miss me."

No doubt, he thought. Olivia Whirlwind was getting under his skin.

Suddenly the corners of her lips tilted. Just a little, just enough to suggest that she could read minds. And then she decided to check on her sister, making him wonder if they'd buried Yvonne's picture in a trunk somewhere.

Like a body that was about to be exhumed.

Olivia found Allie in her studio, staring at one of the crime-scene photos. The younger woman looked up and made a troubled face. "I got paint on this."

"It doesn't matter. I'm sure West brought you his copies. He's probably taking them back to Virginia with him."

"He's leaving?"

"Just for a few days." Olivia moved closer. The paint Allie had speckled on the photograph was red. Like a drop of blood. "Maybe he won't notice." Then again, West didn't miss much. "Did you get Mom's picture?"

"I put it under here." Allie lifted the stack of crime-scene photos. "I can't believe she's dead."

"I know." She wondered if it was significant that

Allie had buried their mother's image. Of course, it had been buried before, stuffed in a box with old keepsake items they never looked at, never touched. "We can't rely on Dad to keep us safe. You know that, don't you?"

Her sister picked at the paint, chipping the deep-crimson color. "Why? Because he couldn't protect Mom? He must have known Mom was dead, and that's what he's been trying to tell us." She stopped picking. "Do you think they're together now?"

It sounded romantic, comforting. But Olivia didn't envision her estranged parents spending eternity together. "We should bring West those pictures."

"Do you think he's going to ask us more questions about Mom?"

"He might not press us for more information today, but eventually he will. It's part of his job."

"What are we supposed to say if he asks us about her personality?" Allie smoothed her dress. It flowed to her ankles, making her look long and lean and mystical. "That she was a bitch half the time?"

Olivia bit back a smile. Her sister never failed to blurt out whatever she was thinking. "We have to tell him the truth. And like you said, she was only a bitch *half* the time. We have some good memories of her, too."

"You're right. West will understand how complicated Mom was. He probably has a sociology degree or something." She paused, then chewed her bottom lip, peeling off the pale pink gloss she wore. "Are you going to sleep with him?"

An honest question, Olivia thought, that deserved an honest answer. "I will if he makes the first move."

Her sister seemed surprised. "That's never stopped you before. You always go after what you want."

"If I come on to him, he'll act superior. He'll have the advantage. He already annoys me."

Allie found the strength to grin, to fall into the humor of the moment, the girl talk that made being female fun. "And Kyle didn't? He's big and dumb. What could be more annoying than that?"

"I like 'em big." Olivia grinned, too. "And all men are dumb."

"West isn't. He knows you want to bang his brains out."

"Gee, thanks." Kyle wasn't dumb, either. He was just shallow. He thought the world revolved around the size of his penis.

Allie sighed. "If Dad can't help us, then I'm going to paint an angel. The most gorgeous warrior that ever existed. Tall and rugged with dark wings."

"Sure. Why not?" She knew she couldn't stop her little sister from expressing her emotions in her art. "Maybe he'll come to life and sweep you off your feet."

"Or bang my brains out," Allie said, making them both laugh.

By the time they returned to the living room, their mood was no longer light. West stood at the window, taking the spot Olivia had abandoned. He looked deep in thought, watching the rain, listening to it pummel the earth.

When he turned around to face her and Allie, his

eyes had taken on that metallic glow. Olivia heard her sister suck in a breath. He was rather breathtaking.

For a special agent with too much attitude.

He came forward to take the pictures out of Allie's hands. He flipped through them, noticed the speck of paint, arched an eyebrow and continued until he came to Yvonne. Her image stopped him cold.

Olivia glanced at the photograph, all too aware of the slant of her mother's cheekbones, the fullness of her lips, the pantherlike prowl in her eyes. She could tell that West was mesmerized. But most men were. Yvonne's effect on the opposite sex coursed through their veins. "She was a dancer when she was young."

"How old was she here?" he wanted to know.

"Forty. It was taken the same year she left."

"So she would be fifty-two now. Around the same age as the killer."

That got Allie's attention. "You've figured out how old he is?"

The killer's age jarred Olivia, too. The LAPD had been working on a profile for months, but the witchcraft elements were making an accurate analysis difficult. She wondered if West had found a way to get past that or if his eyes were as powerful as they seemed, if he could see into the minds of madmen.

She searched his gaze, looking for the answer. "Tell us about him. Tell us what we're dealing with."

"Yes, please." Allie spoke up quickly, just as anxious.

He agreed, and they resumed their seats. Except this

time Olivia took the bentwood rocker. It had been her mother's chair, the place where she had lulled her daughters to sleep.

"In my estimation, the perpetrator is Native American, divorced and lives alone," West said. "He's around five-ten, slim, slightly built. Attractive, dresses well. He appears to be a narcissist, someone driven by self-obsession."

Olivia tried to get a mental image of the killer, but all she could see was the motionless body of her mother, the tattoolike symbol on her skin, the red slashes staining the sheet.

West continued, "I'm not an authority on narcissism, but I'm consulting a psychologist who specializes in this disorder. That's part of my agenda, one of the reasons I'm returning to Virginia. I have a slew of meetings concerning this case."

Allie scooted to the edge of the couch, listening carefully. Olivia asked another question, "What else can you tell us?" She and her sister needed to arm themselves with information, with the power of knowledge.

The special agent smoothed his hair. It was still damp, straight and dark and falling across his forehead. "At one time the perpetrator was connected to the arts, to Hollywood, and he still sees himself as part of that world. He's an urban Indian, raised in the city, with access to money. I'm not sure if he left town and came back or if he's been here all along. But, either way, he considers L.A. his home."

Olivia met his gaze. The rain continued, drumming in her head, pounding between them.

"Go on," she said.

"As you know, he stalks his victims, using his supernatural ability to learn more about them. He's been selecting them carefully, personalizing each woman with the drawing, making it look like a tattoo. That symbol is significant to him."

She shifted in her seat, then stilled the rocker when it creaked. "Is he punishing his victims?"

"Yes. For cheating on their husbands, and in Denise's case, for wanting to have an affair. He's making his victims pay for someone else's sin. A woman he considers a whore. Not his ex-wife, but the woman who destroyed his marriage." He paused to glance at Yvonne's picture. "I think this wound has been festering for a long time. Then something happened recently to set him over the edge, to turn him into a killer."

"How does my mother fit into this?" she asked. "She's a cheating spouse, but she left Dad twelve years ago. Why punish her now?"

Apparently, West had been contemplating the same thing. He had a ready answer, a theory that made sense. "Yvonne is about the right age to have known the killer when he was younger, to have been his lover. Maybe she's the woman he blames, the one who ruined his marriage. Maybe she's the key to all of this."

"Are you sure the Slasher is Indian?"

"In my opinion? Yes. That's why his victims trust him, why they invite him into their homes. And that's why he blended in on the reservation when he went after Denise." West opened his briefcase and slipped the photographs inside, putting her mother's picture on top. "For the most part, his crime scenes reflect organization, but he takes risks, too. Most organized killers hide the bodies, transporting their victims somewhere else. But he leaves them at the scene."

"He has witchcraft on his side," Olivia said.

West agreed. "He's masking evidence, making things disappear, changing chemical compounds. He contaminated his own DNA. In that regard, we don't have squat." He blew out a rough breath. "I'm going to need a list of names from you. Friends, family, old acquaintances. Anyone who knew your mother. Anyone who might be associated with the killer."

"I'll give it to Muncy," Olivia told him.

"What's wrong with giving it to me?"

"You're going out of town tomorrow." And she didn't want to tell him about Glenn. Not yet. She wanted to talk to Glenn by herself, to grill her father's old friend about the secret he was keeping.

"This is important, Olivia."

She bristled. "You don't think I know that?"

His tone softened. "Of course you do. I'm sorry. Is it possible that your vision was a premonition? Something that hasn't happened yet?"

"And my mother is still alive?" She glanced at Allie,

saw the hope in her sister's eyes. "I don't think so. She feels dead to me."

"She's been gone for twelve years," he countered. "Maybe she's been dead to you for a long time."

Olivia shook her head, refusing to let him twist her words. "I already told you, Allie and I didn't wish this upon her."

"Fine. Do you want me to stick around today?" he asked. "I can spend the night, if you want. Crash on the couch."

And do what? she wondered. Play the hero? Slay a dragon? Did he forget that he was in danger, too? That she'd sensed his death? "We'll be fine."

"Promise," he said.

She nodded. "Promise."

Five minutes later she and Allie walked him to the door. Allie reached out to hug him, and he accepted her affection, treating her with gentleness and care.

Afterward, he gave Olivia an anticipatory look. Was he waiting for her to throw her arms around him, too? She stepped back, away from him. He frowned, said goodbye and disappeared into the downpour.

When Olivia turned to look at Allie, her sister was staring at her, upset that she hadn't agreed to let West sleep on the couch.

Interrogating Glenn would have to wait, Olivia thought. It was time to teach Allie that they didn't need a man to keep them safe.

Chapter 6

Kyle's basement had been converted into a gym equipped with free weights, an upright bike, a punching bag and a treadmill. Another portion of the room housed sparring mats. The floor was swept clean, unlike the rest of his house.

Olivia watched the scene before her. She'd told Kyle about their mom, and he'd agreed to train Allie, to teach her how to defend herself.

So far it wasn't going well.

Allie stood with her arms crossed, frowning at Kyle. Instead of changing into workout gear, she wore the same garb she'd had on earlier: a long, flowing dress, a scarf tied around her waist, earrings the size of the solar system. Her hair was fashioned in a single braid, the end wrapped in a leather ornament and decorated with beads.

Kyle studied her as if she were a lost cause. "She's an attack waiting to happen."

Allie snorted at him. "I am not."

"Oh, yeah?" He moved closer, then reached around to tug her braid. "Did you know that in America a woman is raped every two minutes? And did you know the first thing most rapists look for in a potential victim is hairstyle? A way to grab her." He yanked her head back and her eyes went wide. "A ponytail, a bun, a braid. And do know the second thing they look for?" Once again, he answered his own question. "Clothes that are easy to remove. Some men carry scissors to cut pretty dresses off girls like you."

"That hurts!" she yelped, when he pulled her hair a little harder.

"Cry baby." Kyle released her and stepped back.

Allie spun around to glare at her sister. "I can't believe you let him do that to me. Especially now. Especially after everything that's happened."

Olivia didn't say anything. Not a word. She had no idea what Kyle would do next. And neither did Allie. Yet her sister wasn't paying any attention to him.

Lack of awareness. Mistake number one. Allie was blowing it.

He circled her like a vulture. "I always thought you had a sweet little ass." He lowered his voice. "Addle-brained Allie. I'll bet you're a hot lay."

She made a disgusted face. "Screw you, Kyle."

"That's exactly what I had in mind." He lunged, pinning her against the wall. She didn't have time to blink, to draw her next breath.

Olivia waited, watching, praying he wouldn't take it too far. He was already half-naked, his chest bare, his standard-gray sweatpants slung low on his hips. He outweighed Allie by at least eighty pounds.

But size didn't matter. The Slasher was a slightly built man.

With a knife.

Suddenly Olivia saw the blade in Kyle's hand. Allie didn't see it until he held it to her throat. The color drained from her face. Her legs went visibly weak.

"Stop it," she said. "This isn't funny."

"Who's laughing?" Kyle made a malicious sound. "Should I cut you, Allie? Should I slice you up? The way the killer did to your mama?"

Olivia wanted to pound him into the ground. But she didn't. His weapon was a prop. A toy. A piece of rubber that nearly folded against Allie's flesh.

Her sister was too scared to know the difference.

Kyle ended the attack as abruptly as it had begun. He moved away from his victim and waved the knife. It wobbled like a dildo.

When he grinned, Allie went insane. "You bastard! You son of a bitch!"

She came at him full throttle, slamming her fists into his chest. He didn't stop her. He just stood there, six feet four inches of testosterone, allowing a 120-pound girl to pummel him. Allie kept hitting the same area, over and over, trying to bruise him. But that was what he was trying to provoke.

Anger, adrenaline.

Finally he subdued her. "This is called a wrist grab." He clamped his meaty hands around her wrists. "And this—" he turned her like a top, wrapping his arm around her neck, forcing her to bend forward "—is a headlock." He paused, gripped a little tighter. "Now do something about it."

She was trapped beneath his armpit, wrinkling her nose. "You have BO."

He cursed. "I said do something about it."

"Do what?" she creaked. "Find you some deodorant?"

Olivia wondered if her sister really was a lost cause. But Allie redeemed herself. She put her arm around Kyle's waist, turned her face into his body and bit him like a junkyard dog.

The resident rottweiler would be proud.

But Allie didn't stop there. In the midst of the bite, she dropped her free hand and slammed him with all her strength, right between his legs.

Kyle didn't go down. He didn't even flinch. He was wearing a cup, protecting his favorite body part. Infuriated, she bit him even harder, nearly tearing off a piece of his skin.

"Damn." He released her from the headlock. "Not bad, Addle-brain. You've got good instincts."

She spat his blood on the floor, aiming for his feet. "I nearly broke my hand on your armor."

"Yeah, but look." Kyle turned to expose his wound. "You did a number on me." A second later he raised his shoulder and buried his nose in his own hairy armpit. "Do I really have BO?"

Allie sighed, questioning her sister's sanity. "You actually slept with this guy?"

What could Olivia say? That he was great in bed? Allie probably wouldn't believe her. Kyle was sniffing his other armpit now. She shook her head. "Go bandage your bite."

"What?" He glanced up. "Oh, yeah. I'll be right back. Lucky for Allie I don't have any diseases or anything."

As he sauntered over to a cabinet in the corner, Allie wiped her mouth. "I told you he was dumb."

"I heard that." He returned with an oversize Band-Aid slapped on his muscle-bound body. But not just any Band-Aid. It had SpongeBob Squarepants on it. "Ready to continue the lesson?"

"Fine." Allie gave in. Apparently any man who watched cartoons deserved a few minutes of her time. "What's next?"

"How to make a proper fist. You hit like a girl."

"I am a girl."

"Yeah, with a sweet ass."

Her fist shot out.

He shook his head, made some corrections, explained what she was doing wrong. Allie fell into the rhythm. She even looked eager to punch him again.

Olivia relaxed a little. But just a little. There was still a killer out there. And her little sister was a long way from fending off a real attack.

Glenn Sabolich lived in a Spanish-style estate in the Hollywood Hills that presented arched doors and cove ceilings. Elaborate tiled floors and period lighting gave the entryway a touch of Old Hollywood.

Olivia had been here thousands of times. It was her home away from home, a place that made her feel safe.

Until now.

On her way to Glenn's house, she'd glanced up at the Hollywood sign, the larger-than-life letters, the global symbol that represented the glitz and glamour of the entertainment industry.

When she was a child, her father used to talk about Peg Entwistle, a depressed starlet who, in 1932, had climbed the top of the infamous *H* and plunged to her death.

Supposedly her ghost still haunted the area. Eyewitnesses, including a Griffith Park ranger, had claimed to see her, walking in a daze. She normally made her presence known at night, especially when it was foggy and always in the vicinity of the sign, which at the time of Peg's suicide had read Hollywoodland.

As Glenn reached out to hug Olivia, to welcome her into his home, she closed her eyes.

No wonder her father had been fascinated by Peg Entwistle. Hollywoodland had stolen both of their souls.

When Olivia opened her eyes, Glenn was looking at

her. Their faces were only inches apart. She stepped back, recalling how close this man had been to her dad.

Yet he was keeping a secret about her family.

"I'm sorry," he said. "I'm so sorry."

For a moment she couldn't seem to find her voice. She'd told Glenn over the phone about her mother. She'd explained that she'd seen Yvonne's body in a vision, and he believed her. He trusted her ability. He always had.

He escorted her into his living room, where diamond-paned windows reflected Gothic light, remnants of another rainy day. Allie's paintings, along with other up-and-coming artists, graced the walls. An enormous display of silk gardenias sat on an ornately carved table.

Peg Entwistle's ghost was associated with the scent of gardenias, but Glenn had never seemed interested in her tragic story. The 1930s starlet had been her dad's obsession.

These days, alarm systems incorporated with motion detectors protected the Hollywood sign, keeping vandals away. As well as potential suicides who wanted to mimic Peg's desperate leap.

Olivia sat across from Glenn on beige-toned furniture. His housekeeper, a middle-aged Mexican woman who spoke broken English, brought them hot tea and finger sandwiches.

"I'm worried about you and Allie," he said, after his loyal employee left the room.

"We're being careful." Olivia reached for her drink.

He watched her with a paternal expression. "I'm supposed to give the police a list of everyone who knew my mother. And that includes you."

He shifted in his chair. "They're treating your vision like a homicide?"

"They're going to investigate, to see if anything turns up on Mom. But it's not an official homicide. Not yet." She wasn't hungry, but she lifted a sandwich off her plate and took a bite. She knew she needed fuel, energy to keep going. "I'm going to do my damnedest to prove that my vision was real. To find out who killed her."

"I'll help you, any way I can."

Would he? At this point she wasn't so sure.

And on top of that, he didn't look well. Although he was a trim, relatively attractive man, his skin seemed fairer than usual, his blue eyes fading into a watery hue.

"Do you have any idea who Mom ran off with?" she asked.

"No. But I knew it wasn't her first affair. Yvonne had been cheating for years."

Olivia glanced at the silk gardenias. The white spray of flowers seemed virginal, much too delicate for their conversation. "How did you know?"

"All the signs were there. If Joseph hadn't loved her so damned much, he would have known, too. He would have seen through her." Glenn released an audible sigh. "I even confronted her about it. I accused her of taking advantage of Joseph. I was trying to be a good friend, to protect him."

Olivia kept firing questions at him. But what else could she do? They were talking about her family, about her mother's promiscuity, about events that had probably led to her murder. "Did she admit the truth to you?"

"Yes."

"But you never told my dad?"

"No. Never. I couldn't bear to break his heart."

"Is that your secret? Is that what you're so guilty about?"

He caught his breath.

"Is it?" she pressed.

He finally took a sip of his tea, using it as a diversion. She could feel his nerves skittering through his veins, pounding beneath his skin.

"Answer me."

When he replaced his cup on the end table, his hand shook. Mired in anxiety, he fumbled for a cigarette, even though he'd quit smoking over a year ago. She watched him pat down his shirt, tugging at his empty pocket.

Suddenly a blast of betrayal ripped through her, spinning like a tornado.

Oh, God. Dear God.

She shook her head, but she couldn't dispel Glenn's sin. Olivia knew. She could feel what he'd done. "You slept with her. You slept with my mother."

For a moment, for one guilt-ridden instant, he almost denied it. But then he looked at her and saw that she couldn't be fooled.

"Yes," he whispered, his admission raking across his throat, making his voice crack. "I had an affair with my best friend's wife."

Olivia wanted to rip his heart out, to bury it in the dirt and stomp on it until it quit beating. "How could you do that to him?" She clenched her fists. "To me? To Allie?"

"I invited Yvonne over to discuss her marriage, to convince her to stop cheating on Joseph, and—"

"And what? She seduced you?"

"You have no idea how persuasive she was. You don't know how hard I tried to resist her."

Yeah, right. "Am I supposed to see you as some sort of victim? The poor helpless male who couldn't keep his pants zipped?"

"Your mother practiced witchcraft. Black magic. And she used it on me. I know that sounds crazy, but it's true."

"Prove it," she said, refusing to buy his story. He was aware of the witchcraft elements in the Slasher case. She'd discussed it with him months ago, admitting that it was the most difficult investigation she'd ever been involved in.

Once again he searched for a nonexistent cigarette, opening a crystal trinket box on the coffee table. "She belonged to a coven. I can give you the high priest's name. He was one of her lovers."

"Fine. Give me his name."

He closed the box. "Derek Moon."

Olivia blinked. "The producer?" The well-respected

mogul who backed some of the biggest films in Hollywood? Wholesome movies, she thought. Family flicks. "He's into black magic?"

"Yes, but be careful around him. He has powers beyond your comprehension."

"Nothing is beyond my comprehension." She came to her feet, gave him a traitorous look. "Not anymore."

"I'm sorry." He stood, too. But his shoulders were hunched. "I never meant to sleep with her."

"Did Mary find out about your affair?" she asked, questioning him about his ex-wife. "Is that why she divorced you?"

He nodded. "She walked in on us, on Yvonne and me." He made a pained face. "Mary was distraught. She didn't yell. She didn't scream and call us names. She just closed the bedroom door and burst into tears."

"And what did you do?"

He met her gaze, his eyes turning glassy. "I finished making love to your mother. Don't you see? Yvonne was like a drug, an addiction I couldn't control."

She reached for her purse and slung it over her shoulder, hating him, hating his words. "How long did your affair last?"

"A few months. Then she got tired of me. She broke the spell. She let me go."

"And my father never found out? Mary never told him?"

"No. She was worried that it would cause a scandal. That Joseph would come unglued. She didn't want to look like a fool among her friends, to encourage them to gossip about all of us. You know how this town loves that kind of thing. How they look for the worst in everyone."

But not my father, she thought. He'd always trusted the people he loved. "Don't leave town. I'm sure the police are going to want to talk to you."

With that she turned and walked away. She needed to see Allie, to confide in her little sister.

Samantha sat on the kitchen counter, toying with a conversation heart, batting the candy with her paw.

"I don't think Glenn is lying." Allie bustled around, making a pan of black-bean lasagna rolls.

Olivia simply looked at her. She'd expected support from her sister, not contradiction. "You believe that cockamamie story of his?"

"Why not?" The younger woman spread a dollop of ricotta cheese over one side of a noodle, then added a spoonful of the canned beans, rolling the vegetarian concoction. "Mom was selfish enough to use witchcraft as a sexual tool. She thrived on attention. Remember how jealous she used to get whenever your powers outshone hers?"

"Being psychic isn't the same as being a black magic witch."

"Glenn loves us, Olivia. He loved Dad, and he loved Mary. He had a good marriage and then it just fell apart. What other explanation can there be?"

"You're so naive."

"Naive? Believing that our mother was a witch?" She made another lasagna roll. "What Glenn did makes me sick. But think about it? He's the one who stuck by us. Mom ran off and Dad killed himself. In the end, there was only Glenn."

"He could be the Slasher, Allie."

Her sister dropped the spoon. It clanked to the floor, rattling on the linoleum. Samantha darted off like a scaredy-cat. The conversation heart she'd been playing with spun in a pink circle.

Olivia reached for it, read the Page Me inscription. Page whom? Her dead father? No, of course not. That made no sense.

"Glenn isn't a killer." Allie finally went after the spoon, dumping it in the sink. "Your imagination is working overtime."

"He fits the profile." Olivia replaced the heart. The candy company had updated their messages to fit the changing times: Page Me, Fax Me, E-mail Me. It didn't mean a thing, other than kids were more sophisticated these days. "Glenn is around the age of the killer. He's Mom's former lover. He probably blames her for destroying his marriage."

"Glenn doesn't have any supernatural powers."

"How would you know? Have you discussed it with him?"

Once again Allie protested. "That's crazy. Besides, he's white. Blond and blue-eyed. West said the Slasher is Indian."

"West could be wrong."

"He's too good at what he does to make mistakes."

"Now you're really being naive."

The sisters squared off, glaring at each other. But they used to argue like this when they were children. Of course, those disagreements had been silly. They hadn't been fighting about killers, witches and FBI agents.

Allie thrust her hands on her hips. "You should page West. You should tell him what's going on."

Olivia frowned. *Page Me.* "I'll talk to him when he gets back. Besides, I don't have his number."

Her sister stuck her nose in the air. "I do. He gave it to me before he left."

"When?"

"He slipped his card in my belt when I hugged him that night."

"Well, bully for you."

"He knows I'm smart enough to contact him. Unlike you."

Olivia rolled her eyes. "He probably thinks you're a baby who needs protection."

"And he probably thinks you're a bitch. Just like Mom."

Suddenly they both fell silent. Sometimes Yvonne used to pit her daughters against each other. She used to instigate their arguments, taking sides when it suited her. She enjoyed having the chosen one follow her around like a kitten, fawning over her like Mommy's pet.

"I'm sorry," Allie said. "I didn't mean that."

"It's okay. We're both under a lot of stress."

Her sister glanced out the window. "I wish it would stop raining."

"Me, too." She knew what Allie was thinking. Their mother was making it rain. Even dead, Yvonne had the power to control the weather. "Maybe she was a witch."

"Does this mean you're going to stop suspecting Glenn of being a killer?"

"No."

"But he's always been so gentle, so giving." Allie took a clean spoon out of the drawer and went back to her lasagna rolls. "Can you honestly see him slicing up those women? It just doesn't fit."

"Look at Ted Bundy. On the outside, he was handsome and charming and intelligent. But do you know how many women he killed? His last victim was twelve years old."

Allie shuddered. "What about this Derek Moon guy Glenn mentioned? Are you going to tell the police about him?"

"Yes, but first I want to meet him." To delve into his lifestyle, she thought. To see if Glenn was telling the truth, if the G-rated filmmaker really was one of her mother's former lovers.

As well as the high priest of a dark and dangerous coven.

Chapter 7

The following day, Olivia entered the reception area of Moon Dust Entertainment. Plush carpeting, potted palms and glass-topped tables lent the room an airy quality. A floor-to-ceiling, fifth-floor view of Wilshire Boulevard reminded her that this was L.A., the city of angels.

Or demons, she thought.

She approached the front desk, and the receptionist, a thirtysomething redhead in a taupe dress and gold-toned jewelry, glanced up. "May I help you?"

"I'm Olivia Whirlwind. I have a two o'clock appointment with Mr. Moon."

"He's running a little late this afternoon. Have a seat and I'll let you know when he's available." The other woman gave her a professional smile. "It shouldn't be too long."

"Thank you." Olivia sat in a rattan chair and picked up a magazine. Artfully framed movie posters lined the walls, boasting the production company's accomplishments.

Her appointment with Derek Moon had been far too easy to arrange, which meant he was as curious about her as she was about him. A sure-fire sign that he had been acquainted with her mother.

Olivia had dressed carefully for this meeting, choosing a long black dress with leather laces, strips that crisscrossed down the sides of the garment, exposing just a hint of leg. As usual she wore crimson lipstick and smoky black eyeliner.

She wasn't about to change her image for Moon. She wanted to see his reaction to her sex-and-roses look. She'd even added a pair of lace gauntlets for effect, painting her nails a wicked shade of red.

Anxious, she paged through a trade magazine.

Ten minutes later the receptionist introduced her to Moon's private secretary, a young man in a pinstripe suit and fake-bake tan. He led her down a well-lit corridor, where they passed a string of offices equipped with picture windows and chic employees.

Finally they reached the king's quarters. After Moon's secretary escorted her into his boss's office, he departed, leaving her alone with the film-industry mogul.

Derek Moon came right to his feet. Much like Glenn, he appeared to be the estimated height and weight of the killer, around five-ten with a slight build. Well dressed and attractive for man in his fifties, he wore his wavy brown hair neatly trimmed and peppered with gray.

"I'm Derek."

She extended her hand. "And I'm Olivia."

"It's a pleasure to meet you." His hazel eyes all but sparkled. And on top of that, he had a gorgeous smile. But a man in his position could afford cosmetic dentistry.

A beat of silence ensued, then he said, "You're as stunning as your mother."

Surprised, she feigned a polite reaction. She hadn't been prepared for him to mention her mom, at least not so easily. "Thank you."

He guided her to an elegant sitting area, offering her a spot on his overstuffed sofa.

"How is Yvonne?" he asked. "I haven't seen her in ages. Not since before she left your father." He paused. "I'm sorry about Joseph. I sent flowers to his funeral, but you already know that."

Once again Olivia was caught off guard. She didn't recall a bouquet from him. But Glenn had handled most of the details, writing thank-you notes for her and Allie. "I wasn't aware that you knew my father."

"He and your mother attended a few parties at my home. Yvonne and my ex-wife were friends, but only for a short while."

"So that's how you're familiar with my mom?"

"Yes. Would you like a beverage? A soft drink? Juice? Maybe a glass of wine?"

She asked for orange juice and watched him pour her a tall glass. For himself, he prepared club soda with a twist of lime. His office presented a fully stocked bar.

He sat across from her, with a small coffee table between them. "Are you interested in being in the movies, Olivia? Is that why you came to see me?"

She shook her head. "I'm not an actress."

"Then what is it I can do for you?"

She sipped her juice. "Tell me about my mother. Everything you recall about her."

He frowned at a piece of lint on his suit, brushing it away. He'd yet to touch his drink. "Why?"

"Because I have reason to believe that she's dead. That something tragic happened to her. And I'm trying to piece together her past."

"Do you think she was murdered?" he asked.

She took a deep breath. "Yes. I think she was stabbed."

His eyes widened. "Like those Indian women in the news?" He leaned back in his chair, then made a steeple out of his hands, pressing his fingers together, tapping his chin. "I'm terribly sorry, but I'm not surprised that Yvonne met with a violent death. When I was acquainted with her, she didn't lead a very wholesome life."

"I know. I'm aware of her affairs."

"And the negative magic?"

Her heartbeat blasted her chest. "Yes. Glenn Sabolich told me."

"Did he?" Derek dusted his jacket again. "I can only

imagine what else he said. Quite truthfully, I don't have time to discuss this right now. Why don't you have dinner with me this evening? At my home." He met her gaze. "No hanky-panky. Just a meal."

"I wasn't expecting you to seduce me."

He reached for his club soda. "Most young women in this town expect old guys like me to be lecherous."

She tilted her head. Derek Moon was difficult to read. She wasn't able to feel his emotions, to gauge his sincerity. "I'm not most women."

"Not in that dress." He gave her a teasing smile, flashing those dazzling teeth, finally acknowledging her naughty attire. "So, will you have dinner with an old man?"

She wasn't about to turn him down. She suspected he would give her an earful tonight, telling her his side of Glenn's story. At this point she didn't know whom to trust. "I'm looking forward to it."

"Good. I live in Beverly Hills. I know, it's a cliché, but it comes with the territory." He crossed to his desk and retrieved a business card, then wrote his address on the back. "There's a security gate. Just press the intercom and tell the guard who you are. Would eight o'clock be all right?"

She accepted his card. "That's fine."

He walked her to the door, and they lingered for a moment. Was he a black magic witch? The leader of a coven?

Silent, she studied his card, intrigued by the Moon Dust logo, the silver glitter sprinkled across a pitch-black sky.

* * *

At seven-thirty, Olivia stood in front of the full-length mirror in her bedroom, putting the final touches on her appearance. She'd chosen a short white dress, rhinestone jewelry and a studded black belt.

"I can't believe you're going to his house." This came from Allie, who lounged on the bed in a pair of blue sweats and fuzzy slippers.

Olivia reached for her holster and clipped it to her belt. She wanted her Glock to be visible tonight. She wanted Derek Moon to know she was armed. "I don't have much of a choice, Allie. I need to get inside this guy's head. And I want to hear what he has to say."

"I'm going to page West and tell him you're going out with a witch."

Good grief. Her sister was obsessed with telling Agent West every little thing that went on. "I'm not hiding anything from him. Or Muncy and Riggs for that matter. I plan to give all of them a full report."

"Yeah. After the fact." Allie crossed her legs, sitting like a movie Indian chief. "What if Moon puts a spell on you?"

"He wouldn't dare."

"Right. Because you're so tough. You and your gun." The younger woman jumped off the bed to adjust Olivia's belt, angling it just so. "Shoot him if he tries anything."

She met her sister's gaze in the mirror. "I love you, Allie."

"I love you, too."

For a moment they simply looked at each other, re-calling their youth, the games they used to play, the Barbie dolls they used to dress up, the secrets only girls could share.

"He might not be a witch," Olivia said. "Let alone a high priest. Glenn could be lying."

Allie frowned at their reflections. "Glenn isn't the bad guy. He isn't the killer."

Then who is? Olivia wondered, as she drove to Derek Moon's house. Who'd slashed their mother? Who'd sliced up those other women? She wasn't convinced that Glenn was innocent, and Allie's blind-faith belief in him only made those bloody images even more vivid. More gruesome.

She headed west on Sunset Boulevard, following the winding portions of the road and passing the Beverly Hills Hotel.

Derek lived on a well-known, map-to-the-stars street. But that, she supposed, was part of his cliché, a movie-industry luxury he thrived on.

She stopped at the security gate and announced her arrival. After she was granted entrance, she parked in a circular driveway, taking in her surroundings. The Tudor-style mansion didn't look the least bit dangerous. But Olivia had never allowed glamorous things to de-ceive her.

Derek met her at the door. He smiled, flashing his pretty white teeth. "Look at you," he said, glancing at the gun on her hip.

She was fashionably late, but he didn't seem to mind. "A girl can't be too careful these days."

He invited her into his home. "So I gather."

Olivia glanced around, saw the trappings of wealth: elegant furniture, crystal chandeliers, a sweeping staircase. She suspected he had a pool dazzling with tea lights, a fountain that spilled into a hot tub.

He escorted her into a formal dining room, where a bay window presented a mazelike view of his garden. Flowers bloomed at every turn, greenery flourished in mysterious patterns.

"Impressed?" he asked.

She shrugged, which only made him smile. He liked showing off his teeth.

He offered her a chair. The table was set with gilded glassware, a tall orange candle and a bottle of California wine. An enormous painting of a satyr presided over the room. The mythological creature, half man and half goat, danced to a tune only he could hear.

Derek caught her looking at it. "I collect fantasy art." He sat across from her. "Speaking of which…your sister is very talented. I've been following her work."

A chill crept up Olivia's spine. She didn't want him buying any of Allie's paintings. "That isn't her style."

He poured the wine. "No. I suppose not. The satyr symbolizes sexual energy."

And the color of the candle he'd chosen represents attraction, she thought. Physical stimulation.

A moment later, a member of his household staff

served the first course, then left them alone, closing the double doors that secured the dining area.

Olivia tasted her salad. "I heard you were a high priest. And that my mother was part of your coven." She paused, hoping to get a reading on him. "Is that true?"

"Yes, it is." He skewered a cherry tomato, stabbing it with his fork. "But I'm a good witch."

"Like Glinda?"

He laughed. "That's one way of looking at it. Are you familiar with white magic?"

She knew enough to explain the concept. "It's a form of witchcraft used to maintain the delicate balances that exist in the world. White magic practitioners won't cast a spell if it will cause harm or take away someone's free will."

He sipped his wine, made a grand gesture. "See? A good witch."

"And let me guess? My mother was a bad witch."

He drank more wine. "Yvonne was obsessed with self-gratification, in using her magic in negative ways. If someone got in her way, she would make that person ill. Of course, I didn't know that when I first met her. She charmed my wife and me." He tilted his head. "I'm surprised that you weren't aware of her craft. That she practiced black magic. You're her daughter after all."

"Why would I if she was hiding it?"

"Because Yvonne's craft came from her ancestry. All of the women in her family used their supernatural abilities in harmful ways." He studied his fork. "I believe the Chiricahua refer to these kinds of powers as *enti*."

Olivia couldn't think of anything to say. Did he speak the truth? Were her female ancestors evil? She'd never met her mother's family. As far as she knew, they were dead.

"Are you all right?" he asked.

"I'm fine." She took a sip of her water, dousing her discomfort. "Tell me about your ex-wife."

"Beth?" He finished his salad, then dipped his garlic bread into the vinaigrette dressing. "She's beautiful. Classy. Everything a man could hope for."

Olivia remained silent, watching Derek instead.

"Beth was interested in fashion," he said. "So I bought her a boutique on Melrose. It kept her busy."

"How long were you married?"

"Five years. I loved her. I truly did." He sighed, nearly blowing out the candle. "But Yvonne ruined it for us. She was determined to destroy our marriage."

Before she could comment, their server knocked on the double doors, announcing the next course, which included grilled seafood and quinoa-fennel pilaf.

Finally, when they were alone, she asked, "How did Beth meet my mother? How did they get to be friends?"

"Yvonne modeled in Beth's boutique, at an in-store fashion show."

She tasted her shrimp, trying to recall if her mom ever mentioned a modeling gig on Melrose. "Bethany's? Is that the name of your ex's boutique?"

"Yes, that's it." He topped up his wine, noticed her glass was still full. "You don't like the Chardonnay?"

."Alcohol dulls my senses."

"It's supposed to." He lifted his glass, drank. "Oh, of course. You mean your psychic senses."

She looked up, saw him gazing at her, smiling like the satyr in the painting. "You know I'm psychic?"

"Yvonne told me about her children." He ate his shrimp, savoring the herbs, making a show out of enjoying it. "You're clairvoyant. You see images in your head. And you're clairaudient, too. You hear voices and sounds." He angled his head. "But your strongest gift is your empathic skills. You can feel what others are feeling."

"I can't feel what you're feeling."

"That's because I have powers, too."

"You're blocking me?"

"Yes, my dear. I am. I don't like having my emotions read. It's rude and invasive."

"Good magic," she muttered, wondering if Derek Moon was misrepresenting himself. Even his name sounded phony.

"Glenn told me that you were my mother's lover."

"Glenn slept with her. Not me."

She gave him a lethal stare. "Can you prove it?"

"Actually, I can." He rose from his chair and walked around to her side of the table. Then he leaned over. "Ask me if I slept with your mother."

She squinted at him. His face was inches from her. "You're not going to block me?"

"Put your hand on my heart if you don't believe me."

She did just that, knowing it was easier to get a reading if she was physically connected to him. "Did you sleep with my mother?"

"No, I didn't."

She closed her eyes, listened to the rhythm of his heart. He was telling the truth. She could feel his energy. His honesty. He hadn't been Yvonne's lover.

He moved away from her, resuming his seat. "That's all you're going to get from me. The only reading I'll allow you to have." He scooped up a forkful of rice. He looked calm and composed, elegant in the tangerine-tinged light. "You'll just have to trust me with the rest of your questions."

Trust him? At this point, she didn't know whom to trust. Then again, he hadn't gone to bed with her mother, and that put him a notch above Glenn. "Why was Yvonne determined to break up your marriage?"

"Because she wanted me. My wealth. My influence in the entertainment industry."

"But you spurned her advances?"

"I was in love with my wife. Beth meant everything to me. Besides, I don't condone adultery. Your mother behaved like a whore."

And that made him a suspect, Olivia thought. That gave him motive to kill Yvonne, to punish those other women in her likeness.

He finished his meal, leaving a few scallops on his plate, a few untouched morsels. "Any more questions?"

"Yes." She wasn't through interviewing him yet. "How did my mother destroy your marriage? What did she do?"

"She told Beth stories about me."

"What kinds of stories?"

"She claimed that when my wife was at work, I invited other couples to our house and watched them have sex."

"Voyeurism?" Olivia glanced at the satyr, almost expecting it to leer at her. "That would put a damper on someone's marriage."

"It shattered mine. Beth believed every word of it."

When they both fell silent, she looked out the window and noticed the moon was shimmering in the sky, sending a stream of light over the flowers, zigzagging along the shrub-lined paths.

A few minutes later, their server brought dessert, a poached pear drenched in caramel sauce.

Without speaking, she and Derek ate their treats. And then her cell phone rang. She excused herself, walked away from the table and answered it.

"Hello?"

West came on the line. "Hello, yourself."

Olivia pressed the receiver closer to her mouth. "You shouldn't have called."

"Your sister told me you were dining with a witch."

She shifted her gaze, caught sight of the candle, the flame dancing on the wick. Suddenly she felt strangely sexual, aroused by West's voice, by the sloe-gin tone that laced his accent. "I don't need this."

"Need what?"

"Someone checking up on me."

"Yes, you do."

"No. I don't." She could taste the caramel on her lips, and the sticky sweetness made her want more. She glanced at Derek. He watched her from the corner of his eye. Voyeurism? she wondered. Or curiosity? "I have to go."

"I'll be back tomorrow," West said. "You can fill me in then."

"Fine. Whatever." Determined to sever their tie, she hung up on the FBI agent and returned to the witch.

"Was that your boyfriend?" Derek asked.

"No."

He doused the orange candle with his dessert spoon, drizzling caramel onto the wax. "Potential lover?"

"Maybe." She watched the flame go out, but that didn't redirect her desire. Olivia wanted to tear off West's clothes, to rip open his shirt, to unzip his pants, yet he was thousands of miles away.

Too far to satisfy the urgent craving in her soul.

Chapter 8

Ian stood back and watched Olivia blast the hell out of a paper target. He'd driven to what seemed like the middle of nowhere, a patch of sand in the high desert that someone had the nerve to call a town. And, much to his surprise, the address Olivia had given him belonged to an indoor shooting range.

She'd rented the whole damn place. Aside from the range officer tucked away in his control booth, he and Olivia were the only people in the building.

He had to admit that it was an interesting facility, an innovatively engineered modular structure constructed for the remote location. Designed for shooting clubs and other private organizations, it offered ten firing positions for a reasonable hourly rate. But as professional as this place appeared to be, he had a feeling something wasn't quite right.

He moved a little closer to Olivia. In between rounds, she'd told him about Glenn Sabolich and Derek Moon, which included the sordid claims each man had made about her mother.

She fired at the human-shaped target again, nailing it in the heart.

"Who are you trying to kill?" he asked. "Sabolich? Moon? Your already-dead mom?"

"You," she said.

"Me?" Offended, he compared himself to the paper thug, a hard-nosed criminal aiming a pistol at her. This time she'd shot him in the groin, blowing a hole right through his imaginary dick. "What did I do?"

She checked the chamber, then reloaded. Today she was playing cowgirl, firing a single-action Colt. "You called me last night."

"You're still pissed off about that?" He frowned at the back of her head. He could smell her perfume, a seductive mélange of jasmine, lime and ginger. Combined with the lingering odor of gunpowder, it created a heady combination. "I don't understand why it was such a big deal. Not unless you were enjoying Moon's company. Is that it? Did I disturb your fancy-ass dinner?"

She didn't turn to look at him. Instead she raised her revolver and castrated her opponent again. "I thought it was the orange candle. But it wasn't. This isn't a spell. I always feel like this when I'm around you."

Felt like what? Riddling his fly with bullets? "You're not making sense."

She rested her Colt on the bench and retrieved her target, using the automatic control panel. When she handed him the holey thug, he wondered if she expected him to frame it.

"Watch me," she said. "And you might learn something."

"Learn what? How to be psycho?"

"How to take down an FBI agent in your mind."

"I'd rather leave my fellow feds standing."

"Just watch." She put another target in place and reached into her pocket and took out a blindfold.

"What the hell are you doing?" He waited for the range officer to stop her, but the other man allowed her to continue. Ian had been right about this place. They didn't play by the rules.

After she covered her eyes with the blindfold, she reached for her loaded weapon, found it without the slightest hesitation, aimed it in the direction of her target and focused on something she couldn't see. Then she cocked the hammer and squeezed the trigger.

Bull's-eye.

She shot the thug, just as she'd done before, unmanning him.

Ian actually glanced down, making sure his zipper was still intact. "Can you pick on another body part for a while?"

Olivia smiled, took aim. "Like what? His throat? Maybe I'll give him a scar to match mine."

Sure enough, she plugged the paper target. One. Two. Three. Four. As neat as a pin. He'd never seen anything like it.

She fired the last shot, hitting the bad guy in the head. "I guess I'm done with him." She placed her Colt on the bench and removed the blindfold.

When she turned to give Ian a smug look, he merely blinked. Now that it was over, he had a hard-on. A big, raging boner. And considering her penchant for blowing off a man's balls, he wasn't sure why.

She studied his dumbfounded expression. "That was a piece of cake, as easy as pie. Do you want to try it?"

Did she think he was crazy? "No."

"Are you sure?"

"Yes."

"What's the matter? Did I show you up? Shrivel your manhood?"

He bit back a smile. He was still hard, as virile as a pocket rocket on its way to the moon. "Oh, yeah. You emasculated the hell of out me. Do you use blindfolds in bed, too?"

She crossed her arms under her breasts. As usual, she wore an outfit that accentuated her curves. Her stretchy red top was the same notice-me shade of her lipstick, and her low-rise jeans cupped her rear like a man's greedy hands.

"What do you care?" she said. "You're never going to find out."

Liar, he thought. She was just waiting for him to say the word, to admit that he needed her. But Ian wasn't about to grovel for sex.

"Do you want to blow this Popsicle stand?" he asked.

She batted her lashes. "Do I want to blow what?"

He wasn't about to laugh. Sooner or later he would end up groveling. Begging like the divorced, thirty-five-year-old dog he'd never wanted to become. "I noticed a biker bar a few miles back. We could stop for a drink."

"Or shoot some bikers," she said, reaching for her Colt.

"That, too." He shoved the paper thug she'd given him in the trash, even though he was tempted to keep it.

An offbeat memento, he thought, to remember her by.

The bar was a dive, a dingy, smoke-filled cracker box with a dozen or so grungy patrons sucking down beers in the middle of the afternoon. Sunlight glared from the windows, making Ian squint. A battered pool table, a jukebox blaring with Kid Rock, the aroma of greasy pizza. No wannabes here, he thought. No doctors or lawyers pretending to be bikers, shucking their Rolexes for the day. These hard-ass Harley mongers were the real thing.

Olivia turned every head, male and female alike. Or maybe he had caught everyone's attention. With his dark suit and G-man vibe, he didn't need to flash his badge. He had FBI written all over him. But that was how he liked it.

"I enjoy crashing these kinds of places," he said.

"Why?" Olivia led the way, choosing a small wooden table near the front. "Do you have a death wish?"

Did he? Yeah, he thought. He probably did. "I should have hauled you in here in handcuffs. Then we would have looked like we belonged together."

"You can handcuff me now."

"Really?" Damn if he wasn't getting a boner again. He moved his chair next to hers, as close as possible.

She laughed, adjusting her racy-red top. "You can use the blindfold, too."

Okay, now he was really hard. "You're corrupting me, Olivia."

"I aim to please."

A reed-thin waitress with dishwater-brown dread-locks came by to take their order. Her name tag read Bunny. Ian wasn't sure why. Maybe it was the way her teeth bucked in front.

Olivia wanted to try the pizza, making him wonder if she had a death wish, too. They settled on pepperoni and mushroom, as well as a couple of draft beers.

Before Bunny departed, he removed his handcuffs and locked Olivia's wrist to a post on her chair. The waitress's heavily lined eyes went wide.

"She's been bad," Ian said. "But I like naughty girls."

That made Bunny smile. "I've been known to be bad."

No doubt, he thought. But at least she would stop the cook from spitting in their food. As she darted off to fill their order, Olivia glared at him.

For effect, he rattled the steel that confined her to the scarred wood. "You told me I could."

"I didn't even know you had them on you."

"Did you think I'd waltz into a place like this without the tools of my trade? Take a gander, babe. It's infested with outlaws."

Her gaze bore into his, but her lips hinted at a smile. "I'm going to get you back for this. Punish you like no other."

Amused, he shifted in his seat. Then he waved away a stream of smoke that drifted toward them. The California smoking ban wasn't being enforced, but he supposed that was out of his jurisdiction. "Can I blindfold you now?"

"Try it, and I'll blow you to smithereens."

"With your mouth?"

"With my gun, you moron. I still have one hand left."

Their beers arrived, followed by the pizza. Ian didn't unlock Olivia. Instead he watched her eat with the free hand she'd boasted about.

And when she was absorbed in her greasy meal, he crammed his fingers into her pocket and snagged the blindfold. But instead of putting it on her, he slipped it over his own eyes.

She laughed and bumped his shoulder. He felt around for his beer and took a long cold swig.

"Damn. I can't see a thing."

"No shit, Sherlock."

He thought about what she'd done at the shooting range. "How did you pull that off?"

"Pull what off?"

"You know." He raised his finger and cocked his thumb, pretending to fire. "That psychic-sight thing."

"I can feel the position of the target in my mind. Sense where it is."

"Can you do that with moving targets, too?"

"I'm working on it. But not with live ammo. A friend of mine has a laser tag course on his property. So I've been training there."

Ian pushed up the blindfold, wearing it like a headband. "What friend?"

"A guy who lives around here."

"Anyone I should know about?"

She went after her second slice of pizza. "Old lover."

"How old?"

"Too young to be the killer." She motioned with her head. "You shot that biker in the corner."

"What?" He looked up and saw a three-hundred-pound bruiser giving him the evil eye. "Oh, the finger-gun thing." So much for his psychic sight. He shrugged at Bruiser and the other man flipped him off. Ian merely smiled. He wouldn't forget the biker's ugly mug.

"So, what happened in Virginia?" Olivia asked. "Did your colleagues agree with your analysis? The profile in your report?"

"Yes, but they think the killer is fooling me. That there's something I'm missing." He felt that way, too. But he couldn't grasp it. He couldn't figure it out. "Something vital. Something important."

"Maybe it's his heritage."

"No. That isn't it."

"I think it is." She yanked on the handcuffs. "Will you take these off me now?"

He nodded, realizing their conversation had taken a serious turn. They were done flirting, done causing a scene in an already rowdy bar. The billiards game in the back was getting loud, the language and the laughter turning rough.

When he removed the cuffs, she rubbed her wrist. "Glenn could be the perpetrator," she said. "And so could Derek Moon. And neither of them are Indian."

"I already spoke to Muncy and Riggs about that. They're trying to connect Sabolich and Moon to the victims, but with all the witch-tampered evidence, it's next to impossible."

"Those men are connected to my mom."

"True. But we don't have her body." He reached for his beer. "Of course, the killer might have buried her somewhere."

"That's what I've been thinking, especially if he knows the authorities can link her to him. He'd want to cover his tracks." She paused. "I've tried to get a reading on where her body is, but it hasn't worked."

"No vibes?" he asked.

She sighed. "A complete blank."

"Until we locate the man she ran off with, we're grasping at straws." Yvonne Whirlwind's trail had gone cold. No tax records, no valid driver's license, no current credit history. "Maybe he killed her twelve years ago."

"Who? The man she left my dad for?"

"Yeah."

Olivia shook her head. "She looked older in my vision. The age she would be now."

"Which means we're back to square one."

"That's why I've been investigating Glenn and Derek on my own."

He couldn't blame her for that. Nor did he intend to discourage her. "What about Moon's ex-wife? Have you talked to her?"

"Not yet. Do you want to stop by her boutique with me? For all we know, she has powers, too."

"Sure, I'll go with you." At this point, he was game for anything. His grandfather had reared him on ghosts and witches and things that went bump in the night. And this case was chock-full of supernatural occurrences.

Making logic hard to apply.

Bethany's was an upscale boutique on Melrose Avenue, but in Olivia's opinion the fashions were dull and the displays stark and sparse. Headless mannequins with anorexic bodies made an overly chic statement.

"Nice place," West said.

Olivia ignored his comment. He wore a dark suit every day of his life.

A tall, slim woman approached them, mimicking a runway model. Her dyed-black hair, blunt cut and razor sharp, framed an angular face with strong cheekbones and iridescent lipstick. Her two-tone dress, sand and sepia, draped her to perfection.

No doubt this was Beth. The former Mrs. Moon, an ex-Hollywood wife who visited her cosmetic surgeon for regular touch-ups, little procedures here and there that made her look younger than her fiftysomething years.

"Good afternoon," she said, eyeing Olivia's trendy top and slim-fitting jeans with a concerned expression. Obviously, she didn't peg Olivia for a paying customer, someone who would shop at Bethany's.

Good call, Olivia thought. Her gold card would remain in her wallet.

The look Beth graced upon West was altogether different. She assumed he'd dragged Olivia into the shop for a makeover.

Offering him an elegant smile, she stepped closer. "Is there something special you're looking for?"

"We were hoping to speak to the owner," he said.

"That's me." She extended her hand. "Beth Moon."

"Special Agent West." He shook her hand, then flashed his badge and government ID. "And my companion is Olivia Whirlwind."

"Whirlwind?" Beth flinched. "Please don't tell me you're related to Yvonne."

"I'm her daughter."

"And Yvonne is the reason we're here," West said.

Beth agreed to speak with them privately, instructing her sales assistant to watch the floor.

A few minutes later, Olivia and West were seated in Beth's office, a tidy area in the backroom of her boutique. She offered both of them coffee, but she kept her attention focused on West, ignoring Olivia in the process. Uncomfortable, it appeared, by her blood-related connection to Yvonne.

West asked Beth if she knew who Yvonne had left town with, but she shook her head, claiming she didn't keep tabs on Olivia's mother.

"Are you sure?" he prodded.

"Yes." She tucked one side of her hair behind her ear, where a topaz jewel sparkled. "Is Yvonne in trouble with the law?"

"She's missing," West said. "And we suspect foul play."

"Pity," came the cool reply.

He sipped his coffee, then leaned forward, making direct eye contact with the wealthy divorcée. "Did she ruin your marriage?"

Beth raised a manicured hand to the front of her dress. Her nails were painted the same iridescent shade as her lips. "Did Derek tell you that?"

"He told me," Olivia said.

The other woman finally turned to acknowledge her. "What else did he say?"

"He mentioned voyeurism."

"Did he?" Her eyes turned cold. "Derek was obsessed with that type of behavior. And so was your mother."

Olivia couldn't tell if Beth was being truthful. Nothing radiated from her. Nothing but a bitter divorce. "He said they weren't lovers."

"They weren't. But Yvonne used to have sex with other men and let Derek watch. That bitch got off on it."

West glanced at Olivia, and she felt sick inside. The stories about her mom were getting worse.

"Did Derek give you that spiel about him being a good witch?" Beth asked.

Olivia nodded. "He said he practiced white magic."

"Well, he doesn't, not anymore."

"Anymore?"

"After he met Yvonne, he began to explore her magic. The dark things she taught him. Within no time, he was using witchcraft in negative ways, casting spells to advance himself, trying to obtain more wealth and more power."

And he lies about it to protect his reputation, Olivia thought. To stop the media from making scandalous accusations about his squeaky-clean company. "If my mother taught him the things he practices today, then why does he hate her?"

"Because I divorced him over her. He never acted on his voyeurism fantasies until Yvonne came along. She corrupted him. With her supernatural powers, with her sensuality. He isn't the same man I married, and he never will be."

"Do you know Glenn Sabolich?" West asked.

"Yes. He used to be part of the coven, the one Derek started with Yvonne."

Glenn is a witch, Olivia thought. Just like Moon. Lord only knew which man had killed her mother.

Beth continued. "Yvonne called the coven a witch society and referred to Derek as the ceremonial father rather than a high priest. I assume those are Native terms." She heaved a sigh. "I've always been fascinated by other cultures. I suppose that's what drew me to Yvonne when I first met her."

"Will you compile a list of the men and women in Derek's coven?" West asked her. "I'd like to interview them."

"Yvonne was the only woman." She reached for her coffee, frowned into the cup. "As for the men, I'll give you their names, but don't expect them to cooperate. They're all very rich and powerful, and they don't like people poking around in their business."

Olivia scooted to the edge of her chair, dreading her next question. "Did my father know that my mother was involved in witchcraft?"

Beth shook her head. "Not that I'm aware of." She picked up a pen and began making a list of the men in her ex-husband's coven. "But I only saw Joseph a few times."

West asked the next question. "How did you know that your husband was watching Yvonne with other men? How did you know that she wasn't lying to you?"

She handed him the list. "Because she showed me a videotape that he'd filmed, that he'd hidden in his safe. Derek never meant for me to see it. He didn't want me to know what he was doing. Not the black magic or the voyeurism."

The special agent sat back in his chair. "Why was Yvonne trying to break up your marriage?"

"Why else? She wanted Derek and the glamorous lifestyle he could provide. A mansion in Beverly Hills, a thriving production company, rich and famous friends." Beth twisted the topaz in her ear, the amber jewel glinting against her hair. "But in spite of her influence over him, he was still in love with me. She was his playmate, someone to feed his fantasies. Yvonne was the darkness and I was light, the part of himself that he'd lost. That she'd stolen from him." She stopped turning her earring. "Now if you don't have any more questions, I'd like to get back to work."

Olivia and West agreed to end the interview, and when they turned leave, Olivia finally got a reading on Beth Moon.

She hadn't been lying. Everything she'd said had been the truth. But like her ex-husband, she also hated Yvonne enough to kill her.

Chapter 9

Once they were on the sidewalk, Olivia turned to look at West. "Is it possible the Slasher could be a woman?"

"Why? Did you just get a mental confession from Beth?"

"No. But she hated my mom enough to kill her."

"Apparently a lot of people did." He slicked his hair back with his hands. Then he fell silent.

She supposed he was contemplating the female-killer angle. She could almost see the wheels turning in his head.

"Is it possible?" she prodded.

He walked to his car, which was parallel parked a few feet from Bethany's. Olivia's Porsche was around the corner. West had snagged the closer spot.

When he didn't respond, she pushed the issue. "That could be the mistake in your report."

He unlocked the rented sedan and gestured for her to climb into the passenger seat. "I don't think Beth is the offender." They sat in his car, and he rolled down the windows, allowing a small breeze to cool their faces. "I can see her stabbing your mom, but the other victims? It doesn't wash." He leaned against the headrest. "Female killers usually exhibit a preference for victims who can be easily subdued, their own children, an elderly relative. Either that, or they knock off lovers or spouses. They rarely attack adult strangers."

"Maybe she slashed up those other women to make it look like a man committed these crimes. To throw the police off track in case they find my mom's body."

"That's possible. Women are often methodical, eminently lethal in their actions. They don't fool around." He pushed his hair off his forehead again, where the straight, dark strands rebelled from the wind. "And with all the tampered-with DNA, we don't have any gender-specific evidence."

"Plus there was no sexual assault. None of the victims were raped or sodomized." Olivia glanced at the headless mannequins in Bethany's window display. "That could indicate a woman."

"True, but it could indicate a man, too. Thrusting a knife into a body can be a substitute for thrusting a penis. For some killers, sexual satisfaction is derived from seeing the victim's blood spill." He blew out a rough sigh. "This is such a complicated case. One step forward and one step back. We're not getting anywhere."

"Which means what? That you're not ruling out a woman?"

He reached into his pocket for his sunglasses, a pair of *Men in Black* shades that shielded his obscure gray eyes. "At this point, I'm not ruling out anything. But I still have my doubts about Beth."

"She has motive—revenge. And she matches the height of the perpetrator." Something that had been determined by several factors, including the distance between the Slasher's shoeprints. Luckily, the distance between those prints seemed too concise, too real to be considered contaminated, unlike the shoeprints themselves. "Wouldn't a slightly built man be around the same size as a statuesque woman? And wouldn't the victims be more likely to allow a woman into their homes? To not be afraid of her?"

West frowned. "Yes, but Beth isn't a witch, is she? The offender has supernatural powers."

"I didn't get a reading on her spiritual energy. But she's certainly been exposed to the occult. She was telling the truth about her ex. He practices black magic."

"Was she honest about Glenn Sabolich, too? Was he part of the coven?"

"Yes." The man who'd helped shape her childhood was a witch.

"At least we know that much," West said, as sunlight slashed across the windshield.

Silent, Olivia glanced out the open window, where a trio of teenage boys walked along the sidewalk, shoulder to shoulder, displaying their hard-core style and retro-punk attitudes. In the eighties, Melrose had been besieged with studs and spikes and shoes called Creepers. A strangely colorful era, she thought, that had been part of her youth.

But those days were gone, taking her innocence, as well. A father who'd committed suicide. An adulterous mother who'd been murdered. A family friend who'd betrayed the daughters left behind.

If only Allie didn't trust him. If only she could make her sister see that Glenn was dangerous.

West interrupted her thoughts. "Maybe we're dealing with a sophisticated shape-shifter. A man who can morph into a woman. Or a woman who can morph into a man."

"Or a transvestite," she said, making him laugh.

After that, they both turned quiet. Feeling unsettled, Olivia gazed at him, trying to see beyond his masked eyes. She'd become accustomed to the strange color, to their magnetic allure.

The late-day traffic picked up, and cars sluiced past them, zooming through green lights, honking at jay-walking pedestrians.

To abate the noise, West rolled up the windows. And in the stillness of his motionless sedan, she continued to study him. She wanted to touch his face, to graze the texture of his skin, to follow the structure of his bones, the hollow depths that shadowed his features.

"Why are you looking at me like that?" he asked.

Because suddenly his car seemed like a coffin, a reminder that he was going to die. She could sense his scattered energy, the way he would struggle to breathe, his desperate gasps for air. A premonition she couldn't control.

"No reason," she said. What good would her constant warnings do? He would only laugh it off. But maybe that was part of his death wish, the morbid humor that made him who he was.

"I'm going to head over to the station," he told her. "I'd like to reevaluate what we have. Go through those files again. There's got to be a way to zero in on the gender of our killer."

She crossed her arms to avoid a shudder. *Our killer.* It sounded so personal. So intimate.

"Do you want to follow me over there?" he asked.

"No." She wanted to get in her own car and go home, to forget that she was psychic, to ignore her powers and pretend to be normal.

Just once, she thought, curling her fingers around her purse, grasping the inanimate object instead of touching him.

Agent West. The man who was bound to disappear.

When evening came, Olivia still struggled with her emotions. She sat in front of the TV, eating ice cream from the carton, pigging out on chocolate mint.

Allie bustled around the loft, getting ready to go out.

She breezed into the living room to model her new outfit, a flowing black dress that made her look like a dark and dangerous gypsy. Silver hoops dangled in her ears, and her hair, long and loose, exploded in crimping-iron disarray.

"Wow. You look hot," Olivia said.

"I do, don't I?" Allie did a vampish pirouette and laughed. She had been continuing her training with Kyle, and the self-defense sessions seemed to boost her confidence.

Olivia smiled around a spoonful of ice cream. No doubt her sister enjoyed beating up on Kyle.

"Are you sure you don't want to go out?" Allie asked. "A little dancing might do you some good."

Olivia quit smiling. She wasn't in the mood to prowl the club scene, even if she liked Allie's ditzy friends. "Thanks, but I'll pass."

Her sister scrunched up her face. "Did something happen today?"

"No." She didn't want to admit that her deathly premonitions about West were getting stronger. Allie was already too attached to the FBI agent, probably thinking he was a great catch.

The kind of man Olivia needed. She wouldn't put it past her baby sister to try to marry her off, to dream up some grand illusion that Olivia was falling in love with Ian West.

"I'll probably be late," Allie said.

"That's fine. Just watch your back, okay?"

"I won't let any witches get me." The younger woman fluffed her wild mane. Around her neck, she wore a self-designed charm, a wolf claw wrapped in leather and decorated with beads. According to their father, wolves were associated with war, and wolf medicine was used as protection from one's enemies.

Olivia doubted that Allie's charm was strong enough to ward off the witches their mother had spawned, but she wasn't about to discourage her sister's effort.

After Allie left, Olivia remained in front of the TV. Thirty minutes later someone knocked at the door. She climbed off the couch and checked the peephole.

It was West.

With a deep breath she answered the summons. He stood like a sentry in the doorway, tall and strong, with the loft stairs framing him in an architectural backdrop.

"Did Allie call you?" she asked.

He shook his head. "I came on my own."

"Why?"

"To eat some ice cream with you."

She frowned, wondering how he knew she'd been pigging out, then she glanced back and saw the carton on the coffee table. Apparently he'd spotted it, too.

"Do you want to come in?"

His lips tilted in a half smile. "I thought you'd never ask."

Once he was inside, she closed the door. But their conversation didn't pick up. They simply gazed at each other. Stared into each other's eyes.

And then Olivia's knees threatened to buckle.

Déjà vu. This was her vision, the moment West would kiss her.

She fidgeted with her top, with the silk pajamas she wore. West watched her like a predator, and she realized her loungewear was the same color as his eyes.

Had she dragged these pajamas out of her drawer purposely? Or had it been a subconscious effort?

He wore familiar clothes, too. The jeans and tan pullover she'd seen in her vision. She glanced at his feet and noticed his scuffed boots.

"I know why you're here," she said.

"Do you?" He stepped closer.

"Yes."

"Good." He reached out to touch her face, to skim his knuckles along her jaw.

She moistened her lips. There was no point in fighting it. She wanted this to happen. She wanted to feel his mouth against hers, to taste his desire.

His hand slipped, moving down the column of her neck.

She waited, expectation pummeling her body like burning coals.

And then he did it. He kissed her, pushing his tongue into her mouth.

Olivia pressed closer, clawing his shirt with her nails. Somewhere nearby, somewhere in the crowded cavern of her aroused mind, she heard Samantha hissing.

The cat was jealous.

West kept kissing her. But he wasn't gentle. He was fierce and strong, cupping her rear, dragging her pelvis against his.

But Olivia didn't care. This was exactly what she needed, exactly what she craved. Hard-driven lust. His tongue swallowing hers.

She untucked his shirt and reached under it, skimming her fingers along his stomach, dipping her thumb into his navel. He made a rough sound, and she knew he wanted her to unzip his pants. But instead she moved her hand in the other direction, pressing her palm against his heart.

And then she froze. She couldn't feel anything. No life force. No strong, steady beats.

Agent West was dead.

No, she thought, as she pulled away, as she ended the kiss. *No.*

He frowned at her. "What's wrong?"

She couldn't say it. She couldn't tell him that his heartbeat had vanished. That she'd experienced another psychic omen, another warning of his impending doom.

"Don't do this, Olivia. Don't turn me away."

Something told her not to heed his plea, not to get too close, not to be with him tonight. Yet letting him go would only make her ache.

She still craved his touch.

"It's been a while," she said.

"Since you've had sex?"

She nodded. "I don't usually wait this long. When I want a man, I take him."

"So what's stopping you now?"

"My emotions."

"Does that mean you want me to leave?"

"No," she decided, as she grabbed him. "It just means I need you."

Once again they kissed. Only, this time she refused to worry about a heartbeat she couldn't feel.

Ian West was her fantasy, and she wanted to climb in his lap and shudder in his arms. She wanted nasty sex. But she wanted romance, too.

The bad girl who collected bondage belts and blindfolds.

"What color are your panties?" he asked.

"What panties?" she said, making his breath catch in his throat.

Now it was her turn to smile. There he stood, armed with a federally issued firearm and a bulge beneath his zipper.

Talk about a lethal combination.

"Come with me," she said, putting her hands all over him, dragging him to her lair.

As they stumbled down the hall, rubbing and kissing, Samantha hissed like a green-eyed monster, then crossed their path, trying to curse them with bad luck.

Refusing to be distracted, Olivia ignored her sister's pesky pet. She wouldn't let black-cat superstition ruin her fantasy.

West linked his fingers through hers, and she led him to her room, eager to make love.

Together they tumbled onto the bed. She disarmed him, removing his gun, placing it on the dresser. A second later they both went mad, feasting on pent-up passion.

He tore open her pajama top, popping the buttons, baring her breasts. She removed his shirt, scratching his skin, teasing the ripple of muscle.

After he yanked off her pajama bottoms, he shot her a curious look. She was wearing panties.

"I lied," she said.

"So I see." He toyed with the swatch of black lace, running his fingers along the elastic band. "Tell me what you want me to do. Tell me what kind of foreplay you like best."

She gazed at his mouth, at those warm, wicked lips. "You're a smart guy. I'm sure you can figure it out."

"Oh, yeah?"

He discarded her panties, and she arched her hips, letting him know he was doing the right thing. When he pushed her legs apart and lowered his head, pleasure pulsed through her veins.

"Say it, Olivia. Tell me what you want."

She moved closer, as close as she could get. "This," she told him.

"This?" he parroted, licking her sweet and slow.

"Yes." She tunneled her hands through his hair. He looked up at her, and she became fixated on his eyes.

They were glowing. Like moonlight. Like madness. Like a spell she couldn't break.

Lost in the feeling, she rocked back and forth, then

nudged him onto the bed and straddled his face, encouraging him to keep licking her, to keep making her moan.

She liked this position. She liked taking control. "More," she said.

"Much more," he whispered, his words tickling her flesh.

He used his entire mouth, and she nearly melted on the spot. Even the sound turned her on. The saliva against skin. The deep, carnal suckling.

He reached out to hold her, to grip her waist, to make the moment even more erotic. Olivia traced the shape of his lips, and he nibbled her finger, then used his teeth on her clitoris.

Gently, ever so gently.

She couldn't have dreamed up a more perfect lover.

Feeling naughty, she decided to shift their positions again. Only, this time she told him to kneel on the floor. After he did, she scooted to the edge of the bed and hiked her legs over his shoulders.

More bad-girl fantasies.

He indulged her every whim.

Agent West, she thought. Boy toy extraordinaire.

Steeped in sensation, she watched him. And when he looked up at her, his magnetic gaze snaring hers, she came all over his mouth, sweet and thick, warm and syrupy, like caramel dripping over wax.

Olivia wasn't sure how long it took her to recover. She blinked at West, realizing he stood beside the bed, staring at her. Suddenly he seemed like a stranger, a man hiding his soul.

When he turned off the night-light burning in her room, a silvery sheen from the moon bathed his skin. For a moment, she hugged her knees to her chest, protecting her emotions. He looked ominous, deathly in the lunar glow.

Was his heart beating?

Of course it was, she told herself. He was alive. She wasn't losing him.

He unzipped his jeans and took them off. Next he removed his boxers, exposing his nakedness.

Without thinking, Olivia opened her legs and offered herself to him. Like a sacrifice. A woman much too willing to be taken.

He crawled onto the bed and kissed her, his mouth devouring hers. He tasted like her orgasm, like the hot wet flavor of oral sex.

When they separated, she felt empty inside. She wanted him inside her, filling the void.

"Did you bring any condoms?" she asked.

He didn't answer, and she wondered if his mind had drifted, if he'd slipped into some sort of erotic trance. His gaze traveled over her body, lingering at the vee between her thighs.

"Touch yourself," he said.

She shook her head. "I'm not into that."

A small smile ghosted across his lips. "Everyone is into that."

"Not in front of other people."

"Then pretend I'm not here."

Was he serious? There was no way she could forget that a big, tall, gorgeous FBI agent was staring at her, waiting for her to masturbate. "No."

"But I like to watch."

"Too bad."

"You're stubborn, Olivia."

She wasn't giving in, not to something that didn't appeal to her. "It's too much like voyeurism. And that's the last thing I want to think about tonight."

He shrugged, then pushed her down and kissed her. She wrapped her legs around him, and they rolled over the bed, tangling the sheets.

Once again she had control of her fantasy, of the passion she craved. She slid her hand between his legs and stroked him. He cupped her breasts and tongued one of her nipples, bringing it to a hardened peak.

His hair fell across his forehead, making him look rebellious, unlawful, an outlaw who owned a badge.

He was an enigma, she thought. A chameleon. He kept changing the rules.

He tried to thrust into her without protection, but she stopped him.

"Sorry," he said, even though he didn't sound the least bit remorseful.

"You did that on purpose. You're messing with my mind." And she wasn't sure why.

"This is my fantasy, too," he said.

"I'm not having unprotected sex."

"Then give me a minute." He lifted his pants off the floor, dug around in each pocket, checking them over and over again. Finally he came up with a foil packet, almost as if he'd conjured it from thin air.

At this point she didn't care how he'd secured the damn thing. She just wanted him to make love to her, to treat her right.

He rolled on the latex, and she climbed onto his lap and impaled herself, just as she'd imagined doing. He tipped back his head, and she rode him, gripping his shoulders.

In the next instant he pushed her down, holding her arms above her head. He wouldn't let her nuzzle his neck. He wouldn't let her get too close.

He told her he wanted it fast and deep, to make it count. He'd gotten her off, and now it was his turn.

His words stung. She'd expected more from West.

But it was too late to shove him away. He came hard and quick.

When it was over, he discarded the condom and moved to stand beside the window, to stare at the night, at the darkness enveloping the sky.

She studied his naked body, wishing he'd held her. That he'd been just a little bit tender.

But what did she expect? He didn't have a heart.

"I have to go," he said.

She gestured to the door. He wasn't the lover of her sweet, naughty dreams.

And she would never let him touch her again.

Chapter 10

By the following morning, Olivia was fuming. She'd barely slept a wink, and now the sun broke through the clouds and blasted her window.

The same window West had posed in front of.

Heartless jerk.

Even Kyle had treated her with more respect. At least her former lover hadn't played games. Desperate sex was one thing. But yanking her chain was another.

West knew damn well that she'd been emotional last night. That she needed him to care. Or at least pretend that he did.

But, no. He'd lured her right into his Federal Bureau of Insensitivity trap. He'd flayed her to madness, making sweet love with his mouth. Then he'd used his penis like a sword. A blade that had cut bone deep.

Like the knife the Slasher had plunged into his victims.

Olivia checked the clock on her nightstand. She had an appointment with one of her clients this morning. A wealthy widow who relied on her for weekly consultations. But she couldn't handle a private reading today. She couldn't behave like a wise, all-knowing, all-seeing psychic.

How was she supposed to give someone else spiritual advice when her own life was a mess?

Knowing she had to cancel, she called her client and told the gentle-natured lady the truth. Her energy was shot. Her brightly colored, keen-sighted aura had nose-dived, splattering right to the ground.

After she hung up the phone, she showered, applied her makeup and got dressed. Rather than purify her surroundings with sage, she let the negativity consume her.

She wanted West's violation to linger on her skin, to fester into violence.

She closed her eyes and focused on him, wishing she was a witch, wishing she could cast a spell that would shatter his nonbeating heart into a zillion bloody pieces.

He'd raped her soul, ravaged the loneliness inside her, the void that losing both of her parents had caused. Olivia wasn't invincible. Sometimes she needed someone to hold her.

Once again, she picked up the phone. But this time she dialed the Los Angeles Street Station, asking if West was there. The desk sergeant confirmed that the FBI agent was holed up in his borrowed office.

Good, she thought. Adjusting her holster, she decided to pay West a call, to tell him that he was, indeed, going to die.

Maybe even by one of her bullets.

She left Allie a note that read, "I'll be back later." She hadn't told her sister about last night. But Allie had gotten home in the wee hours of the morning, humming like a songbird, and Olivia didn't have the heart to destroy her chipper mood.

After a short, bat-out-of-hell drive, she arrived at the cop shop. Pumped with anger, with male-bashing adrenaline, she swept through the building and barged into West's domain.

He sat at the cluttered desk, wearing a charcoal-colored suit and a narrow tie.

She imagined strangling him with it.

He glanced up. "You could have knocked."

And he could have knocked her up last night, trying to bone her without a condom. "This isn't even your office."

"But I'm using it." He angled his head, looked her up and down. "No leather today? No fishnet stockings? No cleavage?"

"Just jeans and a T-shirt." She thrust her hands on her hips. "And my Glock."

"Yep, your ever-faithful weapon." He tapped his holster. "I've got mine, too."

So what? she thought. They'd faced off before.

He reached for his coffee and took a sip. The fresh-brewed aroma wafted through the air. "As long as you're here, why don't you quit acting so pissy and settle in for a while?" He indicated an empty chair. "I've been going through my notes. Comparing male and female narcissists."

Olivia didn't take a seat. She didn't do anything but stare at him. Did he honestly think she wanted to discuss the case? "Cut the crap."

He squinted at her. "What crap? You don't believe in narcissism?"

"Yes, I believe in it. I think you have it, you self-centered son of a bitch."

"What's with the name calling? I've been working my ass off all night." He squinted again. "I don't need you ragging on me."

"That's why you were in such a hurry to leave my bedroom? To put on your suit and play FBI?" Olivia moved forward and leaned against his desk. "You screwed me. Literally and figuratively. And I'll never forgive you for that."

"What are you talking about?" He motioned to the stack of files in front of him, to his rumpled clothes, to his disheveled hair. "I've been here all night. Do you understand? *All night.*"

"No." She shook her head, fear rising like bile. "You came to my loft. You kissed me, like in my vision. And then I—"

"You what?"

She couldn't say it. She couldn't repeat all those humiliating details. "Nothing."

"Nothing?" He grabbed her wrists, held her within his grasp, locking her in place. "Did you have sex with someone who looked like me? Did you fuck a goddamn witch?" He was nearly shouting now. "We just talked about shape-shifters, Olivia. We talked about them yesterday. Couldn't you tell the difference? Couldn't you—"

She jerked free, pulling away from him, wanting to call him a liar. A cheat. A man who wouldn't admit when he'd treated a woman like a whore. But she couldn't. "It wasn't you?"

"No, it wasn't. You can talk to Muncy. He'll verify that I was here all night. He was here, too. He still is."

She clutched her stomach. "It wasn't a shape-shifter."

"It had to be." He came around the desk and nudged her onto a chair. Then he knelt in front of her, his voice gentle, his tone filled with concern. "Did he hurt you?"

"Not physically." She reached out to touch his face, to tell herself he was real. That this was the man she longed to make love with. "At first he did everything right. He was my fantasy. My boy toy."

West raised his eyebrows, and she realized how ridiculous that sounded.

"Then what happened?" he asked.

"He changed. He stopped being my fantasy."

"He looked exactly like me?"

"Yes, but—" She paused, dropped her hand to his

chest, to the organ pumping blood through his body. "He didn't have a heartbeat."

He searched her gaze. "That doesn't make sense."

"I thought it was an omen. A psychic illusion, another premonition that you were going to die." She kept her palm against his heart, absorbing the warmth, the human contact, the strong, steady pulsation. "Don't you see? It wasn't a shape-shifter. He wasn't even alive."

West raised his eyebrows again. "You banged a dead guy?"

"No." She racked her brain for an explanation, for something that would make the pieces fit, the warning signs she'd ignored last night. "I think he was conceived from an image spell. From a doll."

"Like voodoo?"

"Image dolls are used in all sorts of witchcraft." She blew out the breath she'd been holding. "They're even common among the Southwest tribes." She scanned her mind for bits of information, things she learned as a child, things meant to scare little Indian boys and girls. "Some of the early Native witches used to make clay figures, then pierce them with prickly pear spines." ·

"So it is like voodoo?"

"Yes. But in the Southwest, the most potent dolls were made from a portion of the earth the victim had urinated on."

He made a disgusted face. "I didn't pee on anything."

"Are you sure you didn't take a leak in the bushes somewhere?"

"I don't do that." His expression turned sheepish. "Unless I'm drunk. And you were with me the last time I got wasted."

"So maybe this spell didn't require urine."

He came to his feet, then leaned against the desk. "Someone made an itty-bitty doll of me, but instead of sticking pine needles or pins into it, they used it to create a six-foot clone?"

"Except they couldn't get its heart to beat."

"Who did this to us, Olivia? Who was it?"

She crossed her arms, rubbing the goose bumps that appeared. "Derek Moon." Who else would cast a sexual spell? Who else would prod the clone to say voyeuristic things? "He must have been watching. Viewing the whole damn thing in his mind." She kicked away her chair. "I'm going to kill that pervert. I'm going to rip him in two."

"Not without me, you're not."

"Yes, I am. He won't admit what he did if you're there. He won't talk to the FBI." She held up her hand, stopping West from protesting. "I need to get a confession from him. I need to learn more about his magic."

Because it was time to fight fire with fire. To strengthen her powers.

The malevolence coursing through her veins.

Olivia arrived at Derek Moon's mansion, and the gate was open, the guard tower empty. The Tudor-style house with its charming windows and lush green lawn greeted her with a maniacal leer.

She parked in the circular driveway and told herself the distorted building was an illusion, a trick Derek had conjured.

Things weren't always what they seemed.

She knocked on the door, and when the wood rippled, like water in a blood-dappled stream, she cursed beneath her breath.

Then rubbed the chills that raced up her arm.

No one answered. No one appeared. The house was vacant. She could feel the hollow energy.

A crow cawed in the distance, taunting her with a screeching sound. She glanced up at a second-story window, saw the curtain move.

The house wasn't empty. Not completely.

She tried the doorknob, turned it, heard the hinges squeak. The crow cawed again. Olivia didn't know what the bird was trying to say. In the old days, the Chiricahua feared the black-winged animals. Yet the appearance of a crow before a hunt was a favorable omen.

Was this a hunt?

She looked up at the window again. The curtain had stopped moving.

Olivia kept turning the doorknob. It spun in a circle, like the little girl's head in the *Exorcist*.

Did Derek Moon worship the devil?

No, she thought. This was just part of his game, his theatrics. Irritated, she turned the handle one more time.

The door flew open.

Olivia entered the house, her shoes echoing on marble tiles. Orange candles flickered from every table, from every corner, flames dancing in jest.

Derek had prepared his home just for her.

She glanced around, wondering where the hell he was. She wandered into the dining room and stood in front of the satyr. Refusing to be intimidated, she stared at the jeering beast.

It stared back at her.

The candles smelled like caramel. Sweet and syrupy. Orgasmic.

Olivia wanted to go home and make love with West. The real West, the flesh-and-blood man. She wanted to prove that she was more powerful than Derek's spell.

But you're not, a voice whispered in her head.

"Yes, I am," she said out loud.

She closed her eyes, tried to get a reading on Derek, to locate him in her mind.

But she saw her dead mother instead.

A quick flash, a familiar image. The red-stained sheet, the heart, the arrowhead. Yvonne's motionless body, her beautiful face.

Things aren't always what they seemed.

"I didn't kill her."

Olivia spun around. Derek stood behind her, dressed in a long black robe. Around his neck he wore Allie's charm, the wolf claw, the silver beads.

"You bastard." She reached for the necklace and tore

it off him. The leather thong broke, spilling the beads. They rolled across the floor like tiny marbles.

A second later, they disappeared.

It wasn't Allie's charm, she realized. It was another trick. Another illusion.

Tired of his game, she lunged for his throat and shoved him against the wall, pushing her thumb into his windpipe.

He gasped, his eyes bulging wide.

But Olivia couldn't hold him for long. Something slammed into her, hard and fast and sharp. She fell forward, against Derek, and they both hit the floor.

Pain exploded in her body, blood trailing down her spine. She cursed and crawled away from Derek. He was still gasping for air.

Olivia turned and looked at the painting. The satyr had blood on his hooves.

Her blood.

She drew her gun and aimed it at the canvas, but the half man, half goat did nothing but dance, shuffle its bewitched feet.

Her bullets wouldn't kill it.

She turned the weapon on Derek instead.

He stopped gasping.

Olivia rose, refusing to wince, to give credence to her pain. "I want to learn your magic."

"Why?" Derek didn't move. He remained on the floor, gazing at the pistol aimed at his chest. "So you can bind me? Stop me from casting spells?"

She didn't respond. Her back was still bleeding.

"I won't teach you." He blinked and the candles flickered. "I'm not a fool." Smoke misted around him, rising to the ceiling. "You shouldn't have talked to my ex-wife about me."

"Because she told us the truth?"

"I didn't break my marriage vows. Voyeurism isn't cheating."

Olivia narrowed her eyes. "Your little joke last night wasn't very funny."

He took a chance and stood. "Funny, no. Fun, yes." He smiled at her, even though she was still holding him at gunpoint. "I let you control him. I gave you that much. Your fantasy. Your boy toy. He behaved just the way you wanted him to."

"And then he turned into a creep. He started acting like you."

"Watching rough sex excites me." Braver now, he reached into the pocket of his robe.

Olivia nearly shot off his hand until she saw what he had.

A small cloth figure. The image doll that represented Agent West.

"Do you want to hold it? Kiss it? Put its head between your legs?" He waved the dark-haired figure, making it flop back and forth. "Or should I kill it instead?" When he threw the doll, it sailed through the air, then made a deathly descent.

In one desperate motion, in one gut-clenching instant, Olivia holstered her weapon and lunged for the figure, saving it from the burning candles scattered across the table.

Once it was in her grasp, Derek shrugged and walked away, disappearing into the cavern of his house, leaving her alone with his magic.

A short while later Olivia reclined on West's bed, facedown, with her T-shirt pulled up. While she gazed at the unfamiliar headboard, he dressed the wound on her back. He was no longer staying at the Z-Sleep Inn. He'd moved to another motel on Sunset, leaving her father's ghost behind.

"I knew I should have gone to Moon's house with you," he said.

"I handled it."

"You call this handling it? That son of a bitch kicked you."

"His pet goat kicked me. Derek is too much of a wuss to fight back on his own."

"Then maybe he isn't the killer."

"And maybe he is. He's a powerful witch. He brought that stupid painting to life."

"That's not the same as murdering people."

She sighed into West's pillow. How many whodunit conversations had they had? "I'm exhausted."

"I know. I'm sorry." He bandaged her wound, his ministrations gentle.

"You're good at this." Really good. He even took the sting out of the antiseptic, if that was possible.

"I earned my emergency-medical-technician certification during high school, and I became a paramedic after I graduated. That's what I did to put myself through college."

"Really?" She rolled over to look at him. She hadn't figured him for a healer. "You're a multitalented guy."

"Yep." He pulled her shirt down, adjusting it over her stomach, babying her. "I almost went to medical school, but I changed my mind."

Fascinated, she sat up. "Dr. West became Agent West."

"Yeah, and considering the amount of trouble you get into, you're going to need me." He propped a pillow under her head, making her more comfortable. "As a doctor and an agent."

"Don't get cocky. I saved your ass today."

"You saved a doll." A frown marred his forehead. "Can I see it?"

"It's in my purse."

He climbed off the bed and retrieved her handbag, then gave it to her so she could open it.

Olivia looked inside, then removed the doll, cradling it carefully in her hands. It was dressed in denim pants and a tan shirt, identical to the clothes the clone had worn last night. It even had a tiny gun clipped to its belt. She'd already checked its pockets for miniature condoms, but that was a detail Derek had forgotten, something he'd been forced to conjure from thin air.

"It's cloth," West said. "I expected it to be clay." He

studied it curiously. "Should we torture it and see if I start hurting?"

"That isn't funny." She swiped the little guy away from him. "I already rescued him from a fire."

"Yeah, but this is what Moon used to cast that sexual spell." He took the doll's hand and made it rub her boob. "See? It's a pervert."

"Stop it." She couldn't help but laugh. West had a way of making everything seem funny, no matter how creepy the subject matter was.

"Can I keep it?" he asked.

She gave him a suspicious look. "Why?"

"So I can have my own Mini-Me."

She rolled her eyes. "I should have known you were an Austin Powers fan."

"Yeah, baby." He impersonated the movie character, mimicking a British accent, making a silly face. "Aren't you just dying to shag me?"

She paraded the doll past him. Goofy, sexy, Agent West. "I already shagged Mini-Me."

"Lucky him." He took the cloth figure and placed it on the nightstand. "When the clone was doing everything right, what exactly was he doing?"

"I'm not giving you details."

"Why not? You thought it was me."

"I know, but—"

"Come on, Olivia. Tell me."

"No." She looked around the room, noticed how tidy it was. West never left anything out of place.

When she shifted her gaze back to him, he was staring at her.

Like a dog begging for a bone.

Or a boner, she supposed. He wanted to talk about sex. "You're going to get all horned out about this."

"No, I won't."

"Okay. Fine." She gave in, figuring she owed him that much. He'd been hexed, too. "The clone used his mouth."

He glanced at her zipper. "Down there?"

"Yes, down there." She grabbed the sheet, toyed with a corner of it. "In all sorts of positions."

"Damn." He wet his lips. "Did you do it to him, too?"

"No."

"Why not?"

"Because I didn't think of it."

"You better think of it next time."

She covered herself with the sheet. "Next time?"

He moved a little closer. "When you're with me. We can do it to each other."

Olivia went warm. Woozy and warm. "We've never even kissed."

He leaned over, lowered his head and brushed his mouth across hers, rewarding her with the sweetest, most gentle kiss any man had ever given her.

"Now we have," he said.

She smiled at him. He really was a healer. "I like you, Agent West."

"I like you, too." He smoothed her hair. "But I'm not

going to sleep with a wounded woman. You need to get better first."

Her injury wasn't as serious as he was making it out to be, but she didn't protest. Because the next time he played doctor with her, she would be naked.

And loving every minute of it.

Chapter 11

Olivia couldn't sleep. Thoughts somersaulted in her brain, leaping and jumping, making her head hurt.

Sometimes life was too damn complicated.

She was home in her own bed, and she missed Agent West. Which made her feel stupid. She'd never behaved like a moonstruck female before.

Moonstruck.

Bad word choice, she decided.

Derek Moon. Moon Dust Entertainment.

She was sick of the moon.

To prove her point, she turned her back on the window, snubbing the lunar ball in the sky.

And then a scratching sound caught her attention. A faint noise coming from another room.

Samantha sharpening her claws on the furniture?

No, that didn't seem right. The cat's paws weren't *that* big. She wasn't a mountain lion.

Olivia reached for the lamp and turned the switch, but nothing happened. None of the lights worked.

She sat up and listened.

A rustling motion. Gloved hands. Soft-soled shoes. A person moving with timed precision, invading the loft.

Someone who didn't expect to get caught.

A witch? The killer?

She grabbed her 9 mm from the nightstand, the familiar shape molding to her hand, becoming part of her. Her pistol. Her lifeline.

Trying to get a reading on the intruder, she closed her eyes and concentrated. Male energy, she thought. Dark clothes. A ski mask. She couldn't see him, but she could feel him.

She opened her eyes, preparing to—

A struggle. A muffled scream.

He was in Allie's room.

Olivia took off, running down the hall, her heart pounding in her throat, her bare feet slapping the floor. Samantha raced after her, hissing in the dark. The cat knew something was wrong, too. She stepped on the hem of Olivia's nightgown, panicked and dug her claws into the ebony fabric, tearing it.

Allie's door wouldn't open.

She could hear her sister fighting off her attacker, rolling over the bed, banging into the dresser.

Glass shattered. A figurine of some kind. One of Allie's collectibles.

Samantha hissed again.

Olivia kicked in the door, breaking the lock.

The cat lost her courage, skittering in the other direction.

Mist filled Allie room, making it seem vast, a cavern of endless fog, a dank dungeon.

A magic spell?

Olivia couldn't see Allie, but the younger woman still battled for control, making muffled noises, trying to remove the gag from her mouth, trying to stop the intruder from pinning her arms to the bed.

"Get out!" he shouted, his voice echoing in the blackened chamber, warning Olivia to stay away.

In the next instant Allie broke free. She could feel her sister pulling away from the attacker. But Olivia wasn't going to let him go. She wasn't going to let him escape, disappear like a magician on a smoke-screened stage.

Lifting her weapon, she used her sixth sense, the power she'd been honing. She tracked the male energy, back and forth, through the haze.

She took aim, fired, hit her mark.

He went down, his knees buckling beneath him.

Then the room turned silent.

No movement, no voices. Nothing.

"Allie?" Olivia called in the dark.

"I'm here," came the shell-shocked reply. "But I think you just killed Kyle."

Oh, dear God. "What?"

"I'm not dead," he snarled, his pain-clenched voice sending her heart into a tailspin. "But what the hell did you shoot me for? I told you I was going to do this."

What was he talking about? Suddenly her brain was as cloudy as the room.

A beam of light illuminated the insanity, and Olivia realized Allie had retrieved a flashlight, scanning the darkness, looking for Kyle.

She located him in the corner, an ominous figure shrouded in mist, a ski mask concealing his face, his long hair secured in a ponytail.

Olivia blew out the breath she'd been holding. She'd nailed him in the leg. "I'll call for an ambulance."

"No!" He leaped up and removed the mask, waving it like a flag, clearing the smoke that clung to him. "I'm fine."

Fine? The glaring white orb reflected his injury, the blood that had dampened his pants and dripped onto the area rug beneath him.

"Somebody needs to hit the main breaker," he said. "I turned it off."

"I'll do it." Allie's breath rushed out, her voice quavering with overly spent adrenaline. She left the room, taking the flashlight with her.

Olivia and Kyle waited in the dark, but she managed to open the windows, allowing fresh air to circulate.

"You better turn off the fog machine," he said. "Or it'll start up again. It's on a timer."

Trust him to plant a Halloween device, to trick her into thinking the mist was real. "Where is it?"

"Next to the hamper."

Olivia used her psychic sight, as West called it, to find her way around in the dark. Within seconds she located the machine and deactivated it.

When Allie returned, she flipped on the light. For a moment no one spoke. Beneath the dresser, shards of colored glass littered the floor like rocks in the bottom of an aquarium.

Olivia glanced at her sister. She wore a bandana, the gag Kyle had used on her, looped around her neck.

What a disaster.

"Why can't I call for an ambulance?" Olivia asked.

"Because it's a gunshot wound." Kyle stumbled over to the bed and sat on the edge of it. "And the doctor on duty at the hospital will have to report it to the police." He tossed the ski mask down, made a pained face. "I don't want the cops involved."

She sat next to him, smoothed a stray hair that had come loose from his ponytail. "You'd rather bleed to death?"

He jerked away from her, refusing to let her mother him. "The bullet just grazed me. It hurts like hell, but it's not as bad as it looks."

What if he ended up with an infection? Or what if it was worse than he thought? "At least let me call a friend of mine. He used to be a paramedic."

"Fine. Whatever. Just no hospital. No cops."

Olivia wouldn't dare admit who her friend was. Kyle hated the FBI even more than the police. She used Allie's cell phone and dialed the special agent's motel. He answered on the second ring, and she explained the situation as briefly as she could, asking him what to do.

He gave her a list of instructions, telling her to elevate Kyle's leg and put pressure on the wound to stop the bleeding. Then he promised he would be right over.

Allie helped Olivia with the emergency care, and Kyle scowled at both of them, making Olivia's guilt fester even more.

"You didn't tell me you were going to break in and jump my sister," she said.

"Yes, I did," he argued. "I left a message on your cellphone voice mail earlier. I told you it was part of Allie's training. I mentioned everything, all the details. And I told you to stay the hell out of her room. That I was locking the door."

"There weren't any messages from you today." She pressed a clean pillowcase to his leg, trying to maintain the pressure, while Allie searched for proper medical supplies, getting things ready for West. "You must have called someone else's voice mail."

"No way." He rattled off the number, transposing the last two digits.

Olivia heaved a weary sigh. How brainless could he be? "It's four-five, not five-four."

"Really?" He laughed at his own stupid mistake, and Allie exploded and punched his good leg, shutting him up. Apparently she wasn't amused by the attack he'd staged, even if she'd figured out at some point who he was. But her true anger, Olivia suspected, came from the fear that she'd thought he was dead. Allie had begun to care for Kyle. Not in a romantic way. But she thought of him as a big brother, someone she could count on, even if he drove her nuts.

West finally arrived. Olivia opened the front door for him, and Samantha raced into the living room, meowing nervously at his feet.

He set his briefcase on the floor and scooped up the shivering cat, stroking her fur. Then he gazed at Olivia, snaring her with those gunmetal eyes.

"What am I going to do with you?" he asked.

She frowned at him. "This wasn't my fault."

He set Samantha down, soothing her with one last stroke. "I'll be the judge of that."

They entered Allie's room and Kyle took one look at West and cursed at Olivia. "He's that FBI dude, isn't he? You called a frigging fibbie."

The special agent told Kyle to shut up.

From there, West washed his hands in Allie's bathroom and began treating the wound. He worked diligently, letting everyone know that the injured party would live. Kyle squinted from time to time, looking past the agent to glare at Olivia.

She glared back at him. At least the "FBI dude" wouldn't report it. He would keep their secret.

"What the hell were you doing here?" West asked him.

"Training Addle-brain." Kyle expanded his muscular chest, trying to look macho, in spite of being confined to a frilly pink bed. "Surprise attack."

West continued his medical ministrations. "Addle-brain?"

"Allie." Kyle grinned, finally relaxing in the G-man's presence. "I used a fog machine to make the place seem witchy. I scared the crap out of Addle-brain. Liv, too."

"Liv," West mused, then glanced over his shoulder at her.

She shrugged, trying to seem unaffected by those piercing gray eyes. But she couldn't quite pull it off.

An hour later things were back to normal. Or as normal as the situation would allow. Allie's room had been swept, the bedding changed, the blood droplets on the area rug scrubbed clean. Kyle settled in on the couch, with his leg properly bandaged and the TV remote control at his disposal. Olivia invited West to sleep in her room, where they prepared to retire for the night.

"I'm beat," she said. "It's been a long day."

"No kidding?" He shook his head. "You get kicked by a satyr in the afternoon, then shoot an old lover at night."

"Sometimes Kyle is an imbecile."

"Then why did you date him?"

"He taught me how to fight. And he's got a big—" she paused, saw West raise his eyebrows at her "—heart. He's been a good friend."

He moved closer. "Are you sure you want me to stay?"

"Positive." She removed the torn nightgown, changing into a lighter-colored one, knowing the see-through fabric would catch his eye. "I'm going to seduce you tomorrow."

He roamed his gaze over her. "That's cheating."

"What is? Making you wait?"

"Teasing me with the goods. You look hot."

"You think?" She modeled the slinky garment, turning so he could see every angle, the sheer fabric flowing like a transparent waterfall. When she reached underneath and removed her panties, he lost his breath.

"Now I have a hard-on."

She tossed the lacy thong at him. "I'm sure you'll survive."

He caught her underwear. "Easy for you to say."

She smiled and coaxed him onto the bed, so she could discard his shirt, so he could hold her, so she could sleep in the refuge of his arms and listen to his heartbeat.

Something was wrong. Still groggy, Ian opened his eyes and tried to leap out of bed, but his arms wouldn't move.

Someone had handcuffed him to the slats on the headboard.

Someone?

Olivia had done this. He frowned, rattled the cuffs, then cursed at the absurdity of his situation.

He'd remained awake most of the night, spooning with Olivia, breathing in the fragrance of her hair, holding her, wanting her. Finally he'd crashed hard, falling asleep in his jeans, with her panties in his pocket, a trophy that had aroused him beyond reason.

And now he was at her mercy. She'd unzipped his pants and tugged them down a little, leaving his boxers exposed to her bad-girl whim.

But Ian was far from amused.

A woman shouldn't dominate a man, at least not to this degree. He deserved to keep his pride, to be seduced on his own terms.

When she entered the room in her see-through silvery nightgown, he snapped to attention. Armed with a victorious smile, she carried a plate of food.

He had to hand it to her. She'd managed to lock him up without him even knowing it, and probably with his own cuffs. He'd left them in his briefcase last night.

"You've been parading around the house like that?" he asked.

"No one is here except us. Kyle went home, and my sister had a class this morning." She sat on the edge of the bed and showed him the food: pancakes smothered in syrup, strips of bacon, diced fruit.

He gave her a curious stare, trying to predict her next move. "Why did you fix breakfast?"

"So I can feed you." She cut into the pancakes and held the fork out to him.

He refused the offering. He wasn't about to let her humiliate him. He wasn't a baby. He could feed himself. "Take these damn things off."

"You don't like your punishment?"

"Punishment?" he parroted.

"For using those cuffs on me in the biker bar."

"So that's what this is all about?"

She dipped a strawberry in the syrup and licked it. Her lips were as ripe as the fruit, glossed in a crimson color. "Yep."

He frowned, wondering why she was wearing lipstick first thing in the morning. "Okay, fine. You've had your fun. Now let me go."

"The big bad agent." She ate the strawberry, sinking her teeth into it. "I just might have to pour some syrup over you."

His cock nearly jumped out of his fly. "That isn't funny."

"You're getting turned on."

"I am not."

"Liar." She reached into the pocket of his jeans, aware of the trophy he'd hidden. "You slept with my panties last night. That's kinky, West." She leaned over to kiss him, to slip her tongue into his mouth, to drive him half-mad.

When she tunneled her hands through his hair, he yearned for more, recalling every forbidden thing he'd ever dared to dream.

Including his obsession with her panties.

She pulled back, and he gazed at her, trapped in a web of heat, a tangle of heaven-help-me emotion. For a second, for one masochistic moment, he considered fighting the handcuffs. For the pleasure of trying to grab her, he thought. For the pain of not being able to succeed. But this was her game, her seduction, and suddenly he was willing to play by her rules.

This time, when she offered him a forkful of pancakes, he took it, chewing, swallowing, tasting his own desire. She ate, as well, alternating bites between them.

They didn't speak. They didn't say a word. They just put their mouths on the same fork, using it like a weapon, a sexual tool between soon-to-be lovers.

After the food was gone, his blood rushed to his groin. He knew what came next.

She turned the plate on its side and drizzled maple syrup over his chest, letting it trail down his stomach, marking a path to the waistband of his boxers and the unfastened jeans slung low on his hips.

He all but groaned.

She crawled onto the bed and tasted his skin, starting with his nipples. Her nightgown brushed his body, tickling him, sticking to the syrup.

Ian wondered if he could con her into marrying him. Just for the sex. Just for wild, wicked mornings like this.

After she undressed him, he opened his legs, hoping, praying...

Yes.

He gulped the air that rushed out of his lungs. She went down on him in one fell swoop, that luscious mouth sucking with feminine force.

She didn't mess around. She went for it. All of it, taking as much as she could, using her hands and her throat.

Lost in the feeling, he lifted his hips. "I'm going to propose to you."

She looked up, laughed, then rubbed her face all over him, branding him with her lipstick. Now he knew why she'd worn it.

"You think I'm kidding?" He decided, right then and there, that Olivia Whirlwind was meant to be his wife.

This was the best blow job he'd ever had.

She took him in her mouth again, teasing every inch. He started planning their honeymoon: a bottle of Tequila, a warm ocean breeze, oral pleasure for the rest of his—

She clawed his thighs, and he shivered.

—life. The rest of his I-need-this-woman life.

"Say you'll marry me."

"You're crazy."

His pulse pounded between his legs. "Just say it."

She flicked her tongue over the tip. "No."

"Please."

"Not a chance."

"It'll make me come."

"So will this." Her next bout of fellatio was so fast, so rhythmic, he didn't have a choice.

He ejaculated, hard and quick and liquid hot.

He threw back his head and closed his eyes. Olivia remained there, letting him enjoy the warmth of her mouth, the intoxication of oral sex.

Finally, she peeled off her nightgown and lay on top

of him, her nakedness pressed to his. He longed to hold her, but his wrists were still locked to the headboard.

She nuzzled his neck, breathing softly against his skin. She was sleek and warm and fragrant. Maple syrup and jasmine perfume. No wonder he fantasized about keeping her.

"Are you going to let me do that to you?" he asked.

"Yes."

"When?"

"Soon."

"How soon?"

She snuggled even closer. "You're impatient, Agent West."

"Ian. When we're in bed, you can call me Ian."

She kissed him, and she decided that she liked his name, the English, Scottish and Muscogee roots that made him who he was.

As sunlight dappled the bed, bathing it in rainbow hues, her heart thumped against his.

"Now," she said, lifting her head.

He smiled. He knew what she meant.

She didn't remove the handcuffs. Instead she knelt over his face, bold and beautiful, offering herself to him.

He looked up, anxious to arouse her, to give her everything she'd given him.

Everything and more.

She lowered herself onto his mouth, angling her body so he could taste her. He licked her, sweet and slow, making her warm and wet.

She rocked back and forth, showing him how much she liked it. She wasn't the least bit shy, and that turned him on even more.

Steeped in her flavor, he delved deeper, penetrating her with his tongue. She gasped and threaded her fingers through his hair, riding the wave with turbulent pleasure, clawing at his scalp, thrilling him.

He breathed in her scent, like a wolf claiming its mate. She looked incredibly erotic with her thighs spread over his face. A dominatrix, he thought, forcing him to do wicked things.

No wonder she wore all those bondage-inspired outfits. She got off on taking control, on bending a man to her will. Her kitten-with-a-gun will. He didn't mind a bit.

"Ian," she whispered his name, and their gazes locked.

Deep, real, intimate.

A second later he sucked on her clit, battering her senses, making her moan. Slick and damp, she climaxed, rippling like multicolored wax, melting all over him.

When it ended, she climbed off his face and kissed him, tongue to tongue, tasting herself, making the aftermath of her orgasm even more erotic. He blinked through the haze, through the mind-numbing effect she had on him.

"You're incredible." She removed the handcuffs and set him free.

"So are you." He looped his arms around her, dragging her next to him, holding her tight.

They stayed like that, wrapped in each other's arms, for what seemed like the tenderest moment of his life.

"I borrowed a condom from Kyle," she said.

Ian couldn't help but laugh. So much for tenderness. "He brought a rubber with him last night?"

"He always keeps protection in his wallet."

"Maybe he isn't such an imbecile after all."

"Will you check on him in a few days? Make sure he's healing all right."

"If you want me to." He smoothed her wild hair away from her cheek, wondered if he should be jealous of her old lover. "What kind of illegal activity is he involved in?"

"What makes you think he's doing something illegal?"

"Aside from him not wanting his gunshot wound reported? He called me a fibbie."

"The government lied to the Indians, West."

He frowned. "I'm not part of that government."

"Aren't you?"

"No." He trailed his hand down her back, felt the area he'd bandaged yesterday, the cut the satyr had left on her skin. "I go after bad guys."

"Kyle isn't a bad guy."

"I don't want to talk about him anymore."

"But you're willing to use the condom he supplied?" She held up the foil packet, letting it catch the light.

He took it away from her. "What do you think?"

She smiled and sank her head onto a pillow. "I think you should touch me."

"So do I." He filled his hands with her breasts, mesmerized by her nipples, by the dark-brown areolas.

She was perfect, he thought. Long and slim with golden skin. A woman who lived by her instincts, who exuded passion and beauty and a sense of vulnerability she refused to claim. He wanted to ask her about the scar on her throat, but he knew this wasn't the time, so he caressed her instead, molding her, shaping with his hands, like an artist creating a masterpiece.

They kissed, their mouths melding, their hearts skipping erratic beats. Heat flooded his loins, pulsing through him like a river, a current of need.

After he slipped on the protection, he entered her, slow and sleek and deep. She embraced him, holding him close.

He looked into her eyes and made love to her. Both of their bodies were sticky, glossed with maple syrup, with the sheen of foreplay.

Ian stroked her, the motion as slick and sweet as the sounds she made. The naughty little whispers. The girlish moans.

For now, the dominatrix was his.

He buried his face against her scar and tasted her skin. All his.

Chapter 12

Olivia and West relaxed, drinking sparkling cider from champagne glasses and listening to indigenous music. While incense sweetened the air, they faced each other in a claw-footed bathtub, an old-fashioned luxury that had drawn Olivia to the loft.

The loft Glenn owned.

"What's wrong?" West asked.

"Nothing." She sipped her cider, allowing the bubbles to tickle her throat.

"You always do that. You say 'nothing,' even though something is bothering you."

Did he have to be so observant? Did he have to trap her with those crystalline eyes? "I feel strange living here. I'm concerned that Glenn might have killed my mom, yet I'm renting a home from him."

"Allie trusts him."

"I know. And that makes things even more complicated." She stretched her legs, cautious not to bump his, to let her emotions run away with her. "I just wish this nightmare would end."

"It will. I promise it will."

Olivia sighed. West tried so hard to be her knight in shining armor, but she didn't believe in storybook heroes. He couldn't save her, or himself, from the darkness that loomed in the distance. She could feel it, rolling like distant thunder, waiting to crack across the sky.

"Do you think this was meant to be?" he asked. "Or did we defy fate?"

She tilted her head. His eyes were changing color, going from light to dark to light again. "This? You mean us?"

He nodded. "You had a vision about us kissing, but it wasn't even us."

"I have premonitions about events that are going to happen. Moon didn't plant that vision."

"No, but he conjured the clone you were kissing."

She reached for a washcloth. "That doesn't matter anymore. We're together now."

They sat quietly after that, inhaling the strawberry-scented smoke that curled in the air. She squeezed the washcloth over her body, wondering if they had defied fate.

He interrupted the silence. "Tell me about the scar on your throat."

Olivia looked up, caught his gaze. "There's nothing to tell."

"Is it from a thyroidectomy?"

"Yes, but the tumor was benign. I didn't have cancer." She traced the four-inch mark, slicing her finger across it. "It's no big deal."

"It makes you seem vulnerable."

Troubled, she frowned at him. She preferred to think that the scar made her seem strong, invincible, a woman displaying a war wound. She'd had surgery the same year her dad had committed suicide. The same year she'd started collecting guns, storing them in a case until she'd summoned the courage to learn to fire them.

"I like what it did to your voice."

"I know. You already told me that."

"So I'm telling you again. It's sexy."

"The nerve that supplies my vocal chords was damaged." Feigning indifference, she shrugged. "That's not particularly sexy."

"Yes, it is. Just listening to you gets me hard."

"Then maybe you should go home." She slid her foot between his legs, not quite making contact. "And I'll call you."

"You're not getting rid of me that easy."

"I'm not?"

"No." He took her into his arms. No games, no pretense, just a man who wanted her. "I'll buy a box of condoms today. I'll keep some in my wallet."

She leaned back against his body, wishing she wasn't getting so attached. Forever wasn't in the cards, even if she'd already given him her spare toothbrush. "You won't forget?"

"Are you kidding? It's all I'm going to think about."

She closed her eyes, enjoying the warmth of his skin. "Me, too."

After the water turned cold, they climbed out of the tub and dried off. Standing side by side, they got dressed in her room, using the mirrored closet doors.

"Are you going to the station today?" she asked, watching him tuck in his shirt.

"Yes, but I can't wear this. I have to go back to the motel and change."

She studied his reflection. "Why? Because you slept in your jeans? Or because you still have my underwear in your pocket?"

"You mean these?" He pulled out her panties, waving them like a naughty treasure.

She laughed and tried to grab them.

He laughed, too, fighting for the lace thong, winning the war, shoving them back into his pocket. "Finders keepers, losers weepers."

"Oh, yeah?" She tackled him, knocking him onto the bed. Then an unwelcome premonition exploded in her brain.

Stunned, she pulled back. "You're going to figure out who the killer is."

He sat up, nearly lost his breath. "When?"

"I don't know. But that's what's going to get you in trouble." Horrible trouble. Painful trouble.

"You mean that's what's going to get me killed? Why can't you let that go? Just forget about it?"

Forget about it? Suddenly she wanted to pound some sense into him, slam her fists into his chest. "I'm going to talk to Glenn."

"What for?"

"To find out what he knows. To try to get him to teach me how to use my mother's magic."

"So you can fight forces you can't even see?" West shook his head. "What if Glenn is the Slasher? What if he's the witch we're after?"

"It's a chance I have to take."

"Not without me. Not this time."

"Fine. I'll arrange a meeting for both of us."

"When?" he asked.

"This evening sometime, after Glenn gets home from work." She lifted her chin, felt her pulse go haywire. "Maybe you should resign from this investigation. Go back to Virginia."

"Like hell." He opened his briefcase, inserting the handcuffs she'd used on him. "There's no damn way I'm going to back off, especially now."

"Even if it kills you?"

"Yes," he said. "Even if it kills me."

Silence consumed Glenn's house. Olivia arrived early and, as usual, Glenn's housekeeper had prepared some snacks, placing them on the coffee table. Fresh salsa, tortilla chips, a vegetable platter with dill-seasoned dip. Even the beverage, a pitcher of iced tea, looked enticing.

Glenn filled his glass, but Olivia sensed that he would rather be drinking whiskey.

He was nervous, she thought. Trapped in his own home.

"So," he said.

"So," she repeated.

"Are we waiting for the police?"

She shook her head. "The FBI."

His skin paled a little, and she realized why West enjoyed flashing his badge. Just the name of the agency wielded power.

"How long are they going to be?" Glenn asked.

She glanced at her watch. "Special Agent West will be here soon."

He wrung his hands together. "I wish Allie had joined us."

Olivia had purposely omitted her sister from this meeting. She hadn't even told Allie about it. With a casual air, she reached for a celery stick and snapped it in two. Glenn all but flinched.

The doorbell rang, intensifying the moment even more.

When the housekeeper ushered West into the living room, Olivia and Glenn both rose from their chairs.

Olivia glanced at her lover. He wore a pinstriped suit, a white shirt and a pale gray tie that mirrored the color of his eyes.

He presented his badge and ID to Glenn, making the other man more uncomfortable than he already was.

And then West did something unexpected. He turned to Olivia and brushed her mouth with his. A gentle kiss. A possessive kiss. A form of affection that knocked Glenn for a loop.

He gave up on the iced tea and poured himself a stiff drink from the bar. "You're sleeping with the FBI?"

Olivia smoothed her micromini dress. "Not the whole FBI, just Agent West. But I guess Allie didn't tell you."

"No, she didn't."

"No reason she should," West said. "What Olivia and I do is our business."

She picked up on his cue. "Just like what Glenn did with my mom was his business?"

West unbuttoned his jacket, sat in an overstuffed chair. "No, not like that. Cheating with your best friend's wife isn't the same as two single people hooking up."

Glenn remained beside the bar. "I already explained how that happened."

"Right." The special agent studied the food on the table, eyeing the colorful array of vegetables, the radish rosettes, the vine-ripened cherry tomatoes. "Witchcraft."

Glenn topped his glass. "A love spell."

"Love?" The word made West smile. A cool, malicious smile. "Lust isn't love."

"It isn't?" Olivia ate the broken celery sticks. "And here I thought it was."

West shook his head. "Nope. There's a difference."

"My mistake." She glanced at Glenn. He looked miserable. Mortified. Was he reliving the day his wife had walked in on him and Yvonne? The day his marriage had shattered?

West sat back in his chair, waiting for Glenn to crack.

He did, only a moment later. "What exactly is this meeting about? What is it you want from me?"

"Funny you should ask." This time, Olivia went after a chip. "I want you to teach me everything you know about my mother's magic."

The older man turned toward a diamond-paned window, where a view of the Hollywood Hills lit up the night. "I don't know much. Hardly anything."

"Really?" Olivia ate another chip, taking advantage of the thick, rich salsa. "Beth Moon told us you were part of the coven Derek and my mom started."

Glenn sucked in an audible breath, but he didn't respond. He kept gazing out the window, wishing, it seemed, that the city would swallow him whole. Olivia almost felt sorry for him.

Almost.

"Were you involved in their coven?" West asked.

A cleared throat, a quiet answer. "Yes."

"For how long?"

"Several months. During my affair with Yvonne."

"Then tell us what you know. Help us with this investigation."

"Yes, of course." Glenn glanced at Olivia as if he meant to apologize for dabbling in the black arts.

She tried to gauge his emotions, but she couldn't feel his energy. She didn't know if he was as remorseful as he looked or if he was role-playing. Glenn had done some extra work in his youth. He'd always been drawn to the entertainment industry.

Just like West's profile of the killer.

"All of the women in Yvonne's family were witches," Glenn said. "It was in her blood." He paused to finish his drink, to calm his voice with alcohol. "For the Apache, there are two classes of witch power. The most dangerous is voodoo or sorcery, spells that can make people sick. The second is related to sex and is referred to as love magic. It's only bad when applied in full strength, when normal physical attractions escalate into lust."

"And that's what my mother did to you?" Olivia asked.

"Yes." Glenn turned to West. "Now you know what I meant by a love spell."

The special agent rubbed a hand across his jaw. "What kind of witch were you? What did you practice?"

"I did whatever Yvonne told me to do. I helped her steal personal belongings from her victims, items she used in her voodoo magic, but I never learned how to utilize them. I don't have any power of my own."

Once again, Olivia tried to read him, but she couldn't gauge his sincerity. For all she knew, he was a full-blown sorcerer. "There's nothing you can teach me?"

"Nothing that isn't already inside you. You were born with your mother's power. It's up to you how you use it."

Everyone fell silent for a moment, the impact of

Glenn's statement ricocheting between them, bouncing off the walls.

Olivia was strong enough to be a Chiricahua witch, strong enough to use her ability in malevolent ways.

"Was Yvonne a shape-shifter?" West asked.

Glenn contemplated the question, taking a second to answer. "She claimed that her ancestors could take the form of animals. That they could fly through the night as an owl or become a wolf or a deer or whatever they wanted. But I don't know if she could do it."

"What about Derek Moon?"

"I'm not sure about him, either. But Yvonne taught him everything she knew. She was impressed with his power, even though they hated each other later on."

West leaned forward. "What about taking the form of another human being? Did they ever talk about that?"

"No. But Moon used to clone people with image dolls and make the clones do sexual things. That's his specialty. Warped love magic."

Olivia and West exchanged a quick glance, but Glenn didn't seem to notice.

"Witches like Yvonne are considered monsters in the Apache society," he said. "They bring pain and destruction." He turned to look at Olivia, his gaze boring into hers. "Be careful trying to learn your mother's magic. It might turn you into a monster, too."

After Olivia and West left Glenn's house, West remarked that he was hungry. He hadn't sampled the snacks Glenn's housekeeper had prepared, and Olivia wasn't sure why. Maybe he hadn't wanted to partake in food supplied by a suspect.

She, on the other hand, had enjoyed making Glenn jump every time she'd taken a noisy bite, even if she'd only consumed a few deliberate morsels.

She supposed she was hungry, too.

They agreed to meet at a hookah bar and café in Hollywood. The exotic atmosphere intrigued Olivia, and West was a Middle-Eastern-cuisine virgin. That fascinated her even more. She wanted to deflower the special agent.

They ordered their meals, and their appetizer—hummus—arrived right away.

He spread a dollop onto some pita bread, tasted it, made an undecided face, then went back for more.

"Experimenting?" she asked.

"Seems like the thing to do." He smiled at her, making her feel like part of his experiment.

She figured that was okay, since he was part of hers. She'd never handcuffed a man to the bed. Ian West had been her first.

"Did you get a reading on Glenn?" he asked, interrupting her thoughts.

"No." She glanced up and noticed a charm, an evil eye symbol, dangling from a hook on the wall. "Do you believe in monsters?"

"The kind Glenn spoke of? Of course I do. I analyze violent criminals. Monsters are my specialty."

"What about the other kind?"

"Folklore creatures? I believed in them when I was a kid."

"Like what?" She scooted closer. They sat side by side, rather than across from each other, but the table had been set up that way.

"Like the giants my Muscogee grandfather taught me about. Their eyes open vertically instead of horizontally, and they can daze you, trick you and make you crazy. A temporary insanity. The Little People, fairies, can do that, too."

She tried to picture West as a boy, listening to his grandfather's tales. She imagined him as a serious child, with his angular features and hypnotic eyes. "What else?"

"There's a sharp-breasted snake, a serpent, that can cut through the roots of trees and make them fall over. Another creature is called a *nokos oma,* 'like a bear.' It's about the size of an ordinary brown bear, but it has huge tusks and it keeps its head close to the earth." He drank more of his beer. "A *lohka* is an animal that sometimes appears in the shape of a cat, sometimes in the shape of a chicken."

Olivia wondered if Samantha was a *lohka.* She'd never morphed into a chicken, but sometimes she acted like one.

Ten minutes later the waitress brought their meals, and they dined in the dimly lit café, with Middle Eastern music, the sound of hand drums, flutes and tambourines, playing on overhead speakers.

West seemed to enjoy the seasoned couscous and lamb stew, but she knew he enjoyed her company even more.

Afterward, he agreed to share a pipe with her, so they remained at the table, passing the hookah hose back and forth and sucking on the metal tip. The tobacco had been mixed with the fruit molasses and honey, making the experience smooth and sweet.

When he touched her cheek, she leaned in to kiss him.

"You taste good," he said. "Like the smoke."

"So do you." She'd chosen strawberry-flavored tobacco, like the fruit they'd eaten for breakfast, like the scent of the incense that had burned beside the bathtub when she'd reclined in his arms.

"Is this a love spell?" she asked.

"You ought to know." He brushed his lips against her ear. "You're the one capable of being a witch."

"Then that would make you my victim."

"Your willing victim," he corrected. "You're not taking away my free will."

No, but she wished she could. She wished she could use magic to send him back to Virginia. To keep him away from the killer.

The witch who would send monsters to his door.

Chapter 13

Olivia followed West to his motel, parked beside him and got out of her car. He took her hand and, for a moment, they gazed up at the sky.

"My father used to say that when there are only a few stars out at night, the others are sleeping." She paused, thinking about her childhood, about the way her dad used to tuck her and Allie into bed, the envy she would sometimes see in her mother's eyes. "He never really belonged to us, not completely."

"To who?" he asked. "You and your sister?"

She nodded. "I miss him so much."

"Maybe I should have stayed at the other motel. Maybe he's still there."

"His spirit shouldn't be roaming the earth. That's not how it should be." She moved closer to West, inhaling his cologne, the familiarity of his scent. "We shouldn't even be talking about this. I came here to make love with you."

"Then kiss me." He tipped her face to his. "Under the sleeping stars."

She leaned into him, anxious to touch, to taste, to fill her senses with lust. But as their mouths came together, she shivered.

Desperate, she put her arms around him, searching for warmth, but the chill continued, cutting bone deep, turning passion into pain, making colors twist and turn in her mind.

She stepped back, nearly tripping on a pebble in the walkway. "Monsters."

He blinked. "What?"

"There's something creepy in your room."

A smile tugged at his lips, and she wanted to kick him. This wasn't a game. Her premonitions weren't supposed to amuse him.

"Open the damned door and see," she said.

"Fine." He did just that, using his key-card.

She stood behind him, waiting for something dark and ugly to swallow him, to whisk him off to another dimension, to torture him for not believing her.

He flipped on the light, waited a beat. But nothing appeared. Nothing but an exceptionally clean room.

They both went inside, and he closed the door with a resounding click. "You want to talk monsters?" He loosened his tie, then removed his jacket. "There are some Muscogee creatures I forgot to tell you about."

"What are they?" she asked suspiciously, her gaze darting from corner to corner, assessing the snakelike ties on the drapes, the mouth-shaped handles on the dresser. She knew inanimate objects could come to life.

"I don't know their official name, but they have penises so long, they can reach the tops of trees."

"Very funny." She crossed her arms, refusing to get comfortable.

"I swear it's true. Enormous dicks."

"That's not going to help you get laid."

He laughed and opened the closet, but nothing jumped out at him. No monsters. No porn-king creatures.

"I'm not taking off my clothes." She looked around again, imagining a fifty-foot penis sliding between her legs. "Not here. Not tonight."

"That's crazy."

"No, it isn't." She stood like a statue, wondering when the monsters would strike.

He changed into a pair of sweats and a novelty T-shirt with FBI, Female Body Inspector, written across the front. West's idea of a joke, no doubt.

She watched him, then caught an image in the mirror.

A human-size owl, its unblinking eyes boring into hers.

"There!"

He spun around and stared at the glass. "What? Where?"

She stood next to him. "Right in front of you."

"I don't see anything but you and me."

The creature angled its head, making a mockery of her. She considered shooting the mirror, shattering it with a round of hollow-point bullets, but she knew it wouldn't do any good. To the Apache, an owl was the materialization of a ghost, of a bad spirit. A dead witch could enter the body of an owl, hurting people, making them sick.

"You can't stay here," she told him.

West remained where he was, facing a monster he couldn't see. "Come on, Olivia. Give it a rest."

The owl moved from side to side, placing finger-size talons on West's shoulder, holding on to his reflection, like the ghosts in the Haunted Mansion at Disneyland.

Olivia shivered. "Move in with me."

"Are you serious?"

She nodded, breathing deeply, inhaling, exhaling, trying to stay calm. The owl tore West's shirt, piercing his skin. "Just until this case is over."

"So you can protect me?"

"Yes. There's a monster in the mirror and it's hurting you."

"Then how come I·don't feel anything? Whatever you're looking at isn't real," he told her. "It's just an illusion."

"Stay with me, anyway."

"Will I get laid?"

Olivia almost laughed, almost cried, wishing he

could see what the entity inside the glass was doing to him. The marks on his body, the poison sluicing through his veins.

Did it matter that it was an owl? A witch could make any animal attack its victim. Real animals. Supernatural beings. There was no escape.

She watched his blood fall, running in scarlet rivulets. "Just pack your damn bags."

He grinned. "What if those creatures with the big dicks show up?"

Frustrated, she tore a pillow off the bed and threw it at him. He caught it, then tossed it at the mirror. It rattled the glass and plopped to the floor.

His reflection returned to normal.

"Is it gone?" he asked.

"Yes," she said. But now the pillow was bleeding, dying right before her eyes.

He picked it up and placed it back on the bed, fluffing it just so, unable to see the crimson stain on his hands.

Walking past him, she opened the closet and began folding his clothes, forcing Agent West to come home with her.

"Am I safe now?" West asked.

"Don't be a smart-ass." Olivia lay next to him in her bed. Didn't he realize the sacrifice she was making to accommodate him? She'd never lived with a man before. She'd never shared her space, her belongings or her freedom with a lover. "You're just damn lucky to have me in your corner."

"Oh, yeah. This is every guy's dream. Being protected by a woman."

"Get over the macho crap, West."

"Screw you."

"Screw you, too." Angry now, she rolled on top of him, pinning him beneath her. "Female body inspector, my ass."

He smiled, and she knew she'd been had. He was trying to rile her, trying to get her in the mood for some down-and-dirty sex.

She did her damnedest not to return his smile. "You're such a jerk."

"Yeah, but that's why you love me."

Love him? "Dream on, FBI man."

"I will if you let me inspect your bod." He turned the tables, rolling her onto her back and climbing on top of her, taking the position of power.

She looked up at him. Tall, dark, Agent West. Somewhere in the back of her mind, she could still see the owl clawing his skin, making him bleed. "You need to get over your death wish."

He lowered his head to kiss her, to rub his mouth against hers, teasing her, promising more. "Don't blame that witchy stuff on me."

"You're an easy target."

"Because I'm not afraid of dying? That's not why the killer is after me."

"I know. But it makes you more susceptible to a spell. Every time you scoff at the magic, you're putting yourself in danger."

"Yeah, but you said it yourself. I'm the one who's going to identify the Slasher. And that gives me power."

She glanced at the mirrored closet doors, but there was nothing there. No human-size owl, no talons, no blood.

Shifting her gaze to West, she released the air in her lungs. He was still straddling her. Big and strong and unharmed. "Your power is between your legs."

He grinned and lifted her nightgown, peeling the garment over her head. Then he attacked her panties, tugging the swatch of lace. "Me and those Muscogee penis monsters."

Naked, she arched against him. "Don't start."

"I wasn't making them up." He explored her body, molding her like clay, roaming her curves. "They really are part of my culture. Part of the folklore."

She spread her thighs, taking what he offered. "What a legacy."

He used his fingers, making her wet. "Yeah."

Aroused, she cupped his jaw to kiss him, to push her tongue down his throat. They rolled over the bed, whispering erotic things in each other's ears.

He used his teeth, nibbling, biting, leaving marks on her shoulders. She dragged off his shirt and put her hands all over his chest, over hard planes and male muscle, over flesh that was warm and solid and real.

She looked into his eyes, and their gazes locked. Iced

metal, she thought. Smoked steel. He confused her. He made her head spin.

His hair fell in licorice disarray, more black than brown, an optical illusion in the shadowed light.

When he kissed her, he tasted like mint, like a tooth-paste-flavored liqueur. She deepened the kiss, trying to get drunk, to lose herself, to teeter on the edge of sanity.

Mindless, she wanted more, as much of him as she could get. Stripping off the remainder of his clothes, she went down on him, taking him in her mouth.

He grabbed her waist, maneuvering her, shifting her body. Within seconds her legs were sprawled over his face, so he could pleasure her, too.

Sixty-nine, she thought. The ultimate foreplay.

She glanced at the mirror and saw their reflections. They were like acrobats, arching and stretching, the low-burning lamp showering them in midnight hues. He painted her with his tongue, his saliva warm and moist.

She shuddered under his touch, knowing he was more than a lover, more than a vehicle for her desire. Somewhere along the way, he'd become part of her emotions, part of something that mattered.

For a moment she wanted to end their relationship, to stop giving a damn about him, but she climaxed instead, coming all over him.

He tasted her release, sipping her like wine. She blinked, tried to clear her senses, then realized his erection still filled her mouth.

Heaven help her, she thought. Down-and-dirty sex.

He didn't let her bring him to oral fruition. He was more than ready to make love, to battle the condom box he'd stuffed in her nightstand, to grab a foil packet and tear it open.

Olivia was ready, too. She wanted him inside her, pumping hard and fast.

He sheathed himself and thrust full hilt, leaving her breathless. When his hands sought hers, they held each other, fingers locked, bodies joined. He didn't move. He just stared at her, his strange gray eyes absorbing every angle of her face.

"Do something," she said.

"Do what?" he asked.

She reared up to kiss him, to bite him, to tell him to pound her into the bed.

He smiled, still clutching her hands.

Then he went mad.

Wicked, wild sex. A craving to mate. A man hell-bent on giving her what she wanted, what they both couldn't live without.

She gripped the headboard, blood roaring in her head, soaring through her veins. He drove himself into her, over and over, a rhythm that had her digging her nails into his skin.

Restless, edgy, she fought to stay focused, to stop the delirium. But she couldn't.

Olivia climaxed, breathing in the scent of their love-making. The sweat. The pheromones. The anticipation.

She looked into his eyes, watching, waiting, urging

him on. And then it happened. He came, too, holding her close, his heart pounding next to hers.

Like a storm, she thought. Like rain exploding from a dark and deadly sky.

Before dawn, Olivia's cell phone rang, jarring her awake. West awakened, too, flinging his arm in her direction.

"It's probably one of my clients," she said, nearly knocking over the alarm clock to find the noisemaker.

He grumbled, making a sour face, covering his head with a pillow. "Hell of a time to call someone."

She flipped open the receiver, walking away from her lover, taking the phone into her bathroom. Having a bedmate, even a man she cared about, was a pain in the ass.

"Hello?"

"What took you so long to answer?" a male voice asked.

She turned on the light. "Who is this?"

"Derek Moon."

She started, then caught her tired reflection in the mirror. "What do you want?"

"To meet with you this morning."

"Why?"

"To discuss your mother."

She leaned against the sink and glanced out the window, where twilight peeked through the bubbled glass. "You're going to teach me her magic?"

"Just meet with me. As soon as you can."

"Where?"

"Peppermill Park."

"Fine. I'll get ready now." She closed the phone, ending the call, not quite sure what Derek had up his sleeve. And that meant she wasn't about to tell West where she was going. She didn't need him insisting on coming with her, not with the dark cloud hovering over his life. He was safer at home, away from Derek and his bag of tricks.

She returned to her room and sat on the edge of the bed, removing the pillow from West's head. "I have to go out."

He squinted at her, the light she'd left on in her bathroom illuminating him in a hazy glow. "At this hour? Why?"

"Client emergency."

He sat up, the sheet slipping to his waist. He was naked, with his jaw unshaven and his hair falling across his forehead. All male and all rumpled. She had the sudden urge to kiss him, to nudge him onto the bed and straddle his lap. He was already half-hard, a mindless condition he didn't seem to notice. That made it even sexier.

But Derek Moon was expecting her.

"What kind of client emergencies do psychics have?" he asked.

Witch trials, she thought. "I'm a consultant. People need me."

He scratched his head, messing his hair up even more. "If you say so."

"I do." Just to satisfy her craving, she gave him a quick kiss.

He rewarded her with a smile. "You're going to miss me when I'm gone."

"You wish." She pushed him down and covered him with the sheet. "Now go back to sleep."

Within no time, he rolled over and conked out. The big bad agent and his big bad boner.

Olivia got ready as quickly as she could, leaving the house in a red sweater and threadbare jeans, her boots sounding on the stairwell.

She arrived at Peppermill Park just as daylight broke through the clouds, marking the dawn. Parking her Porsche on the street, she noticed the carnival rides and decided they were part of Derek's plan.

She located him at the chain-link fence that surrounded the lifeless carnival. He stood with his hands in his pockets, dressed as casually as she was.

He turned and flashed a straight, white smile. "Olivia. Lovely as ever."

"This place isn't open yet, Derek. The gate's locked."

"So it is." He took a small black bag out of his pocket, removed a pinch of glittery dust and blew it at the fence, making it turn watery, like a door to another dimension. "Abracadabra. Now we can go inside."

"Impressive." And creepy, she thought, as she followed him into the carnival, the fence solidifying behind her.

"What's your favorite ride?" he asked.

She looked around, deciding the Ferris wheel, the

Tilt-A-Whirl and the Scrambler looked dangerous, particularly with a black magic witch at the helm.

"The merry-go-round," she told him.

"Really? How sweet." He escorted her to the canopied carousel, where pretty little ponies waited.

She gave the fiberglass figures a suspicious glance. "They don't bite, do they?"

He chuckled. "They could, I suppose. But I didn't ask you here to teach you your mother's magic." He gestured for her to take a seat, to straddle a white horse with a golden mane.

She climbed into the saddle and watched him mount the polka-dotted equine next to her. "Then what's this all about?"

"The man Yvonne ran off with."

Her heart nearly stopped. "You know who he is?"

"Yes. I've known for a while. But I didn't want to tell you before now."

The merry-go-round started moving, turning in a circle, her horse going up and down, the brass-ring music chiming in the morning air.

She told herself this wasn't as bizarre as it seemed. "Who he is?"

Derek's pony bobbed, too, in an opposing rhythm. While she went up, he went down. "His name is Taylor Campbell. He's a writer, dabbling in supernatural fiction. Wealthy by way of an inheritance. Eccentric. Reclusive. Bought an old castle in Ireland." He held on to the gold pole in front of him, the merry-go-round still moving. "Yvonne admired his work. His creature-feature stories. She wrote to him, using a P.O. Box address. They started making plans to be together. He wanted her for his mistress."

"She's been in Ireland all this time?"

"Yes, under an assumed name. Taylor helped her change her identity. To become someone new." Derek stroked his horse's colorful mane, leaning forward to gaze at its frozen expression. "I didn't know about this when it first happened. I found out about six months ago."

"How? Who told who?"

"Taylor did. He contacted me, asking me to help him get rid of Yvonne. He was sick of her and her selfish ways."

"Get rid of her?" A chill clawed Olivia's spine. "You mean kill her?"

"No, dear." Derek waved his arm and lowered the volume of the music. "He wanted me to cast a spell, to make her lose interest in him."

"And did you?"

"No. I didn't want to get involved, but I guess I should have. Things didn't turn out too well."

"Why? What happened?"

"Taylor got sick a few months later, and Yvonne disappeared with a bundle of his money."

"Is he still sick?" she asked.

Derek shook his head. "He's dead."

"From his illness?"

"Yes." He stopped the carousel, bringing it to an abrupt halt. "Witch sickness, if you ask me. I think Yvonne killed him."

Olivia didn't know what to believe. At this point, her head was reeling. "She killed him, then someone killed her?"

"So it seems."

"Why did Taylor contact you to begin with? How did he know about you?"

"He said Yvonne told him who I was. She talked about everyone from her past. You and Allie, too."

She tried to picture her mother living in a castle in Ireland, wandering the dungeon, contemplating the family she'd left behind, describing them to Taylor Campbell. "Why are you sharing this information with me? Why the sudden change of heart?"

His smiled, exposing a thin, sharp hint of his dazzling teeth. "Because I decided that I like you. You and your FBI lover. The least I could do is cooperate with your investigation."

She narrowed her gaze, shrinking him down to size. "And what do you expect in return? An invitation to our bedroom?"

He shifted in his saddle, moving closer to the pole. "A ringside seat would be nice. You're an erotic couple."

"Go suck a duck."

He chuckled, amused by her bravado. "You can't blame a voyeur for trying."

"Are you done?" she asked. "Or is there more?"

He made an empty gesture. "That's it. I've told everything I know."

"Then let's abracadabra out of here."

"Fine." He climbed off the polka-dotted pony, and the merry-go-round started turning again, only a little faster this time.

She vacated her horse, too. "That's not funny, Derek."

His eyes grew wide. "I'm not doing this."

Yeah, right. Him and his witch humor. "Then who is? Me?"

"How would I know? You—" He stopped in midsentence. "Look at your horse."

She turned her head, saw that it was shifting, changing, morphing into a robotic tiger. Not a real jungle animal, but one that was alive just the same.

The tiger growled at Derek, baring its teeth. He took a step back, his face going pale.

The merry-go-round twirled even faster.

Olivia drew her weapon.

Then lost sight of Derek.

A pane of double-sided glass slammed between them.

Within an instant, funhouse mirrors appeared out of thin air, zigzagging, bolting to the floor of the ride, distorting everything, making grotesque images out of the carousel horses.

The tiger roared.

Olivia spun around. Nothing but horses, warped shapes going up and down.

Laughter sprang in the air.

And then a man screamed.

Derek?

She called his name above the music. Was he doing this? Had he tricked her? She started darting through the maze, following contorted paths, doing her damnedest to find him, to separate mirrors from reality, but she kept bumping into glass.

The merry-go-round changed direction, moving backward making her dizzy.

Oh, God.

She turned, froze, nearly stumbled over Derek's mutilated body on the ground. Bile rose in her throat. Half of his head had been chewed off, his mangled brain oozing at her feet, sticking to her boots.

An eerie sound. A low, warning growl.

She took a deep breath, looked up.

And saw the owl from West's motel room staring right at her.

Chapter 14

The owl didn't move. It simply watched her. A human-size raptor calculating its prey. But wasn't that what it was? Owls were raptors, birds of prey.

Olivia stepped forward, refusing to be intimated. The gunk beneath her boots made a squishing sound.

Derek's brains.

"I'm not afraid of you," she said to the owl.

In response, it angled its head.

She tried to get a reading on who or what it was, but nothing happened. Moving closer, she caught her own reflection. The owl was inside a mirror, the way it had been in West's motel room.

Was that the creature's shield? Its protection?

Coward, she thought. "Why don't you show your true colors?"

Within an instant, the raptor accepted Olivia's challenge and started shifting, changing, morphing into a woman.

The beak became a full, sultry mouth and the wide, unblinking eyes narrowed into an exotic shape. Feathers lengthened into long black hair, coiled with a leather ornament. The only owl-like features that remained were the golden color of her eyes and two streaks of silver hair that framed her face, giving her a moonlit quality.

Tall and slim, she wore a long-sleeved blouse and a full skirt, reminiscent of an Apache woman in the early twentieth century.

She was in her midtwenties, Olivia surmised. A stunningly beautiful shape-shifter, a witch from the past.

Drawn to the other woman, Olivia moved even closer. She reminded herself that this was the same entity who'd hurt West's reflection in the motel-room mirror. Yet somehow, she seemed too compelling to be evil.

"Who are you?" Olivia asked.

The shape-shifter didn't speak. Instead, she pressed her hand against the glass, inviting Olivia to touch the mirror, to enter the realm in which she lived.

"What will happen if I go with you?" Tempted, so very tempted, she gazed at the witch, wanting to know her, wanting to feel her touch.

The beads around her neck dazzled, like stars that refused to sleep.

"We're connected," Olivia said to her. "I can feel your blood in my veins. I can feel—"

The merry-go-round changed direction, spinning forward again, making Derek's mutilated body roll at Olivia's feet.

The shape-shifter smiled.

Oh, God. Olivia swayed, knowing she was being bewitched.

Fighting the feeling, the overpowering seduction, she took a deep breath and closed her eyes. But the need was still there. She hungered to step inside the glass, to become part of the magic.

Laughter ripped through the air.

The shape-shifter was winning.

Olivia opened her eyes and glanced down at Derek's body, which was reflected in the funhouse mirrors that surrounded her, magnifying his mutilated flesh, making it look even more distorted.

Help me, his voice whispered in her head.

Stunned, she backed into a carousel horse. Olivia wasn't a medium. Aside from her father's ghost, she'd never conversed with the dead. Yet Derek was communicating with her.

"I can't," she told him.

Yes, you can. Deny her. Don't let her take your soul.

"Who is she?" Olivia asked.

He didn't respond.

The entity in the mirror beckoned.

Once again, a sensation of kinship overpowered her. A haunting affection. A twisted bond.

But a bond just the same.

With her heart pounding like a Native drum, Olivia lifted her gun, aimed it at the mirror and pulled the trigger.

The glass didn't shatter. Instead the bullet ricocheted, coming back at Olivia. She dived to the ground, landing on top of Derek's mangled body. Even when she'd fired, she'd known the bullet wouldn't harm the shapeshifter or damage her protective shield. But it was a symbolic gesture, a denial.

Olivia intended to keep her soul.

She crawled away from Derek and drew her knees to her chest. Holy Mother of God. His brain started squirming back into his head, the stuff that had been sticking to the soles of Olivia's boots squiggling like worms to catch up. Wide-eyed, she watched fragments of his skull snap into place, like pieces in a puzzle. The rest of him, the parts that were missing, reappeared, completing the process, restoring his body.

The entity in the mirror finally made a sound, screeching like an owl, becoming a human-size raptor once again.

An angry raptor, its yellow eyes flashing like embers.

"Run!" Olivia told Derek. "Run!"

He jumped to his feet, then wobbled like Dorothy's scarecrow and grinned at her.

Stupid male witch, she thought, shoving past him.

The merry-go-round picked up speed, moving a little faster, the carousel horses bobbing like pogo sticks.

Olivia ignored the disturbing motion. Somewhere in the distance, the robotic tiger growled, its mechanical footsteps echoing behind them.

"That damn thing wants to chomp on me again," Derek said, stopping to look over his shoulder.

"Then quit stalling." Every time Olivia bumped into a mirror, she kicked it, shattering it with her boot, grateful the funhouse glass was breakable, unlike the shield that protected the shape-shifter.

Derek followed her lead, and together they smashed their way out of the maze, determined to find the edge of the merry-go-round.

But when they did, the ride spun so fast, Derek insisted he was going to vomit.

Too bad, she thought, pushing him over the side. A second later, Olivia jumped, too, landing on the grass with a painful, wrenching thud.

For a while, the world kept moving, turning in a dizzying circle. She spied Derek from the corner of her eye. He was, indeed, vomiting. Hunched over, regurgitating whatever he'd eaten for breakfast that morning.

Finally Olivia stood up and looked around. The merry-go-round was no longer moving. No music, no funhouse mirrors. The owl and her magic had vanished.

Derek stumbled over to a water fountain and rinsed

his mouth, spitting onto the ground. When he approached Olivia, he looked pale.

Like death warmed over.

Which was exactly what he was.

"I brought you back to life," she said. "Could I have done that if you weren't a witch?"

He shook his head. "It was both of our powers that did it."

Suspicious, she crossed her arms. "How?"

"My soul was hovering over my body, so my spirit was still functioning. And your soul—" he paused to blow out a windy breath "—was hovering, too, on the verge of being taken. Together we were strong enough to fight the owl, to reverse her spell."

"Is she an ancestor of mine?"

"Probably." He sniffed the air. "Dead witches are the worst."

"You and your damn carnival." She glanced at the colorful rides, the concession stands, an atmosphere that was supposed to be fun.

"How did I know that she-bitch was going to show up?" He took a step back. "I'm not helping you with this investigation anymore."

"Helping me? For all I know you're responsible for that whole merry-go-round thing."

"Yeah, right. I killed myself."

She narrowed her eyes. "Maybe your mutilated body was an illusion. Maybe you were alive the entire time, hiding behind a spell."

"And the owl? You think I conjured her, too?"

"It's possible."

"That's bull and you know it. I'm not the Slasher, Olivia. I'm not the witch who murdered your mother."

"Then who is?"

"Ask Agent West," he said. "He's the FBI profiler. The guy who's supposed to figure this out."

Later that day Olivia sat beside Detective Riggs at a conference table at the Los Angeles Street Station. Detective Muncy was there, too, wolfing down an early dinner, the fried aroma of take-out chicken scenting the air.

West, the ringleader, had called this meeting. He stood at the front of the room, dressed in one of his dark suits.

Riggs leaned toward Olivia. "He looks pissed."

Olivia nodded, and West spun around to glare at them.

"If you ladies have something to say, I suggest you share it with the rest of us."

Unimpressed, Riggs squared her shoulders. "I told her that you looked pissed."

"Really?" He put his hands on the table. "Well, let me clarify that for you. I'm beyond pissed. Olivia had no business gallivanting off to see Moon without telling me."

"I did tell you," she protested.

"Yeah, after the fact."

Muncy cut in. "At least Moon gave her some accurate information." He picked at the crispy coating on his chicken, wiping his hands on his pants before reaching for the report he'd prepared. "Yvonne was in Ireland with Taylor Campbell for the past twelve years. And Campbell did die from an illness. An unidentifiable virus of some kind."

Olivia frowned. "What about the money? Did she rip him off?"

"Not exactly, no. She disappeared with a bundle, but it was from an account that he'd set up for her."

"What was her alias?" Olivia asked. "What name was she using in Ireland?"

"Coyote. Yvonne Coyote." Muncy turned to look at her. "Is that significant?"

"It could be. Coyote is a trickster. He can't be trusted."

"And neither can you," West said.

Olivia lifted her chin. "I was trying to protect you."

"I don't need your goddamn protection."

"The hell you don't."

"Oh, that's right. You're the belle of the witch's ball." He leaned on the table, pinning her with his gaze, nailing her right to her seat. "You put Moon's mutilated head back together."

"He said we both did it."

"Which means what? That you won't be able to do it for me?" He practically crammed his face next to hers, stealing her oxygen. "I'd rather be dead anyway. I don't want the daughter of a witch messing with my mind."

"You mean your heart?" Riggs asked.

He rounded on her. "What?"

"Your heart," the female detective reiterated. "You're so in love with her, you can't even see straight."

Olivia caught her breath.

And so did West. Before he told Riggs to go straight to hell.

Muncy cleared his throat, trying to ease the tension. "Can we get back to the case?"

"You mean the case I'm going to solve?" West dragged his hand through his hair, spiking the straight, dark strands. "At the moment I don't really give a damn."

That wasn't true, Olivia thought. He cared. But that didn't mean she could save him. She could still feel the danger that awaited him.

"I don't understand why your ancestor is involved in this," Muncy said to Olivia, trying to steer the conversation back on track. "What does the owl lady want? Besides your soul?"

She gave him a hard stare. "Isn't that enough?"

He fumbled with his chicken. "Yes, of course, but it doesn't explain how she ties into this case."

"Maybe she doesn't," Riggs put in. "Maybe she's a separate issue."

"What do you think?" Olivia asked West.

"I don't know." He smoothed the hair he'd spiked, then sat in a wooden chair and scraped his booted feet on the linoleum.

He looked restless, troubled. A man with too many disturbances on his mind. Olivia wanted to place her hands on his shoulders, to offer comfort, companion-ship, but she couldn't bring herself to touch him.

"Where did Yvonne go when she left Ireland?" West asked Muncy.

The detective didn't need to glance at his notes. He had a ready answer. "Here. She came to L.A."

The special agent frowned. "How long ago?"

"A few months before the first murder."

West clasped his hands behind his neck and stared at the wall. Olivia stared, too. Her mother had come home, yet she hadn't contacted her or Allie.

"Is Moon still a suspect?" she asked.

"He is as far as I'm concerned." This came from Muncy, who resumed eating the greasy chicken. "If he's the killer, then the owl lady going after him makes sense."

Olivia sighed. "Why? To punish him for killing my mom?"

Muncy nodded, his mouth full of fowl.

Riggs shifted in her seat. "It's a pretty good theory. It explains why the owl lady would want Olivia's soul, too. All the females in her family were witches, and now Yvonne, the last witch, is dead. They need someone to carry on the tradition."

"Me," Olivia said.

West still stared at the wall. "That's all fine and dandy, but why does the owl lady want to hurt me? If I'm going to solve this case and discover who killed Yvonne, then why am I a threat?"

For a moment no one answered. Then Riggs pursed her lips and looked at Olivia.

"Don't say it," Olivia said.

West rose from his chair. "Don't say what?"

Silence.

"What?" he pressed, snaring Olivia's gaze.

She drew a deep breath, noticed his eyes were glowing. "My ancestors think you're a threat because you're in love with me. That the women in my family will have a better chance of taking my soul if you're not involved in my life."

"Why would that matter?" He gave her cynical smile. "Unless you're in love with me, too."

"But I'm not," she told him.

"Neither am I," he said.

Riggs looked at Muncy and they both shook their heads.

The meeting went downhill from there. But it didn't matter because Olivia knew West wouldn't rest until he solved the case.

Until his life was hanging by a thread.

The man she didn't love.

"I can't believe you won't admit that you love him," Allie said.

Olivia blew out a weary breath. It was after midnight and West still wasn't home. "I care about him. He means a lot to me. But that's not the same thing."

"You're so full of it your eyes are turning brown."

She gave her sister an exasperated look. They sat in the living room, waiting for a man who might not show up. He wasn't answering his cell phone, wasn't responding to his pages. "My eyes are already brown."

"And his are gray."

"So?"

"So every time those eyes connect with yours, you get all fluttery."

"I do not. And fluttery is a stupid word."

"If the shoe fits."

"Enough with the phrases. They're annoying."

Allie reached for a pillow. She was curled up on the couch, wearing a gypsy-style nightgown, the satiny fabric embroidered with blue and yellow flowers. "I know why you won't admit how you feel."

"Please, spare me your psychological evaluation. I'm edgy as it is." She glanced out the window, where rain drizzled from the heavens. The weatherman had predicted clear skies and, to Olivia, that was a bad sign.

Was this a witch-driven rain? Had the owl lady killed a horned toad? Or snake, placing the animal on its back?

At this point, too much rain in California made her suspicious. And soon, she thought, it would start pouring, water flooding the earth.

Allie fluffed her pillow. "You're afraid of admitting that you love him because of your premonitions. Your fear that he's going to die."

A shiver drilled its way through Olivia's bones, nearly rattling her teeth. She didn't want to think about

West's impending doom. "I told you to spare me, Dr. Addle-brain."

"Addle-brain, my butt. I even figured out why West is denying that he loves you."

Much too curious, Olivia reached for her tea, an herbal blend of oranges and mint, a hot drink to ease the chill. "Okay, smarty-pants. Let's hear it."

"Pride." Her sister tucked her hair behind her ears. "If you would have told him that you loved him, he would have admitted it, too. But he wasn't about to say anything after you shot him down."

"And you know this because?"

"Of the way he looks at you. Even Samantha can tell."

Olivia clutched her tea and glanced at the cat. The feline napped on top of the DVD player, her front paws draped over the machine, her hindquarters scooped into a little ball.

"Right, Sam?" Allie said.

At the mention of her nickname, the cat lifted her head, gave both women a sleepy-eyed expression and went back to sleep.

Olivia sighed. "I can see that she knows exactly what's going on." Frustrated, she glanced out the window again. Where was West? The rain was starting to pick up speed, falling a bit more heavily. "This is driving me crazy."

"Maybe we should try his cell phone again," Allie said. "Or check with the station one more time. Maybe he's there now."

"He isn't. I asked the desk sergeant to call if he

showed up." West had left the cop shop hours ago, disappearing into the night.

"What about the FBI field office?"

"He isn't there, either."

"Then we'll wait. Do you want to play Monopoly or something?"

Olivia smiled. Trust Allie to come up with a time-consuming diversion. "No. But thanks, anyway." She listened to the rain, praying the owl lady hadn't hurt West. "I wish we had an Ouija board."

"What for?" Her sister made a perplexed face. "You're already psychic."

"I was thinking that maybe Dad could help." The conversation hearts were still on the counter, but the dialogue on those stale candies was limited, making communicating with their father difficult. "I'm not a very strong medium. I've only had a few experiences in that realm. If we had an Ouija board—"

"We can make one." Allie hopped up. "We can use a wineglass for the pointer. Or whatever it's called."

"It's called a planchette. Or an indicator. And it's worth a try." Olivia carried her tea into the kitchen and poured the rest of it down the sink.

Allie searched for a cardboard box, found one and cut out a flat piece. Sitting at the table, Olivia wrote the letters of the alphabet across the center, arranged in two lines. Below that, she inscribed the words *Yes* and *No* in each corner. Then she added numbers.

"It looks pretty good," her sister said.

"Yes, but it's supposed to be smooth. This is a bit bumpy. We should place it under a glass surface."

"I can tape it under the table."

"Sure. That will work."

Allie retrieved a roll of package-sealing tape and attached their makeshift device, faceup, to the underside of the glass-topped table, close enough to their chairs that they would both have access to it.

"The man who invented the Ouija board was a cabinet maker," Olivia said. "But he made coffins, too."

Her sister looked up. "Really?"

She nodded. "He sold his invention to a friend, who marketed it. But later that man took his own life."

"Like Dad." Allie secured the tape. "I haven't finished the painting of him, but he won't be ready to travel the Ghost Road until all of this is over."

They took their seats. "Are you ready to talk to him?"

"If you are."

"Then let's do it." Olivia turned the wineglass over and put her fingers on the rim, placing it in the center of the board. Either it would work or it wouldn't. Neither she nor Allie would falsify a reading, moving the indicator on her own.

The younger woman placed her fingers on the inverted wineglass, too. "What should we ask him?"

"First, we should make sure it's Dad. If a spirit shows up at all. We might not reach anyone."

"Are you kidding?" Allie managed a smile. "We have powers. What able-minded ghost would ignore us?"

They sat for a while, channeling their energy. The scent of vanilla candles, Allie's favorite fragrance, sweetened the air.

And then the indicator moved, a featherlight motion, sliding in a slow circle, taking their hands with it. They looked at each other. They hadn't asked a question yet.

"Someone's anxious," Allie whispered.

"Dad?" Olivia said.

The wine glass moved to *No*.

"You're not our father?"

Once again, a negative response. A silent *No*.

"Who are you?"

Nothing happened. The indicator stalled.

Olivia and Allie waited. Then the glass shifted slowly across the tabletop to the letter *Z*. The indicator continued moving, until the name Zinna had been spelled.

"That's pretty," Allie said. "Are you a woman?"

The wineglass slid to *Yes*. Then it started spelling again.

O.

W.

L.

Olivia sucked in a breath. *Owl*. "Do you know who the owl lady is?"

"Yes," came the Ouija board reply.

The sisters exchanged a glance. Then Allie asked, "Who is she?"

The glass moved to *G*.

Outside, the rain continued to fall, showering the roof, making heartbeat sounds.

Finally the indicator slid to another letter, then another. By the time it stopped, it had spelled *great-grandmother.*

For a moment Olivia and Allie remained quiet. Then an image flashed in Olivia's mind. A demented shape: white-tipped feathers, long black hair, a face that was part human, part raptor.

The spirit they'd channeled.

Dear God. She looked at the indicator, felt her fingers tremble. "It's her."

Allie gave her a dumbfounded stare. "What?"

Olivia pushed away from the table. "*Her.* Zinna is our great-grandmother. The owl lady. That's who we're talking to."

"Oh, shit." Allie tore the tape off the bottom of the Ouija board and ripped the cardboard, trying to tear it in two. "We shouldn't have done this. We shouldn't have messed with the dead."

The lights flickered.

"Shit," the younger woman said again.

"Don't panic." Olivia helped Allie destroy their homemade device. "Just don't give her your soul."

"Oh, sure. No problem. That makes me feel a lot better."

Thunder cracked in the sky.

Then the front door rattled.

Allie's eyes grew wide. "Someone's trying to get in."

"Maybe it's West."

"But what if it isn't?" The door rattled again, harder this time. So hard, they realized the being on the other side was trying to force its way in.

West wouldn't do that.

Olivia took her sister's hand and raced into the living room. Steeped in anxiety, she opened the gun case, knowing there wasn't time to grab her Glock from her nightstand. The rest of her arsenal would do. Unless, heaven help them, the thing Zinna had conjured was already dead.

Samantha leaped off the DVD player and hissed. But a second later she made a beeline for the noise.

"No!" Allie shouted, trying to stop her cat.

Too late.

The loft door flew open, stealing Olivia's breath.

Chapter 15

West froze in the entryway. "What's going on?"

Olivia lowered the weapon in her hand. Her trembling hand. She wanted to throw her arms around him, to thank the Creator that he was safe. But she wanted to shoot him, too. To teach him a lesson. "We were expecting a monster. You scared us half to death."

He frowned. "The door was stuck. And why were you expecting a monster?"

Allie dropped to the edge of a nearby chair. "Because the owl lady is here." She opened her arms, gesturing to an entity they couldn't see. "She talked to us on a Ouija board we made."

He eyed the loft suspiciously. "What the hell for? Why did you conjure her spirit?"

Allie responded, "We were trying to contact our dad."

"And got our great-grandmother instead," Olivia interjected. "Her name is Zinna."

"Wonderful. Perfect. Now you're on a first-name basis with a shape-shifter."

Olivia set her gun on the coffee table, realizing it was the Magnum her dad had used. "Don't you dare reprimand us. We were worried sick about you."

Samantha finally butted into the conversation, meowing at West's feet. She'd been waiting all this time for him to acknowledge her, to baby her the way he usually did.

He left his briefcase in the entryway and picked her up, giving her the attention she craved, carrying her into the living room. "I'm sorry if I scared you, if I made you worry." He looked at Allie, then stole a wary glance at Olivia. "But I wasn't expecting either of you to be up. It's—" he paused to glance at his watch "—almost one in the morning."

"No kidding." Olivia crossed her arms, warding off a chill. The heater in the loft hadn't come on, in spite of the weather. "We thought something happened to you."

He set the cat back on her feet. "I'm fine."

He didn't look fine. His hair was soaked, falling onto his forehead, and his clothes were damp. And on top of that, he had faint circles under his eyes. "Where have you been?"

"I went to Kyle's house earlier."

"Why?"

"To check on his wound. I promised I would, re-member?"

"Yes, of course." But she hadn't expected him to do it this evening. And not without telling her first. Of course she hadn't told him that she'd met with Moon until later, but that was different. "Is Kyle healing all right?"

The special agent nodded, then removed his damp jacket and hung it on a vintage coatrack. He still wore the suit he'd had on earlier, but his tie was gone. Folded in his briefcase, no doubt.

"What did you do after you checked on Kyle?" Olivia wanted to know.

"Drove around, mostly. Stopped at a lookout point in the desert and watched the rain."

"Why didn't you answer your cell phone or respond to your pager? I've been trying to reach you since nine o'clock."

"After I left Kyle's house, I turned them off. I needed some time alone. I wanted to think, to go over some things in my head."

"Things?" She studied his troubled expression. "You mean the case?"

"Yes." He shoved his hands into his pockets, his posture tense.

Olivia glanced at Allie and saw that her sister was watching West, analyzing him, trying to gauge his emotions. She probably thought he was still smarting over Olivia's rejection.

The I-don't-love-you remark.

But, hey, he hadn't gone off to brood. He was consumed with his job, with the Slasher investigation. The way he should be.

Allie, Olivia decided, was a hopeless romantic. And so was Samantha, she supposed. The cat was slinking between West's legs, rubbing against his ankles, looking for attention again. Either that or giving herself a kitty thrill, getting orgasmic over him.

Which, Olivia knew, was easy to do.

"I suppose it's better that you're both awake," he said. "I was going to talk to you in the morning."

"About the case?" Allie asked.

He nodded, and a second later thunder echoed through the house, intensifying the storm.

Olivia looked around, wondering if Zinna was watching them.

"I figured it out," he said.

Olivia's heartbeat blasted her chest. "You know who the killer is?"

"Yes." He blew out a heavy breath. "But this isn't going to be easy. For either of you." He pulled a hand through his rain-sloshed hair. "This is going to hurt."

"Oh, God." Allie started to rock forward. "It's someone we're close to, isn't it?"

"Yes," he said again. "Someone who matches the profile. But I haven't told Muncy and Riggs yet, either. I was going to wait until morning for that, too."

An image flashed across Olivia's mind. A painful vision. Blood on her bedroom floor. West struggling to breathe.

She held up her hand, saw her fingers shake. "Don't say it! We need to get prepared first. We need to get ready."

He blinked. "For what?"

"A fight. The minute you say the killer's name, all hell is going to break loose." Because Zinna was protecting the Slasher. Olivia knew that now.

But even so, it didn't make sense. Why would Zinna protect the witch that had killed Yvonne? Her own granddaughter?

West shook his head. "I can't withhold this information. It's a murder investigation. I have to report my findings."

"I'm not asking you to withhold it. I'm just asking you to wait." She reached for the Magnum on the table, shoving the gun at Allie, trying to arm her sister. "Take this, damn it. And if anything tries to hurt him, shoot it."

Allie's dark skin paled, goose bumps freckling her arms. "It's Dad's gun."

"Yes, and Dad would want you to use it." She took a moment to show her sister how to load the Magnum, how to fire it. Then she glanced at West.

"Calm down, Olivia." He tried to grab her, but she pulled away from him, removing pistols from the gun case, as well as police-style holsters.

"Knives," she said. "We need knives, too." She dug through the arsenal and recovered a handful of blades, scattering them on the coffee table.

"Are you armed?" she asked West.

"Yes."

She forced a backup weapon into his hand, making sure he clipped it to his belt. "You're going to need all the artillery you can carry."

"What the hell is wrong with you?" He gestured to their surroundings. "Nothing is popping out of the woodwork to hurt me."

"Not yet, but something will."

"Zinna?" Allie asked.

"Yes. Our great-grandmother is protecting the Slasher. But I don't have a clue as to why."

"I do," West said, proving how much danger he was in.

Olivia took a deep breath, wishing he'd resigned from this case, wishing he hadn't uncovered the truth. "There are creatures coming. Monsters. I can feel them."

He moved closer, as if he meant to kiss her. But he didn't. He just looked into her eyes and made her pulse turn fluttery.

Fluttery. Like a woman in love.

Oh, God.

Allie clutched the Magnum. "West shouldn't tell us who the killer is. He shouldn't tell anyone."

Trying to stay focused, Olivia fought the fear, the weakness in her heart. "That won't do any good. The information is in his head. He'll never be safe, not until the Slasher is apprehended." She strapped a holster to her body, then clipped a row of pistols, extra ammo and a knife sheath onto it. Next she buckled the same type of holster around her sister. "West has to tell us who the killer is, and we have to battle the enemy. We have to end the madness."

"Then we should be wearing shoes." Allie sprinted down the hall and came back with a pair of boots for herself and Olivia. She'd even grabbed Olivia's Glock.

And then they gazed at each other, two women dressed in flowing nightgowns and heavy boots, weapons attached to their hips.

"These creatures won't be after us. It's him they want," Olivia said to her sister. "They're going to try to detain us so they can get to him."

Allie made a face. "But if he tells us who the Slasher is, won't we be in danger, too?"

"Yes, but not like him. I can't explain why. It's just something I feel." Her psychic sight, she thought. Anxious, she spun around to look at West. "Fight for your life. But try to stay close to me. Or to Allie. If you don't, we won't be able to protect you."

"Are you ready?" he asked. "Can I say the killer's name?"

Olivia glanced at Allie, and her sister nodded. Even Samantha seemed prepared. She crouched in a corner, blending into the shadows, like a jungle cat waiting to strike, to take down the first evil thing that came her way.

"We're ready," Olivia said.

West frowned, took a rough breath and opened his mouth to speak.

But he never got the chance.

A gust of wind hit him like a tornado, spinning his body, sending him crashing against the wall, rendering him unconscious.

And then lightning flashed, streaking across the living room like fire. Olivia grabbed her sister, and they hit the deck, taking cover behind the sofa. Samantha remained in the corner, her green eyes darting wildly.

Boom. Boom. Boom.

While thunder crashed in the sky, three enormous beings, dressed like Indian warriors, materialized, their feet rattling the floor. A supernatural sentry, they surrounded the special agent, guarding Zinna's prey.

"We're in trouble," Allie said.

Olivia studied the giants. Although they weren't armed, they were at least seven feet tall, with hulking, mutantlike bodies and vertical eyes. "They're from West's culture. Mythic creatures his grandfather used to tell him about when he was young." She paused, steadied her weapon. "Zinna probably created them from West's imagination. The way he envisioned them when he was a boy."

"Why are they just standing there?"

"I think they're waiting for us to make the first move."

"They're not hurting him."

"They daze their victims. They make them crazy. But it's only a temporary insanity."

Another flash of lightning lit up the room.

"Look!" Allie shrieked.

"I know. Keep your voice down." West was regaining consciousness, stumbling to his feet. Although he was barely visible, Olivia could see him, searching for her and Allie, gazing through a narrow space between two giants. "I think he's already starting to feel it. He's already getting dazed."

"He probably has a concussion, too," her sister whispered. "He hit his head pretty hard."

Olivia wanted to charge through the monster brigade and put her arms around him, hold him, protect him. He was struggling to unholster his gun, struggling to think clearly. A trail of blood dripped from his hairline, running down the side of his face. He wiped it away, blinked, retrieved his weapon and aimed it at the back of one of the giants.

"He's going to open fire," she said.

"Should we do that, too?"

"Yes. On my command." Olivia waited, watching her lover. He swayed on his feet, pulled the trigger, then managed to duck for cover, zigzagging between the giants, running, jumping, landing behind a chair.

"Now!"

Thunder roared. Bullets popped, blasting like firecrackers. Olivia shot the creatures full of holes. Allie's wasn't faring so well. The recoil on the Magnum startled her, knocking her on her butt. West was having problems, too. From her vantage point, Olivia could see him, fighting dizziness, struggling with his aim.

Olivia kept firing. But the giants were barely fazed by the bullets. She switched to a higher-caliber weapon, hoping, praying, to take them down.

But her effort proved in vain. Penetrating their skin was next to impossible. They reacted like elephants being pelted with BBs.

Angry, annoyed.

Then the lights went out. Even the streetlights were gone. A blackout, Olivia thought. But she knew it was witchcraft, not a result of the storm. The flames on the candles had been vanquished, too.

"Olivia?" Allie's voice quavered in the dark.

"It's okay. I have a flashlight." She removed it from her holster, but the damn thing didn't work. "The supernatural energy must have drained the batteries." She touched her sister's shoulder, reassuring her. "I can handle this. I can sense where things are."

"Well, I can't. It's pitch-black in here."

Something growled.

Allie caught her breath. "What was that?"

Silent, Olivia zeroed in on the energy. Gray fur, pointed ears, fangs.

A bewitched canine.

"It's a wolf." She paused, steadied her weapon. "A lone male. There are bats hanging from the ceiling, too."

Her sister all but squeaked.

Silence.

Then thunderous footsteps. Objects crashing to the floor, splintering, rolling.

Allie squeezed Olivia's leg. "What's going on?"

"It's the giants. They can't see in the dark, either." She froze, felt the wolf creeping across the room toward West.

She turned, fired, missed.

The lights came back on, sending the bats into a tail-spin. Wings flapped in fury, filling the living room. Allie screamed, waving her arms.

Olivia struggled to reach West, to stop the wolf from reaching him. But the bats were everywhere, blocking her path, diving, darting, careening into each other, making hellish sounds. Irritated, she fired at the winged creatures, dropping them like oversize flies.

Still crouched on the floor, Allie grabbed the Magnum and starting firing, as well. She took out a few of the birdlike mammals, but she hit a window, too, shattering it, sending a gush of rain into the loft.

In the midst of the chaos, Olivia spotted Samantha. The cat attacked her share of bats, swatting them with her claws. But then she slid on a stream of water and bumped into another cat.

A tabby that morphed into a chicken.

A *lohka*. Another being from West's culture.

Allie screeched, and Olivia spun around. One of the giants had pinned her to the floor, putting his ugly face next to hers. Allie froze, sucked in a panicked breath, then reacted on instinct, kicking him between the legs.

He let out an excruciating bellow, his painful cry rattling the walls.

Olivia's breath rushed out. Kyle had taught Allie well. Males, no matter what breed, had a vulnerable spot. Something Olivia had forgotten to consider.

Within no time she located the other two giants. They

guarded the hallway, telling her that the wolf had dragged West into another room.

Focusing on the enormous duo, she took Allie's maneuver a step further. In the blink of an eye, she fired her weapon and blasted them in the balls, grateful they weren't the beings with the fifty-foot dicks.

The moderately endowed monsters toppled like bowling pins, roaring in agony.

And then they disappeared.

Leaving nothing but the sound of rain.

Even the bats were gone.

Allie came skidding around the corner, with Samantha on her heels.

"Now what?" her sister asked.

Olivia couldn't help but smile. Allie had bat shit in her hair, and Samantha had chicken feathers sticking out of her mouth, but they were ready for another battle.

A second later her smile fell. "The wolf is still here." She motioned to the trail of blood. "He took West into my room." And from what she could see, West had struggled to get away.

"How badly is he hurt?"

"He's in trouble. But not just from his wounds." She could feel her lover's pain, the ache in his chest as he tried to breathe. "The wolf is stealing his oxygen. Making him weak. He can't fight back anymore."

"I might be able to help," Allie said. "The charm I made is in my room, in my jewelry box."

"The wolf claw?"

"Yes. If we can get to West, if we can put it around his neck, it might protect him. What could be stronger against a bewitched wolf than its own medicine?"

"You're right." And at this point, Olivia was willing to try anything. "You get the necklace, and I'll—"

The lights went out again.

"Damn it." Zinna's idea of a joke, Olivia thought. "I really hate that bitch."

"Me, too."

"I'll help you get the charm." She wasn't about to let Allie stumble around in the dark by herself.

"I was hoping you'd say that."

Together they made their way into Allie's bedroom, where her sister bumped into the edge of the dresser, bruised her knee and cursed like a sailor.

By the time they secured the necklace, Olivia's heart thumped frantically in her chest. West was getting weaker. She could feel him losing consciousness. "We have to hurry."

She guided her sister across the hall, and they stood outside of Olivia's room. Rain pounded on the roof, intensifying the atmosphere. Samantha hissed in the dark.

"What should we do?" Allie asked.

"I'm going in there," Olivia said. "I'm going to shoot the wolf."

"What about me?"

"You can wait until it's over."

"No way." The younger woman refused to remain

idle. "I'll stay behind you. And as soon as the wolf is down, I'll find West. I'll put the necklace on him."

"It's pitch-black, Allie. How are you going to find him?"

The lights returned.

Her sister puffed out an excited breath. "That's how."

"Fine, but leave the wolf to me. You're a terrible shot. You might hit West."

"Look who's talking. You're the one who plugged Kyle."

"Yeah, but I meant to do that." She moved closer to Allie, touching her hand, needing the connection, the sibling bond. "If the lights go out again, you could get hurt."

Allie met her gaze. "I'll be fine. I trust you. You'll get that beast, even if it's dark."

Samantha meowed, lending her support. Olivia had no idea how the cat intended to help, but she wasn't about to discourage her. "Then let's do this."

Olivia opened the door a crack, and the wolf growled, sending shivers along her spine. She could see him, crouched in the corner, guarding West. The FBI agent lay on the floor, as motionless as a rag doll.

She stepped into the room, Allie creeping in behind her. Samantha ran past them, darting under the bed.

So much for the feline's bravery.

Another step closer. Another growl.

"Shoot him," Allie said.

"I can't. He's too close to West. I'm going to have

to wait until he tries to attack me. Until he abandons his prey."

The wolf remained right where he was, so Olivia kept moving, threatening him.

"When that beast charges you, I'm running toward West, okay?"

"Okay. But what if he charges *you?*"

Allie's footsteps stalled behind her. "That's not funny."

Olivia stepped closer to the wolf. His yellow eyes followed her. She could see him preparing to strike. He bared his teeth, ready to tear her flesh.

Then the lights went out again.

Olivia fired, but the wolf sprang forward, knocking the gun out of her hand, sending the shot into the air, the bullet hitting the ceiling.

As Allie ran toward West, the wolf slammed Olivia to the ground. She wrestled with the snarling beast, asking the Creator to protect them.

All of them. Her, Allie and West.

The wolf sank his teeth into Olivia's arm. Her nightgown tangled as she rolled, as she struggled to grab a weapon from her holster.

Any weapon.

"Are you hurt?" Allie screamed out in the dark. "What should I do? Tell me what to do!"

"Just take care of West!"

A moment of silence, then a frenzied, "The necklace broke. I tried to put it on him, but the leather snapped."

Olivia recited a prayer in her head. Black Elk's Earth Prayer. The words of a Lakota holy man.

Allie spoke again, her voice edged with fear. "The pieces scattered. I can't find the claw."

The lights came back on, but not completely. They flickered, creating eerie shadows, haunting the room.

"Oh, dear God." Another frantic cry. "He's not breathing!"

Olivia latched onto her knife and slit the wolf's throat. His blood ran warm and thick, spilling all over her. When she shoved him away and stood up, her legs wobbling with the effort, tears sprang to her eyes.

Allie attempted to revive West, tilting his head back, pinching his nose, covering his mouth with hers, blowing air into his lungs.

Olivia ran to his side, falling to her knees.

His skin was blue, ghostly in the blinking light.

Allie began chest compressions, pushing, pumping, struggling to keep up. She'd never taken a CPR class.

And neither had Olivia. But she tried to save him, too. While Allie pumped, she leaned over him, breathing into his mouth the way her sister had done.

But he wasn't responding.

Nothing happened.

Allie burst into tears.

Desperate, Olivia scrambled to find the broken charm. But as she gathered the beads, searching frantically for the claw, she knew it was too late.

Agent West was dead.

Chapter 16

The rain pounded even harder, the sound echoing in Olivia's ears. Feeling like a zombie, she sat on the floor, stringing the beads she'd recovered. The leather strap on the necklace had broken near the knot, so it was still long enough to tie around West's neck.

If she couldn't protect him in life, then she hoped to protect him in death.

She glanced at Allie, who clutched her knees to her chest. Her sister had stopped crying, but the rain had become her tears.

"I still haven't found the claw," Olivia said. She couldn't even sense where it was. Her psychic sight wasn't working. But then, her ability wasn't foolproof, especially when her emotions got in the way.

Allie's breath hitched. "He doesn't look peaceful. He looks cold."

Olivia nodded. The lights had stopped flickering. The lamps in her room burned bright, showering West with an icy glow.

Samantha poked her head out from under the bed and hissed.

Olivia kept stringing the beads, her fingers numb, her heart empty.

"Your arm is bleeding," Allie said suddenly.

"It's okay. It doesn't matter."

"Yes, it does." Her sister climbed to her feet. "West would want you to bandage it." The younger woman stepped over the dead wolf, gathering medical supplies from the bathroom.

Samantha hissed again.

Allie returned with the first-aid kit. Olivia glanced at West and noticed he wasn't bleeding. There wasn't a wound on his body, not one scratch, yet the hallway had been marked with his blood. There were droplets by the bedroom door, too, but the trail had become smeared farther into the room, where Olivia had killed the wolf.

Confused, she reached out to touch West's hair and noticed it was bone dry. No dampness lingered from the rain.

Samantha watched Olivia through curious eyes, then pinned her ears and growled like a wildcat.

Allie tried to shush her, but Sam extended her claws and batted West's shoulder, attacking him as if he were a stranger instead of the man she adored.

"Something's wrong," Olivia said.

"Do you think she's angry at him for leaving her?"

"No. It's—" Olivia paused. She didn't know what it was. Her power still wasn't working. "West doesn't have any wounds. That doesn't make sense."

Allie bandaged Olivia's arm, silent for a moment, contemplating her words. "I don't understand."

"Neither do I. But his clothes are too tidy, too neat. He doesn't look like he was in a struggle."

"But we know he was."

"Exactly." Olivia shifted her gaze. Samantha had stopped attacking West, but she was still growling under her breath, treating him like a threat.

The cat didn't trust him.

A stream of panic sluiced through Olivia's veins. Was Zinna preparing West for the ghost world? Was she transforming his body? Healing his wounds? Turning him into one of her creatures? "We need to find that claw."

They scoured the room, searching every inch of the floor, checking under furniture. Samantha started nosing about, too, sniffing at dust bunnies. Then she hissed at the mirrored closet doors.

Olivia spun around, afraid she would see Zinna in the glass. But no one was there.

The cat pawed the rail. Cautious, Olivia moved closer. The door was slightly ajar, so she inched it back.

And found the claw.

She picked it up, holding it carefully in her hand. Had Zinna tried to suck it into the mirror?

With deep, anxious breaths, Olivia finished stringing the necklace. Allie handed her the rest of the beads, making sure the pattern was correct.

When the charm was done, Olivia tied it around West's neck. Unable to help herself, she skimmed his cheek, felt the chill of his skin.

"Oh, my God. Look!" Allie backed away from the wolf.

Only it wasn't a wolf anymore.

It had morphed into another canine, a much smaller breed: a coyote. A trickster in Olivia and Allie's culture.

Although the animal was still dead, it had reverted to its true form. The coyote had only been pretending to be a wolf, and the charm had exposed him.

So what had the charm done to West?

Olivia glanced at Allie, and in one simultaneous move, both women turned toward the special agent's body.

But he was gone.

In his place was an image doll, a tiny clay figure, the wolf charm far too big for its neck.

Allie gasped.

Olivia's knees went weak. "That wasn't West we were trying to revive. Zinna must have replaced him with a clone right before we came into the room."

"So where is the real West?" Allie rubbed the goose bumps on her arms. "What happened to him?"

"I don't know. I—"

The lights went out.

"Not again," Allie whispered.

Olivia froze. Her psychic sight had returned. She could feel the presence of another being in the room. Wary, she turned around, sensing the identity of the intruder.

The closet-door mirrors lit up, reflecting Zinna's image.

"She took him," Olivia said.

By now, Allie had caught sight of the lighted mirror. She, too, stared at their great-grandmother's reflection.

Suddenly laughter echoed through the loft, as eerie as the screech of an owl.

Anger pummeled Olivia's chest. "She wanted us to figure this out. She wanted us to know that we'd been tricked."

"I still don't understand where West is."

Olivia stepped closer to the glass. Zinna didn't move. She stood like a statue, her golden-colored eyes shining like amber jewels. "He's in the mirror. He's in her world somewhere." And Olivia intended to find him, no matter what it took.

Zinna finally moved. One simple motion. One noticeable change in her expression.

The owl lady smiled, her lips tilting in a thin line.

When the lights came back on, she'd disappeared, taking the dead coyote and the image doll of Agent West with her. Even the crimson stain on Olivia's nightgown vanished.

The only blood that remained belonged to West.

And so did the knowledge that he was trapped in another dimension, at the mercy of an ancient witch.

* * *

At daybreak the loft was filled with people. Olivia had called Muncy, Riggs, Kyle and Derek to help her and Allie with a game plan. An eclectic group, at best. But everyone was skilled in his or her own right.

Muncy and Riggs sat at the kitchen table, discussing the case. Sorting through West's briefcase, they paged through his notes, hoping the special agent had left behind some clues. Something, anything that would prove who he believed the killer was. At this point Glenn was the primary suspect. West had claimed that the killer was close to Olivia and Allie, and Glenn fit the bill. Yet there wasn't any evidence linking him to the murders. Or to an alliance with Zinna.

Unimpressed with the police work so far, Kyle rolled his eyes. He'd assigned himself cleanup duty, boarding up the shattered window in the living room, sweeping the broken glass, then mopping the rainwater that pooled at everyone's feet.

Every so often, he took a moment to slant Detective Riggs an I-don't-like-you glance. And she, in turn, checked out the renegade warrior with the same screw-you interest.

If Olivia hadn't been steeped in her own problems, she would have found the sexual energy between them amusing.

Kyle didn't trust officers of the law. Nor did he find white women appealing. But the lady cop had caught his eye, just as he'd caught hers.

And they were both good and pissed about it.

Derek was another enigma. At first he'd refused to come over to help Olivia. But he'd caved in soon enough. She suspected that deep down he was still swayed by good magic, by doing the right thing. Of course, given his penchant for Peeping Tom sex, he would probably never be the noblest witch on the block.

But he was all she had. Her best hope.

He occupied the war-torn sofa, with Allie sitting next to him, taking notes. Olivia sat in the rocking chair, picking his brain.

"Can you get me into the mirror?" she asked.

"Yes, but you can't go leaping into your great-grand-mother's realm unprepared." He shifted in his seat, blowing out a tired breath, drinking the coffee Allie had prepared. "Once you're in the same dimension with her, she can steal your soul faster than you can blink an eye."

"So how do I prepare to face an ancient witch? What should I do?"

"You'll have to arm yourself with Apache medicine. Green malachite wards off evil. And just in case Zinna creates any beings for you to fight, you should attach some malachite to all of the guns you bring. It'll make the weapons shoot straight."

Olivia wasn't about to argue that she was already a crack shot. She'd made some mistakes lately, and she wasn't taking any chances, not with West's rescue. "What else?"

"Eagle feathers and turquoise beads are used for protection. You can tie them onto your clothes. You'll need cattail pollen, too. You should keep it in a buckskin bag."

"For healing?" she asked.

"Yes. From what you said, Agent West was injured before Zinna took him. He's probably extremely ill by now." Derek glanced at Allie, who'd stopped taking notes to listen. "Mortals can't survive in a witch dimension for very long, not unless they give the dead witch their soul."

Olivia thought about her lover. How hard he worked to make the world a better place, to put violent offenders behind bars. "West wouldn't do that. He wouldn't become one of the bad guys."

"Then you'll have to heal him. Make him well enough to travel, to return to this dimension."

"Olivia isn't a shaman," Allie said.

"She could be," Derek countered. "Her power is strong enough. But just the same, it won't be easy. She needs instruction from a medicine man, someone who can train her, but there isn't time. She's going to have to wing this on her own."

"Why can't we solicit a shaman to go with her?" This came from Kyle, who leaned against his mop, his shirtsleeves rolled up, a cloth headband securing his hair. "It doesn't make sense to send her in there alone."

Derek made an exasperated sound. "That's a novel idea, but if it were possible, wouldn't I have suggested it by now? Zinna had the opportunity to kill West last night. But she took him instead."

"So she's using him as bait?" Kyle asked. "To lure Olivia into her realm? To try to turn her into a witch?"

"Precisely. And there's no way she would allow Olivia to bring a shaman with her."

Allie doodled on her notepad. "What about me? Doesn't our great-grandmother want me to be a witch, too?"

"You?" Kyle hooted a laugh. "Remember Aunt Clara on those old reruns of *Bewitched?* How she was always goofing up her incantations? That'd be you, Addle-brain."

Derek smirked. "What about that other bumbling character? Esmerelda. She botched things up, too."

Allie shot both men the bird. She didn't appreciate them making jokes at her expense. But Olivia knew that Kyle, and maybe Derek, too, were only trying to protect her, to keep her away from Zinna.

Allie wasn't ready to enter a witch realm. She was just learning the strength of her power.

Olivia took a deep breath and thought about her own situation, her own power. She wasn't even sure if she was ready. But she didn't have a choice.

"What else should I bring with me?" she asked, directing the conversation back to the business at hand.

"Anything that transcends your medicine," Derek said. "That makes you feel strong."

"What about conventional medicine? Like aspirin or penicillin? Would that help West?"

Derek shook his head. "Not with a witch sickness.

You'll have to fight magic with magic, with remedies a shaman would use."

"I have a tape in my car you can take with you," Kyle told her. "Southwest singing and drumming. You can use it for the healing ceremony." He shifted his attention to her sister. "Write that down, Addle-brain. And a mini tape recorder, too."

"Her name is Allie," Riggs said, pushing away from the kitchen table and reprimanding Kyle in one attention-grabbing swoop. "She shouldn't have to take that crap from you."

He gave the lady cop a lethal stare. Then he glanced at Allie, who sided with Riggs, making him hate the female detective even more.

But instead of telling her off, he crossed his arms and brooded like a six-foot-four baby.

Olivia sighed, wondering if she and West had behaved that foolishly when they'd fought their attraction. "What if I can't save him?" she said suddenly, putting an uncomfortable hush over the room.

Muncy finally joined the somber group, offering Olivia the comfort she needed. He stood next to her chair, putting his hand on her shoulder. Tears burned her eyes, but she refused to let them fall. Instead she squeezed Muncy's hand, recalling how she'd cried in his arms on the night her father had died.

"Can you put a binding spell on Glenn?" he asked Derek.

"Why? Because you think he's the killer? Yes, I can

bind him, but it won't matter. He was a lousy witch, nothing more than Yvonne's lackey. He's not the Slasher."

"Then who is?" Muncy challenged, still wary of the other man.

Derek shrugged. "You're the detective, not me." He turned to look at Olivia. "You better get ready. We can all help you gather the things you need."

"What's a witch realm like?" she asked. "What can I expect?"

"Honestly, I have no idea. Dead witches create their own dimensions. And I've never been in one."

She came to her feet and took a deep breath, preparing for her journey. A supernatural abyss, she thought. A bottomless pit.

A world of the unknown.

Hours later the same group of people gathered in Olivia's bedroom. Allie and Riggs sat on the edge of the bed, and Kyle and Muncy stood back, looking out of place next to each other.

Olivia waited, her backpack filled with supplies, several guns attached to her belt, a knife sheath and bone-handled blade tucked into her boot. On her shirt she wore eagle feathers that had belonged to her father.

Derek ran his hands over the surface of the mirror. "I've never done this before. I've never opened a portal."

Olivia glanced around, hoping the ritual was safe,

hoping it wouldn't put anyone in danger. "Then how do you know it will work?"

"Zinna wants you to enter her realm. She won't stop this from happening."

"Will we get to see her?" Kyle wanted to know. "Will her reflection appear in the mirror?"

"No." Derek drew an enormous circle on the glass, using a red marker. "She won't risk coming that close, not if the portal is going to open." He dabbed some ointment he'd prepared in the center of the circle, smearing it into an ancient symbol. Candles burned in every corner, lending an eerie glow.

When Derek rubbed the ointment onto Olivia's arms, she flinched. Her skin turned red, her pores tingling. "What is that?"

"Poison," he responded much too casually. "But only if it's taken orally."

He continued his ritual, placing a handful of crystals on a makeshift altar.

Allie heaved a nervous breath. "How is Olivia supposed to come back through the portal? Will it stay open?"

"No. But the ointment I put on her is connected to this world, and if she places her hands in the center of the circle, it should open from the other side."

"So the circle you drew is the door?" Olivia asked.

"Yes, but I don't know if you'll be able to see it once you've crossed over. You might have to use your psychic ability to find it. And on top of that, the potency of the ointment will fade."

"How long do I have?"

"Three or four hours at best. You'll have to make this a timely mission."

"Or I'll get stuck in Zinna's dimension?"

"Unless she lets you out. It's her realm. She controls it."

"We're going to wait for you," Muncy said, frowning at the mirror. "All of us. We won't leave this house until you and West are back. Safe and sound."

Olivia smiled at the detective, putting on a brave front, but her stomach was doing somersaults.

Derek addressed everyone. "Say your goodbyes now. Before I finish the spell. Once the portal opens, there won't be time."

Kyle stepped forward first, taking Olivia in his arms, brushing his mouth across hers. She held him for a moment, enjoying the power of his body, drawing from his physical strength.

Riggs shooed Kyle away, using her tough-girl charm, whispering words of encouragement in Olivia's ear.

Muncy simply kissed her forehead, and Allie...

Olivia gazed at her sister. "Don't you dare cry."

"I'm not. I won't." Allie placed the wolf charm around her neck. "To keep the coyotes away," she said, her eyes watering.

The sisters embraced, holding each other close. After they separated, Derek completed his magic, behaving like the good witch he still longed to be.

Olivia could feel the energy in the room, the magnetic force electrifying the air. She glanced at the crystals and saw them reflect the light.

When the circle on the mirror began to spin, Derek gave her a silent nod. She stepped forward, watching the glass ripple. The ointment on her arms seeped into her pores, making her heart race.

Without looking back, she stepped through the portal.

And experienced the sensation of flight.

Darkness sped past her eyes, then little pinwheels of light, twirling in an endless sky. Finally her feet touched the ground, and she realized she was encased in a bubble, like Glinda in the Land of Oz.

Was this Zinna's idea of a joke? Or a side effect from Derek's good-witch spell?

Cautious, Olivia stepped through the circle, but there wasn't a munchkin in sight.

Directly in front of her was a Gothic-style mansion. The towering building had been constructed in the middle of a densely wooded area, with wild brush and gnarled trees creating a moss-draped fortress.

She approached the porch, a brick structure surrounded by fanciful woodwork. Lavish patterns trimmed the front door, delicately swirled, like frosting on a wedding cake.

A strange setting for an ancient Apache witch, she thought. But Zinna was always full of surprises.

Olivia tried to focus on West, on his energy, but she couldn't feel anything. She had no idea if he was here.

She glanced back and noticed the bubble remained where it was. Was it waiting for her?

When she entered the house, nothing stirred. Not one sound, not one sign of life. The interior was pure white: the carpet, the walls, the furniture.

Beautiful. Chilling.

Like freshly fallen snow.

She wandered through the hallways, noticed the arched ceilings and embellished chandeliers, the etched opal glass twinkling with flame-tipped lights. As she stepped into the parlor, her feet sank into the carpet, leaving an impression of the soles of her boots.

"My home is lovely, isn't it?"

Olivia spun around. Zinna stood before her in a flowing skirt and a cotton blouse adorned with shell necklaces. Her raptor-colored eyes burned bright, but her body had a waterish quality, tangible yet transparent.

A spirit. A corpse.

Wary, Olivia touched the wolf claw Allie had given her. She had been prepared to face her great-grandmother, to ward off her magic, but she hadn't expected to socialize with her, to engage in small talk. "I don't think being in a witch dimension is lovely."

Zinna tilted her head, her bluish black hair enhanced with a beaded bow, a Chiricahua ornament from days gone by. "I was hoping you'd choose to stay a while, to get to know me."

"After what you've done?"

"We're family, Olivia. Surely you can make peace with me." She moved forward, her skirt sweeping the floor. "Did you know I was a prisoner of war? That I lived most of my life at Fort Sill? That's where I died, almost a hundred years ago." She paused, heaved a sigh. "It was a dreadful existence, much more difficult for me than the others. I was a witch, scorned by my own people, but still living under the government's thumb. Of course, I've come a long way since then."

"How? By taking your own prisoners?"

"You mean Agent West?" The owl lady removed a rose from a cut-glass vase, inhaling the fragrance of the white flower. "I offered him redemption."

No matter how hard she tried, Olivia still couldn't feel his presence. She couldn't get a reading on her lover. "For what? His loyalty? His soul?"

"It's a fair exchange, but he's too stubborn to know better." Still holding the rose, Zinna sat in a velvet settee. Behind her, two clover-shaped windows offered a view of the woods, of the thick brush and moss-festooned trees. "He reminds me of someone I used to know. A man I once loved."

Was this part of Zinna's ploy? Part of her enchantment? Was she trying to make herself seem human? Vulnerable? A woman who'd lost her heart?

"He wasn't the man I had a child with," the witch said. "He wasn't your great-grandfather."

Olivia remained where she was, standing in the middle of the room, armed with supplies, with Apache medicine, with the weapons she still expected to use. "Then who was he?"

"His name doesn't matter." Zinna placed the rose

beside her, where it withered and died. "But I've never forgotten him." A slow, deliberate smile tilted her lips. "And I'm certain he's never forgotten me." She brushed the dead flower petals onto the floor, scattering them like ashes. "Not after I cursed him."

"That's not love."

Zinna rose from her seat. "Don't mock me. I may look young, but I've survived for nearly a century."

"Here? In the fortress you created?" Olivia glanced out a window, where the wind had begun to howl. She knew there were creatures lurking in the forest, entities spawned from Zinna's magic. She could feel them, whispering their demented praises to their mistress.

Was that where she was keeping West? In a dark, dank shelter in the woods?

"Yes," Zinna said.

Olivia shifted her gaze, felt a chill rack her bones. The owl lady had just read her mind. "I want to see him."

"Not yet. There's someone else I want you to see first."

"A person? A human?"

"Yes." Zinna escorted her up a flight of stairs, a spiral path leading to the second story. Olivia held on to the banister, gripping the slick, polished wood. Was this a trick? Was there really someone here besides West?

Her great-grandmother was being far too civil, far too ladylike for a witch who screeched like an owl.

They walked down a hallway, where mirrors of every shape and size glinted on the walls.

"This is it." Zinna opened a door at the end of the hall. With a hard nudge, she sent Olivia sprawling into the elegantly furnished room, snapping the door closed behind her.

She landed on her hands and knees, then glanced up and saw the crimson-stained bed.

And the woman who lay upon it.

She crawled to her feet, her breath lodged in her throat. This was the image she'd seen in her mind. The vision she'd had about her mother.

Only she wasn't dead.

Yvonne opened her eyes and smiled, even though she was bathed in blood.

Chapter 17

Confused, Olivia took a step back. Her mother couldn't be alive. Could she? "This can't be happening. You're not real. You're one of Zinna's tricks."

"No, darling. It's me."

"But the Slasher killed you."

Yvonne, or whoever she was, sat up and smoothed her hair away from her face, smearing blood across her cheek. She wore a lacy bra and a pair of matching panties. On the right side of her abdomen was the mark of the killer, an arrowhead encased in a heart. Only, unlike the other victims, the symbol hadn't been drawn onto her body with a black marker. It was a tattoo. The real thing.

"I'm not dead." Yvonne held out her red-stained

palms. "This is stage blood. See?" She gestured to her exposed flesh. "I don't have any wounds."

Dizzy, Olivia sank into a nearby chair.

Her mother walked to an adjoining bathroom and came back with a stack of damp towels. Silent, she began wiping her skin, bathing herself. Although the terry cloth absorbed most of the thick red substance, a few watered-down streaks remained on her underwear. When she dropped the towels to the floor, they stained the virginal carpet.

Olivia took a deep breath. "Why did you douse yourself with blood?"

"Because it makes me feel good." She opened an antique armoire and chose a silky pantsuit. Amber. The color of the owl lady's eyes. "It purges my pain."

"Your pain? You're the one who left us. Who walked away."

"I know. But I came back." She removed the soiled sheet and tossed it onto the floor, where it landed on top of the towels. Then she went after the pillowcases. "I ruined my marriage for Taylor Campbell. I went to Ireland with him, spent all that time as his mistress. And when I got older, that bastard didn't want me anymore." She sat on the edge of the barren mattress. "I should have known better. Taylor was half the man your father was. Joseph would have never done that to me. That's why I returned to L.A. I wanted to reconcile with your dad, to start over."

After twelve years? After her rich lover got tired of her? "You didn't know Dad was dead?"

"No." Yvonne smoothed her hair again. She wore it long and straight, much like Allie's. And although she'd aged, she was still beautiful. "I had no idea that he'd committed suicide. Can you imagine how I felt when I discovered what he'd done? I wanted to die, too."

Olivia glanced at the red stain on the carpet, the towels, the sheet, the pillowcases—evidence of her mother's morbid ritual.

"I was staying in a motel near the beach, mourning my loss," Yvonne told her. "And that's when Zinna first appeared to me. There she was in the mirror, beckoning me to come to her. So I did. But I was still suicidal."

"So what are you saying? That Zinna saved your life?"

"Yes." Yvonne slipped on a pair of gold heels. "She even created this house to cheer me up. The one she had before wasn't Gothic, but I've always been partial to European architecture."

Olivia didn't respond. She simply waited for her mom to continue.

"But I was still depressed," Yvonne said. "I moped around this big, beautiful house, missing Joseph, feeling like a whore for all the times I'd cheated on him. I was even too upset to get in touch with you and Allie."

An excuse, she thought. A reason to ignore her daughters, to wallow in self-pity. "So what happened?"

"Zinna told me to stop blaming myself, and I knew she was right. I had to find a way to alleviate my pain. To stop contemplating suicide."

"The fake blood?" Olivia asked, hoping, praying the

story would end there. Even though, God help her, she feared her mother's crime went beyond forging her own death.

"No. I didn't start doing that until later." Still perched on the edge of the barren mattress, she adjusted the straps on her shoes. "Until I started punishing those women for their infidelity."

Feeling ill, Olivia rose from her chair and opened a window, needing air, needing an escape. Her stomach roiled, and she clutched her middle, doing her damnedest not to vomit.

Her mother was the Slasher.

She looked at the woman who'd given her life and felt her heart go numb.

Yvonne reached for a diamond bracelet on the nightstand and slipped it on, admiring the way it looked on her wrist.

Olivia fingered the crudely made charm around her neck, remembering what Allie had said. *To keep the coyotes away.* No wonder their mother had chosen Yvonne Coyote as her alias. She'd been a trickster from the beginning.

And now Olivia understood how West had pieced together the puzzle. Yvonne doused herself with phony blood to relive the murders and mime her own death. She transposed herself with her victims, fantasizing, giving herself a sick thrill.

Hadn't the clues been there all along? "The first time I had a vision of you covered in blood, I'd been trying to get an image of the killer, trying to get a reading from a picture Allie had painted. But I'd misinterpreted what I saw. I'd assumed you were a victim. Not the Slasher reliving her crimes."

"Don't let it upset you, darling. Those women deserved to die. I learned the error of my ways, but they were still behaving like whores, still hurting the men they'd married." A pause, a reflective expression. "I even stopped the last one, Denise, before she could cheat. Before the damage was done."

Dear God. Olivia closed her eyes. West had claimed the Slasher was narcissist. And Yvonne had committed unspeakable acts to make herself feel better. She'd punished other women for *her* mistakes. *Her* guilt. *Her* supposed pain.

And not only that, but she'd probably killed Taylor Campbell, too. Casting a spell and afflicting him with an illness.

Olivia opened her eyes and turned to the window. A crisp breeze blew, billowing the lace sheers, making them look like a ghost.

Was this what her father had been trying to her warn her and Allie about? Had he been trying to tell them that their mother was the Slasher?

"You can frame Glenn," Yvonne said.

Olivia shifted her gaze. "What?"

"You and Agent West. You can frame Glenn for the murders. The police already think he did it. And he's such a spineless weasel. I never liked him."

At a loss for words, Olivia clutched her stomach again.

"Just think," her mother went on to say. "If you convince West to take our side, the two of you can come here as often as you like. The way I do. And Zinna will give you anything you want." She stood, smiled, moved closer. "We can be a family. With Allie, of course." She reached out to hug Olivia, to embrace her . "Allie will follow your lead. Your sister adores you."

"No." She put her hands on her mother's shoulders and pushed her away. "I'd never frame an innocent man. And neither would Allie nor West."

Yvonne stumbled, nearly tripping on the soiled linens. "Damn you!"

"Go to hell, Mom."

"Listen to you. Miss High-and-Mighty. If you don't convince Agent West to get his priorities straight, he's going to die."

"No, he isn't. I'm going to heal him. And then I'm taking him home."

Her mom laughed. "Heal him? Who filled your head with that nonsense? You're not a medicine woman. You're a witch."

"No, I'm not. I'm my father's daughter, not yours."

Yvonne's narcissism sparked like fire. "Joseph is dead. And he killed himself because of me. I'm the one who mattered to him. Not you. Not your sister."

"Nothing you say will sway me. Nothing you say will make me betray my own soul."

"Then your lover won't survive."

Olivia held her ground. "I already told you, I'm going to heal him." And capture her mother, she thought. Turn her over to the police.

"I know what you're thinking," Yvonne said. "But Zinna would never allow it." She tossed back her hair and smiled. "This is my sanctuary. I'm safe here."

"Are you sure about that?" Olivia reached for her gun and aimed it at her mom. "You're still human. My bullet can still kill you."

"Yes, it could. But you're a fool to even consider such a thing."

In the next instant the owl lady materialized, shielding Yvonne. And within a heartbeat, the house disappeared, leaving Olivia standing in the middle of the forest.

With the wind howling at her back.

There was nothing but endless foliage: trees dripping with moss, zigzagging brush, vines creeping across the ground, twisting and turning into narrow paths.

Olivia didn't know which way to turn.

West was being kept in a shelter in the woods. Or, at least, that was what she'd been led to believe. But now that she was here, she couldn't feel his presence.

She was lost.

And so was he.

Even the bubble was gone.

No, she told herself. Don't give up. Her medicine had worked so far. Hadn't it? Zinna hadn't tempted her. She hadn't even come close to stealing her soul.

And neither had Yvonne.

Olivia swayed on her feet. Just thinking about her mother, imagining her sacrificing those women, sent a wave of nausea sloshing through her system.

West had told her the truth would hurt.

And now she had to find him, to heal him, to rescue him from this hellhole. Still battling a bout of queasiness, she reached for the water she'd packed, and took a small sip.

Then something moved at her feet.

She looked down, saw it shimmer beneath the brush, like a piece of garland that had fallen from a Christmas tree.

She watched it slink through the ivy, making leaves quake in its path. Cautious, she followed it. In her hand, she carried the gun she'd aimed at her mom.

She knew that nothing pure of heart lived in this forest, no birds or bees or mammals that hadn't been bewitched, nothing that dwelled in natural settings. The only beings that lurked in the shadows were Zinna's creatures.

Yet somehow this shimmering entity seemed chaste. A white light.

But how could she be sure?

It kept moving, slowly, allowing her to keep up, to make her way through low-hanging branches.

Suddenly the wind stirred, sweeping a chill through the air, lifting the eagle feathers attached to her shirt.

She stalled, squinted through a copse of trees and noticed a thatched roof in the distance.

West.

Finally. She could feel him. He was here, about a hundred yards away. Olivia took off running, heading for the rugged shanty, cypress limbs scratching her arms, moss tendrils attacking her hair like spiderwebs.

Her shimmering companion sped through the forest, too, racing ahead of her. She tripped, nearly stumbled, afraid the tiny building would disappear before she reached it. But by the time she got there, the white-light entity was already guarding the door.

It had to be her protector.

Anxious, she searched the one-room shack and found West in a dingy corner. He lay on the floor, his clothes torn, dried blood and dirt caked on his skin.

She knelt beside him and touched his cheek. "It's me," she whispered, removing a bundle of sage from her backpack.

He didn't open his eyes; he didn't respond.

She smudged herself and West, then purified the stagnant air. With quaking hands, she arranged the items she'd brought with her.

Would Zinna interfere with the healing? Or had the ancient witch backed off purposely, believing Olivia would fail...convinced she would be forced to give up her soul in exchange for West's life?

Determined to prove otherwise, Olivia played the Southwestern drumming-and-singing tape, letting the Native chants fill the room.

While she cleaned and bandaged West's wounds,

his eyelids fluttered. His skin was hot, feverish. She bathed his body with a liquid herbal mixture, trying to cool his skin.

And then she noticed the object beneath his flesh, on the left side of his chest. She traced the shape and realized what it was.

An arrowhead in the vicinity of his heart.

A calling card from the Slasher.

Distraught, Olivia gazed at her lover. Her mother had done this to him. Clearly, this had come from Yvonne. Olivia had heard of object-intrusion spells, where the sorcerer inserted a witch weapon into the victim's body. But she had no idea how to remove it.

Taking a chance, she used the cattail pollen on West's forehead. As far as she knew, curing ceremonies were long and detailed, with friends and family by the patient's side. But Olivia did her best to make him well, to use her medicine, to utilize her power.

Yet her efforts proved in vain.

The arrowhead remained. And so did his fever.

She glanced at her watch, saw how much time had passed. She held his hand and said a prayer.

He opened his eyes and looked at her. She caught her breath. His eyes were glazed, as foggy as a misty night, but he was moving his lips, attempting to speak.

"Dreaming," he said.

She smoothed his hair away from his face. "You're awake. I came here to take you home."

"Happy to see you."

"Me, too." She propped up his head and offered him some water, holding the plastic bottle for him. His lips were parched, blistering from the heat within his body.

"We should go now," he said.

"But you're still sick."

"Better," he told her.

Olivia pressed her palm to his cheek. He still had a fever, but it wasn't nearly as high as before. She frowned at his chest, at the arrowhead imbedded in his skin. How long would his recovery last? A few minutes? An hour? She hadn't broken the object-intrusion spell.

"Don't want to stay here," he said.

She checked her watch again. "You're right. We need to go." She gathered her supplies, getting ready to take him home.

He sat up, and she knew he was dizzy. She could sense the room spinning before his eyes. He leaned his head on her shoulder, and she drew him close.

Finally she got him to his feet. She held on to him at first, but he insisted that he could make it to the door on his own. Male pride, she thought, grateful for his determination.

The white-light entity was still outside.

But so were the forces of evil. The forest had come alive with dark, demented creatures. Olivia couldn't see them, but she felt them. Waiting, watching.

Zinna wasn't about to let them leave without a fight. Olivia's medicine had taken them farther than the owl lady had anticipated, which meant they had a chance.

A chance Zinna intended to destroy.

"We have to find the portal." Olivia tried to use her psychic sight to locate the bubble, but nothing happened.

Damn it, she thought. Why couldn't her ability be infallible?

"Which way should we go?" she asked the white light.

It turned in a circle, unsure of what path to take.

Curious, West moved closer. "What is that?"

"Something that's trying to help." But now she wondered why it was staying so low to the ground. Was it struggling in this dimension? Unable to rise to its full power?

"I need a weapon," West said. "They took mine."

They. Her mother and Zinna. Olivia placed a backup gun in his hand. "I know who the Slasher is. I saw her. I spoke to her."

He met her gaze. "I'm sorry it turned out this way."

Her heart clenched, ashamed of her mother, of what she'd done to him. "So am I." And before it was too late, she had to take him home.

Once again she tried to get a reading on the bubble. And this time she sensed what direction to take. "We need to go that way." She gestured to the opposite path from which they'd come.

As they traveled, Olivia monitored their time. They moved at a steady pace, but she worried about West. A cool breeze no longer blew. The terrain had become moist and slippery, and the temperature had reached a brutal height. The air was thick, humid with the scent of water. A harsh environment for a man battling an illness.

Something flew over their heads, and Olivia raised her weapon to the sky. One of Zinna's pets. A vulture, a buzzard waiting for West to die. Angry, she shot the bird, blasting it to the ground.

"Good versus evil," she said, trying to keep their spirits up, trying to surround them with positive energy. "How can we lose?"

West gave her an appreciative smile, and an instant later, a trio of winged monkeys—like the Wicked Witch of the West's mischief makers—flew out of a tree, leaping on Olivia's back, clawing her shirt, pulling her hair, yanking her head back.

Stunned, she fought off the twisted attack. Did Zinna think this was funny? Was she watching from a crystal ball? Or had it been Yvonne's idea?

West had been ambushed, too. She saw him rolling on the damp ground, struggling to fight back, leafy plants and broken branches scratching his arms.

While the beasts on Olivia's back continued their assault, she fired at West's monkeys. The creatures keeled over, dropping like flies.

"Shoot mine!" she yelled, as one of the winged primates stole her gun.

He squinted at her, and she knew his gaze was blurry. Wrestling with the monkeys had drained the last of his strength.

The white-light entity zigzagged, alerting Olivia to a new danger.

An alligator was approaching.

"Shoot!" She screamed at West again.

He fired, killing the monkeys in three successive shots, even though his aim was severely off. The malachite had worked, making the gun shoot straight. Score one for the good guys, she thought, focusing on the alligator.

Olivia retrieved her weapon and plugged the reptile full of holes, then spun around and saw the swamp from which it had come. "The bubble is in the water. I can feel it."

The protector didn't move. And Olivia knew why. West remained on the ground, drenched in sweat.

She knelt beside him, wanting to tell him that she loved him. But afraid, so very afraid, to say the words out loud. Instead, she got into her backpack and sponged his face and neck with the herbal mixture, trying to cool his skin. His fever had spiked once again. "We have to swim for it."

He lifted his hand, touched her cheek. "I'll try."

"I know you will." She blinked, told herself not to cry, then offered him some water, knowing he needed fluids to survive. "I'll hold on to you. We can do this together."

She helped him to his feet, and he leaned against her the entire way. When they reached the edge of the swamp, they both stalled.

"Might be more alligators," he said.

"I know." But they were running out of time, out of options. She considered diving in on her own and bringing the bubble to the bank. But if it was heavy enough to sink, then it was too cumbersome for her to move.

The protector hit the water first, gliding like an electric eel.

"Our turn," she said to West. "But I might have to let go of you, just for an instant. I'll have to use both hands to open the portal."

He nodded, and she prayed they didn't drown inside the bubble, that it didn't absorb the water when it opened.

Taking West with her, Olivia swam across the swamp, laboring to keep him close, using the protector's shimmering image as a beacon. They located the portal about thirty feet from the bank, immersed six feet under. The depth of a grave, she thought. She searched for evidence of the drawing Derek had made, the door to the other dimension, but there was no visible sign of where it was.

She used her psychic sight, found the right spot and released West, allowing him to swim on his own. She felt horribly disconnected letting him go, as if one of her limbs had just been severed, but that wasn't the only thing that panicked her.

The portal wouldn't open. The ointment on her arms wasn't working. Had the water deactivated it? Had—

She caught movement from the corner of her eye and noticed the white-light entity was spinning like a maniac.

Another alligator.

She dived for West, but the four-foot reptile grabbed his arm. She punched the beast's snout, and it opened its mouth and retreated. A maneuver she'd seen on *Animal Planet*. But West had already been bitten.

She propelled him to the surface so he could gulp some air. He hadn't lost consciousness. But she feared he might. How much could he endure? He was too sick to be in this situation.

Yet she had to submerge him again. She had to find a way to open the portal and get him inside.

But how?

Olivia clung to West, then glanced at his arm, at his blood seeping into the water. What if she wasn't strong enough to save them?

What if Zinna and the Slasher had already won?

Chapter 18

No, Olivia thought. She wouldn't lose hope. Not in the middle of a swamp with a man who seemed determined to stay conscious, no matter how ill he was. West's death wish had long since passed. Now that it was a reality, he wanted to survive.

Cradling him, Olivia swam toward a log, grabbed it and used it as a flotation device. She helped him put his arms around it, and he held on. The arm the alligator had attacked was still bleeding, but the wound didn't look serious. Maybe it was the smaller size of the gator. Of course that did little to ease her mind. Even a minor bite could get infected.

"The magic that was supposed to open the portal

isn't working," Olivia said. "But that doesn't matter. We can do this on our own."

West squinted at the sun. "How?"

"By holding on to each other. By using our medicine." She looked into his eyes, those strange gray eyes. "Our power. Good versus evil."

He leaned his head against the log. "Fearless leader."

"Who? Me?" She touched his cheek and felt the heat raging in his body. His lips were still blistered, and his breathing was labored.

"Trust you," he said.

"Thank you." Her eyes misted, but she blinked away the emotion. "We're both going to place our hands on the portal door. And I'm not going to let go of you this time."

"No more gators."

"No. No more attacks." Or so she prayed. She looked at her protector. "We need your energy, too. Your power. Just stay with us when we try to open the portal."

It didn't respond, of course. But she knew it understood. That it cared.

"Ready?" she asked, gazing at her companions.

West nodded, and she put her arms around him, hoping that he could hold his breath long enough to remain underwater. She removed the wolf charm from around her neck and slipped it over his head.

He gave her a tender smile, and she decided he had to be the most determined FBI agent on the planet.

Federal Bureau of Inspiration.

"Let's go," she said, submerging him below the surface.

The white-light entity made the dive, too.

West shivered in her arms, but she kept him close to her body, close to her heart. She wasn't going to lose him.

When they reached the bubble, she braced herself against the back of West's body, holding him in place. Then she lifted his hands and put them on the portal door. Next she placed her hands right below his.

Her protector started spinning.

Suddenly there were alligators everywhere, coming at them from all sides.

Zinna was trying to stop them.

Olivia pressed closer to West. Soon the gators would be close enough to bite.

Just then, the white-light entity touched Olivia's hands, showering her with every ounce of power it had, letting her draw from its energy.

The door to the bubble opened, taking her and West inside. She blinked, felt her skin tingle and realized her protector was gone.

Darkness sped before her eyes, and she reached for West. He slumped against her shoulder. Did he see the sudden pinwheels of light?

When her feet touched solid ground, she gazed at her own bedroom, looking at it from inside her closet-door mirror.

Strange. Surreal.

The image of home.

"Ian," she said, using his Christian name. "We're here."

West mumbled and pitched forward, falling through

the spinning circle on the mirror. He'd finally lost consciousness, giving up the fight.

Olivia stepped through the portal and took him in her arms. The glass solidified, closing off the world to Zinna's dimension.

She could hear voices in other parts of the loft. But there wasn't anyone else in her room. For now it was just her and West.

She removed his shirt and traced the arrowhead under his skin.

The nightmare wasn't over yet.

Olivia still hadn't saved him.

The silence was deafening. The people gathered around West's bedside were at a loss for words, especially after Olivia had told them who the Slasher was.

Allie looked ill, but Olivia understood how her sister felt. She'd wanted to vomit when she'd first learned the truth, too.

Muncy and Riggs hadn't discussed how they were going to apprehend a woman hiding out in a witch dimension, but it was on their minds. It was on Olivia's mind, too. She couldn't—*wouldn't*—let her mother go free.

But first things first.

West was still unconscious.

"How do I remove the arrowhead?" Olivia asked Derek.

"You? You're not strong enough to do this."

"Why not?" she challenged. "Before I went to the witch dimension, you told me I could heal West. So what's changed? What's different?"

He blew out a heavy sigh. "I knew West would be ill, but I hadn't counted on an object-intrusion spell. Even if an experienced shaman sucks it from his body, it's extremely dangerous."

"For who? West?"

He nodded. "And the shaman. If the medicine man fails, the witch weapon will enter his body and he'll die right along with the patient."

Olivia smoothed West's towel-dried hair and felt her heart constrict. She'd already stripped off the special agent's wet clothes and bathed him with the herbal mixture again. But it hadn't done any good. He lay on her bed, wearing a pair of boxers and burning up with a fever.

She, too, had changed into dry clothes, needing to free herself of the swamp. She glanced at Kyle, who was tending to West's arm, wrapping the disinfected wound with gauze and adhesive tape.

"I can help you find a shaman," he said. "I can go back to my rez—"

"No." She interrupted her former boyfriend. She wasn't about to allow a medicine man from Kyle's reservation to get involved. Or any rez for that matter. "I'm not going to ask a shaman to risk his life for something my mother did."

Allie moved closer. Up until now, she'd been gazing out the window, rubbing the chill that racked her bones. "*Our* mother," she said. "Yvonne gave birth to me, too."

Olivia met her sister's gaze. "Then you understand why I won't ask a medicine man to do this?"

"Yes. But that doesn't mean I'm not afraid for you."

"Hold on. Wait." Derek watched Yvonne's daughters with wariness in his eyes, objecting to their conversation. "I just said Olivia wasn't strong enough."

"And you're wrong." Allie let out the breath she'd been holding. "My sister can remove that object, but only if we support her. If we believe in her."

"West trusts me," Olivia said. "Don't you see, Derek? I'm the one who's meant to do this."

"Maybe." He frowned at the mirror, at the circle he'd drawn onto the glass. "But there's more at stake than West's life. Or yours, for that matter. If the healing is successful, the witch who inserted the object will suffer. So that means this affects Yvonne's fate, too."

Muncy and Riggs perked up. Both detectives gazed at Derek. "How will it affect her?" Riggs asked. "What exactly will happen?"

"I'm not sure. There's no 'exactly' in situations like this. First of all, she's in a witch realm, so for all I know, she could be immune. But if she isn't—" He paused, made a thoughtful expression. "It will probably kill her."

The lady cop looked at Olivia. "Are you prepared to take your mother's life?"

She thought about the gun she'd aimed at Yvonne. "If that's what it comes down to." She turned to Allie. "Are you still going to support me, even if Mom dies?"

Her sister frowned. "Yes, but—"

"But what?"

"I'll be really upset if you and West die instead. If Mom gets away with all of this." Allie crossed her arms, chilled again. "You can't fail, Olivia. I can't bear to lose you."

"You won't."

"Promise?"

"Yes." She leaned forward to embrace her sister, wondering if she had a right to make such a confident vow. There were no guarantees in life. But even so, Olivia had to believe in her power. She had to trust herself. "I'm stronger than Mom. I know I am."

When they separated, Olivia addressed everyone in the room. "Allie was right about me needing your support. If anyone can't handle this, then he or she should leave."

"We can handle it," Kyle said. He turned, looked around. "Right?"

Muncy agreed and so did Riggs. But Derek wasn't ready to commit.

"How did you return from Zinna's dimension?" he asked Olivia. "The ointment I put on your arms wasn't waterproof. So how did you open the door?"

"I did it with positive energy."

"Was West involved?"

"Yes. And another entity. A spirit guide, something that was trying to protect me. But it's gone now. It used up all its strength in the witch dimension."

"And that's what you plan to accomplish here? A mass of positive energy?"

"Yes," she said again. "Is that a problem for you?"

"I'm still torn between white and black magic," he admitted. "And that could create an adverse effect. I don't think I should stay. But I can still help."

When she walked toward him, her shoes sounded on the floor, echoing lightly. "How? What can you do?"

"I can contact the members of my coven, and we can try to put a binding spell on Zinna, to keep her from retaliation."

"Why haven't you done that before?"

"Because if it doesn't work, it will piss Zinna off even more."

"And if it does work?" she prodded.

"It won't last. Eventually she'll regain her powers. But for now it's all we've got."

Yes, Olivia thought. It was better than nothing. And Derek, in spite of his inner struggle, was trying to do the right thing. To her, that made a difference. "Then I should wait to remove the arrowhead. Wait until you cast your spell."

He nodded. "I'll call you when it's done."

She offered him a hug, thanking him for caring. He shrugged and stepped back, but his skin was flushed, warmed by her sentiment.

"I'll call you," he said, gathering his supplies, breaking down the makeshift altar he'd used earlier, giving Olivia a chance to prepare for the object-intrusion ceremony.

She decided to ask Glenn to come over, to be part of

the healing. He was, after all, the man her mother wanted to frame for the murders. And in spite of his affair with Yvonne, he deserved Olivia's forgiveness. He'd only been a pawn, another person Yvonne had tried to destroy.

She got Derek's attention before he left. "How will I know if my mother died? How will I know if removing the arrowhead affects her?"

"You'll hear an explosion," he said. "And then it will be over. She'll be gone."

"And if not?"

"Then it didn't work."

But it will, she thought. It had to. Because Olivia wasn't about to let the Slasher get away with her crimes.

Derek kept his word. He called her several hours later. Of course, there was no way to know if his spell had been successful. Only time would tell.

West was still unconscious. The witch dimension had taken its toll. He didn't have anything left to give.

Olivia glanced around, then locked gazes with Glenn. He'd arrived just a short while ago, bringing his heart with him. He was grateful for Olivia's forgiveness, for her apology. Even now, after they'd embraced, they kept looking at each other, shedding the pain between them.

Finally she shifted her gaze. Along with Glenn, Allie, Kyle and the two detectives gathered around West. Family and friends. Positive energy. Even Samantha had joined them. The cat watched West through protective eyes.

But even so, this wasn't a proper ceremony. Olivia wasn't a shaman skilled at removing witch weapons nor had she employed Apache singers to assist her, to sing and drum. But she delved into her soul, chanting her own words. Whispering them in the sage-scented air.

She used cattail pollen on West, then put some on herself, as well. Her father's eagle feathers remained close by. They'd survived the witch dimension. They'd protected her in the most unholy of places. She knew they would protect her now.

Olivia turned down the lights, and the candles on the nightstand flickered, shadowing West's face, intensifying his features. If only he wasn't so pale.

She sat next to him on the bed, leaned over and pressed her mouth to his ear. He didn't stir, but she could feel his heart beating beneath his chest, thumping against the arrowhead.

"I love you," she whispered. "You're worth the risk."

Ready to break the spell, to fight the battle between good and evil, she placed her lips on his skin.

And tried to draw the witch weapon from his body.

Nothing happened at first. But then he started to shake, violently, like a seizure.

The people gathered around West didn't try to touch him. They knew it wasn't their place to interfere, to interrupt the healing, no matter how traumatic it was.

Olivia held West while he shook, held him until her own body began to tremble, until the arrowhead tried to suck the life out of her.

West opened his eyes and stared at her.

She gazed back at him. She knew they were caught in the magic, trapped by the witch weapon that threatened to destroy them both.

But she refused to be afraid, to let fear consume her.

When West shot up and tried to reach for her, she went flying off the bed and hit the mirror. The glass rattled, jarring her, making her head hurt.

Colors burst in her mind, like a kaleidoscope exploding into a million pieces.

The arrowhead was trying to pierce her skin.

A woman screamed. A death-defying yell.

Was it her? Was she rebelling? Or was it a voice in her head?

She could still see her lover, like a faraway dream, reaching for her. But she couldn't go to him.

She was pinned against the glass.

Olivia focused on West, on the intensity of his emotions, the depth of his need. As a silvery light surrounded her, she knew it was his energy, the struggle inside him.

He was trying so hard to be with her, but he wasn't strong enough to move, to fight the magic. He was glued to the bed the way she was cemented to the mirror.

Death was only a breath away.

But was so was love. The warmth of family and friends. The belief that she was powerful enough to break the spell.

And she was.

She pulled free, rushing into West's arms, letting him hold her, letting him draw from her strength.

It was over. They'd survived.

West didn't speak. He just kept her close, their hearts pounding in unison. A man and a woman who'd defied the odds.

Olivia touched his cheek. His skin was cool. His fever had broken. But he needed to rest. She could see the exhaustion in his eyes.

A moment later the candles went out. The flames stopped burning. Allie turned up the lights, and they waited for the explosion. The sign that their mother was dead.

But there was nothing but silence.

"I'll go back for her," Olivia said. "I'll bring her to justice."

"Is that possible?" Allie asked.

"Mom said it wasn't. But I have to try." Olivia looked around, expecting resistance. But no one argued. No one debated what needed to be done.

"I'll help you," Allie said. "I'll help you capture Mom. We'll—"

Suddenly the room vibrated. Pictures rattled on walls; furniture teetered; the alarm clock fell off the nightstand.

And then the circle on the mirror spun, the door to Zinna's dimension opening.

But it wasn't the ancient witch who crashed into the room, who flew right at Olivia. It was Yvonne, and she was very much alive.

She dragged her oldest daughter onto the floor, trying to pull her into the witch dimension.

But Olivia knew it wouldn't work. The arrowhead had brought Yvonne back. Her own magic had cursed her. It hadn't killed her, but it had stripped away her powers.

"You can't win." Olivia rolled on top of her mother and aimed a gun at her head.

The room fell silent. The portal closed.

And for one horribly painful moment, Olivia and Yvonne stared at each other, childhood memories assaulting Olivia's brain. Good memories, bad memories, a connection they shared.

But even so, she wanted to pull the trigger.

"Don't do it," a man said.

Olivia ignored the voice of reason. She knew it was Muncy. She could feel him moving closer, trying to defuse her emotions.

An eye for an eye, she thought. A tooth for a tooth. Why couldn't she end it here? Why couldn't she take the law into her own hands?

She looked up and saw Allie. Her sister had a gun aimed at Yvonne, too. The Magnum their father had used.

But Allie wouldn't shoot, not unless Yvonne didn't give them a choice.

Olivia couldn't do it, either. Not like this. She couldn't commit a cold-blooded murder.

She wasn't like Yvonne.

"Take her," she said to Muncy. "Get her out of my sight."

The detective put Yvonne in handcuffs. She cursed

her children, screaming that she should have killed them, too. That they deserved to die, just like the women she'd stabbed.

As the police arrested their mother, Olivia stood next to Allie, shoulder to shoulder, comforting each other without words.

A united front.

No matter what, they would always have each other.

The following morning Olivia awakened next to West. He slept soundly, as he'd done all night, looking beautifully rumpled. She smoothed his hair away from his face, and he swatted her hand, unaware of her affection. He probably thought she was a mosquito.

"You big lug." She kissed his forehead and let him sleep.

Ready to start fresh, she reached for her robe and glanced at the closet door mirror. The circle Derek had drawn, the portal to the witch dimension, was gone. Erased, like a teacher's chalkboard at the end of the day.

Anxious to see Allie, she went into her sister's studio, where she knew the younger woman would be.

Allie stood quietly, gazing at the buffalo hide painting of their dad. Olivia moved forward, studying it, as well. Joseph looked magnificent in his traditional Sioux regalia and war weapons. Allie had done him proud.

"I finished it this morning," her sister said. "Do you think he's ready for the Ghost Road? Do you think it's time?"

Olivia didn't know. "I hope so."

"Me, too." Allie turned away from the painting. "How's West?"

She thought about the way she'd held him last night, listening to him breathe. Grateful, so incredibly grateful that he was alive. "He's still sleeping."

"But here we are. At the crack of dawn." Allie stretched, rolling her shoulders. "Zinna hasn't tried to retaliate. Derek's spell must have worked."

"So it seems." Of course, how could they be sure? Their great-grandmother was an extremely powerful witch. Even Derek admitted that he couldn't bind her forever. That her magic was nearly impossible to contain.

Allie tucked her hair behind her ears. She wore it loose, falling like ebony silk, spilling over a white nightgown. "I've been wondering about the man Zinna cursed."

"That was almost a hundred years ago."

"I know, but I can't help but think about him."

"He's got to be dead by now, Allie."

"What if he isn't? What if Zinna cursed him to a hell dimension somewhere?" She frowned, then sighed. "Maybe he needs someone to save him."

"And maybe it's a curse that can't be broken." Olivia gazed at her sister, noticed how pretty the embroidery on her nightgown was. Flowers the color of cotton candy, leaves as green as a clover-dotted countryside. "Why don't you focus on your angel instead? Have you started painting him?"

"My winged hunk? No. But I will." She grinned. "He's supposed to bang my brains out, remember?" Her smile fell. "I'm going to be ready for Zinna. I'm going to fight her the next time."

Impressed, Olivia admired her sister. Her strength. Her determination. The female warrior she was sure to become. "Maybe your angel will help."

Then again, who knew what the future held? Olivia's premonitions only took them so far, and at the moment she had no idea when Zinna would return or what would happen when she did.

But Allie would be prepared. The thought gave Olivia comfort. "Do you want some breakfast? I can fix—" She stopped speaking.

A light caught her eye. She turned toward it and saw that the painting of their father was glowing.

"He's here," Allie said.

"Yes." Their dad's spirit was in the room, swirling around the picture, making the buffalo hide shimmer. Yet there was more, so much more, that captivated Olivia.

That warmed her heart.

"It was him," she said, tears gathering in her eyes. "My protector in the witch dimension. That was Dad." She could feel the connection, the same energy.

Allie didn't move. She kept gazing at the painting. "That must have been difficult for him."

Extremely difficult, Olivia thought. "That's why I didn't know it was him. He was being careful not to reveal himself. To keep Zinna and Mom from discovering who he was. From letting them mess with his soul."

Allie gasped. "Look!"

The shield in his hand moved, just a little, just enough to make his image come to life. And then the painting remained still, the glow around it fading, disappearing softly.

"Is he gone?" Allie asked. "Did he leave for the Ghost Road?"

"I don't think so. I think he's going to wait for you, with the weapons you gave him. In case Zinna comes back."

"Then I'll wait for him, too." Her sister took a deep breath. "I'll wait as long as I have to."

"Just be safe." Olivia hugged Allie, then left her alone in the studio, where she was destined to create more magic.

Olivia decided not to fix breakfast. She returned to her bedroom instead, wanting to see West, to watch him sleep.

Only, he wasn't asleep. He sat up in bed, braced against the headboard, the sheet falling to his waist. He looked strong and healthy, a sight to behold.

"Hey," she said, studying his features, those compelling eyes, the angle of his cheekbones, the beard stubble shadowing his jaw. Then she glanced at his stomach, fascinated by the ripple of muscle, the indentation of his navel.

"Hey, yourself." He looked at her with same sexual interest, up and down, all over.

Lust, she thought. Amazing, beautiful lust. She shed her robe and climbed into bed with him.

"Have I thanked you for what you did?" he asked.

"You don't have to. I know you appreciate it." She moved closer, inhaling his herbal scent, the medicine that lingered on his skin. "And you would have done the same thing for me."

"I heard what you said to me, Olivia." He took her hand and held it. "When I was unconscious, I could still hear you. Like a dream in my head."

Her heartbeat turned fluttery, much too girlish. "Oh, that." Those three little words. She couldn't take them back, not even if she wanted to. "It's no big deal."

"Yes, it is." The sun bathed the bed in a golden hue, drifting across the sheet, dancing in the air. "And I love you, too."

A jangle of nerves rose to the occasion, tingling her skin, making her pulse jump. "Thank you. I mean…I'm glad you feel the same way."

"So, what happens now?" he asked.

"Nothing spectacular." She feigned a casual air, wishing her heart would stop flapping its wings. "We go on with our lives."

"Just like that, huh?" He still held her hand. "How about this? We can keep working together. Seeing each other as often as we can. I'll request to have you on my cases."

Her lips twitched. "Why? So I can save your ass a few more times?"

"Yeah, but it's such a great ass." With strong, possessive arms, he grabbed her, dragging her against his body, making her sigh. "I'll bet you're obsessed with it."

"I am not."

"Liar." He nuzzled her neck, and they nearly melted in each other arms.

It was a feeling she wasn't used to. But she let it happen. Because she loved him. Because he was worth saving.

"I'll be your boy toy," he said.

She laughed and snuggled closer. Special Agent West. Friend, lover…

…sex slave.

That sounded pretty darn good.

Better than good, she decided, when he offered her his handcuffs.

Much, much better.

* * * * *

Look for Sheri WhiteFeather's
BETRAYED BIRTHRIGHT,
coming in July from Silhouette Desire.
And watch for Allie Whirlwind's story,
coming soon from Silhouette Bombshell.

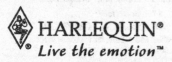

COMING NEXT MONTH

#29 PERSONAL ENEMY—Sylvie Kurtz

When security specialist Adria Caskey's undercover plan to ruin the man who had destroyed her family went awry, she found herself protecting the man she loathed most in the world. But as a cunning stalker drew them into a trap, her sense of duty battled her desire for revenge....

#30 CONTACT—Evelyn Vaughn
Athena Force

Anonymous police contact Faith Corbett had been a psychic all her life, but now her undercover work had put her in a serial killer's sights. As she raced to save innocent lives, she had to confront the dark secrets about her psychic gift, her family and the skeptical detective who challenged her at every turn....

#31 THE MEDUSA PROJECT—Cindy Dees

Major Vanessa Blake had the chance to be part of the first all-female Special Ops team in the U.S. military through the Medusa Project. Only trouble was, the man charged with training the women was under orders to make sure they failed. But when their commander disappeared in enemy territory, Vanessa and the Medusas were the only people the government could turn to to retrieve him and expose a deadly terrorist plot.

#32 THE SPY WORE RED—Wendy Rosnau
Spy Games

When Quest agent Nadja Stefn accepted a mission to terminate an international assassin and seize his future-kill files, she had another agenda: finding the child who was ripped from her at birth. But she hadn't counted on working with her ex-lover, Bjorn, agent extraordinaire— and unbeknownst to him, her child's father.

SBCNM0105